Readers love the Tales from Foster High by JOHN GOODE

Tales from Foster High

"This story was awesome. You could really get behind the feelings these young men had for each other and their lives in their small Texas community."

—Mrs. Condit & Friends Read Books

"Brilliant. A truly phenomenal piece that took me right back to the halls of my youth, and made me remember the reality of what it was like."

—Rainbow Book Reviews

End of the Innocence

"John Goode writes one hell of a book. His way with words is just almost sensual. He weaves not just a story, but threads that seem to wrap around your entire being."

—Gay Romance Writer

"It is easily one of the most outstanding examples of realistic Young Adult fiction I've ever had the pleasure to read."

—The Novel Approach

"You have to read this novel. Its twist and turns will leave you wanting more."

—MM Good Book Reviews

151 Days

"This book and this series is important to read to really understand what some kids are going through in high school."

—Hearts on Fire

By JOHN GOODE

First Time for Everything (anthology)
Going the Distance

LORDS OF ARCADIA
Distant Rumblings
Eye of the Storm
The Unseen Tempest

TALES FROM FOSTER HIGH
Tales from Foster High • To Wish for Impossible Things
End of the Innocence • Dear God
151 Days

Published by HARMONY INK PRESS
http://harmonyinkpress.com

GOING
THE DISTANCE

John Goode

Harmony Ink

Published by
HARMONY INK PRESS

5032 Capital Circle SW, Suite 2, PMB# 279, Tallahassee, FL 32305-7886 USA
publisher@harmonyinkpress.com • http://harmonyinkpress.com

This is a work of fiction. Names, characters, places, and incidents either are the product of author imagination or are used fictitiously, and any resemblance to actual persons, living or dead, business establishments, events, or locales is entirely coincidental.

Going the Distance
© 2014 John Goode.

Cover Art
© 2014 Paul Richmond.
www.paulrichmondstudio.com
Cover content is for illustrative purposes only and any person depicted on the cover is a model.

ISBN: 978-1-63216-619-7
Library Edition ISBN: 978-1-63216-620-3
Digital ISBN: 978-1-63216-621-0
Library of Congress Control Number: 2014949324
First Edition November 2014
Library Edition February 2015

Printed in the United States of America
∞
This paper meets the requirements of
ANSI/NISO Z39.48-1992 (Permanence of Paper).

This is dedicated to every single gay athlete who played even though they knew their teammates might not accept them.

CHAPTER ONE:
TIP-OFF

MY NAME is Daniel Devin Monroe, and I'm eighteen years old.

I was born on January 24 in the Naval Hospital at Camp Pendleton to John and Mary Monroe, who had been married for only six months at the time. My dad was a newly minted PFC fresh out of boot and spent exactly three days with me as an infant before being shipped out. Later that month Mom and I joined him at Kaneohe Bay in Hawaii, where we lived until I was five years old and she was killed.

A drunk driver blindsided her on her way back from the store just outside of base. I was being watched by family friends on base and had no idea what had happened until a chaplain came to collect me. My father was deployed when it happened, and it took the brass almost a week to get him back home. Neither of them had any relatives living nearby, so I stayed with a family on base. It was the longest week of my life. I was pretty sure my parents had given me back. I cried, screamed, begged the people watching me to tell Mommy and Daddy that I would do better if they gave me another chance. No one wanted to be the guy who told a kid his mom was dead, so instead they kept trying to reassure me that I hadn't done anything wrong.

To this day I walk around feeling like I have done something wrong even when I haven't.

I can vaguely remember my dad standing there in his uniform, sobbing violently as they gave him the details of what had happened. Up to that moment I'd had no clue how bad the situation was. I thought Mommy had gone to Daddy and they were leaving me forever. Seeing him break down was the instant I knew our life as it had been was over. That might seem like a very complex thought for a five-year-old, but little kids see and understand more than a lot of adults think. I knew that Mommy was gone and she wasn't coming back.

After that I don't remember much besides an endless stream of covered dishes from the other families on base and the nights lying awake in my bed hearing my dad cry in the next room. I didn't know it at the time, but my dad's life was crashing around him also. He was the sole caretaker of a child he barely knew. I never asked him if he had the desire to send me off somewhere else to live. I knew he had a sister he never talked to, so it wasn't like he didn't have options. I never asked him because I was always afraid of the answer. I'm sure he was given the chance to get out of the service, but he didn't take it. He was twenty-three years old, a widower raising a child on his own, and I figure he didn't want to add "unemployed" to the words that described him.

We moved around a lot after that. The Marines assigned him to mercy billets, which were postings in CONUS—Contiguous United States, meaning the lower forty-eight—he could fill while raising me. We never stayed anywhere more than a year and a half. The only housing I knew was on base. I grew up with a high and tight and an oversized USMC sweatshirt on wherever I went. I was a base brat in a bad way, and it never occurred to me that people lived any differently than I did.

When I was ten, Dad sat me down and explained that we had a chance to transfer to Germany for an actual posting. The Marine Corps had been more than patient with him, and he repaid them with what would become a willing lifetime service commitment. Five years was a long time to not have a steady post, and at ten I was more than old enough to weather an overseas billet. My dad was now an MP, and there was a posting in Stuttgart he could take, providing I was okay with it. I didn't understand at the time what going overseas meant or why he was asking me for the first time if I wanted to go somewhere. I simply agreed, thinking being in Germany meant another base school I wouldn't like in a new place I'd never see.

I have never been so wrong about something before or since.

The thing about military bases is that they have a consistency that is comforting to a young child in ways an adult can't understand. I never learned the difference between Oklahoma and Virginia, since the bases in each state looked exactly the same to me. The same steel gray tones coupled with the overwhelming sense of order made me oblivious to the concept that one place could be different from another. So when I stepped off the plane in Germany and was, for the first time in my ten years of life, confronted with something new and not the same as everything else, I did what any world-wise child would do.

I threw a fit and screamed, begging to go home.

The sad part was, I had no idea where home was. Home was a series of half a dozen names sprinkled across the country. Home was the identical four walls that made up my bedroom in each place. I was a military gypsy and was crying for a place that didn't exist. I couldn't verbalize to my father what I wanted. I'm sure he knew he was screwed. He had committed himself to the posting, and there were no other options. The Marines had given him more than enough leeway, and now it was his time to pay them back. The feelings of a ten-year-old had no impact whatsoever in their feelings, and he'd known me long enough by then to deal with me as best he could. In Germany.

On the other hand, I felt my dad was unfair, a jerk, and doing this just to make my life miserable. I hated the base, the school, the other kids who lived there, everything. My level of loathing knew no bounds. As time passed the loathing just increased. The first month sucked, since my dad had an inordinate amount of training and paperwork to complete in order to be brought up to speed with his assignment, which meant the horrible place with nothing on TV was made even worse by the fact I had to suffer it alone.

I hated the people who lived there, and I hated the weird language they spoke. I hated the different uniforms people wore on base, and I hated that we had to learn different things in school. I had gone from being an average student to the slow guy overnight when I found the difference between US-based schools and German schools to be devastating. I didn't want to learn about Europe or Germany or anything new. I hated it more and more and blamed my dad for landing us in Stuttgart. I became surly, mouthing off to teachers, refusing to do schoolwork, generally being a spoiled fucking brat of the highest order. I say that now, looking back at how impossibly hard it must have been for my dad. He spent a twelve-hour shift in a new place with different regulations and a different culture and then came home to me and my problems. Me not liking the school and hating the language and not having good TV programs must have seemed petty to him.

If anyone knew life was not fair, it was my dad. He had been cheated out of a lifetime with my mother because one idiot asked for another round before leaving the bar that night. He had been forced not only to be a Marine but to be a single parent as well, and there was nothing he could do about it. My father knew very well life was not fair, and hearing the fact proclaimed loudly and often by a child who had no concept of what unfair meant must have been excruciating.

Around then we started fighting.

We had always gotten along before, and this was new territory for us. I had done what he said without complaint, and he had never felt the need to raise his voice at me. In Germany, things changed. I hated him for stranding me there, and he hated me for blaming him. Every night we would end up in a screaming match that more times than not included something getting thrown at a wall or the floor in anger and/or frustration. Things devolved into not talking at all, which didn't make the feelings subside, of course. I began to wander around the base instead of going home after school, hoping in vain to find some part of this alien world that might seem normal even for a little while.

That was when I met them.

To say they were cool kids would be an insult to people who are truly cool. They were simply other kids. They were older than me, which meant they were automatically better in every way. A few belonged to the civilians who worked on base; others were fellow military brats who hated Stuttgart too. They had longer hair, cursed, and smoked constantly, which was a trifecta of epic to me. They hung out near the bowling alley just outside the base perimeter, their frayed jeans cuffs rolled up while they tried desperately to look apathetic about everything. I was tall for my age; in fact I was a freak for any age. At eleven I was almost six feet tall and looked like an oversized puppy with huge ears and feet I constantly tripped over. I was horribly skinny in a really noncool way. I was all elbows and ribs and no matter how much I ate, I only grew taller and stayed scrawny.

I'm not sure if they knew how young I really was and didn't care, or if they had mistaken me for their age, but either way they accepted me into their little group. I pretended to smoke by dangling a cigarette out of my mouth and made "fuck" every other word in my sentences to be like them. They seemed to think I was funny as hell. My dad, on the other hand, didn't. He forbade me to hang out with them, but because he was on duty for half the day, he had no way to keep an eye on me.

As we approached the end of our first year in Stuttgart, I had learned to inhale properly and knew every word you could never say on television plus a few that wouldn't even make it into movies. We were a pack of rabid dogs thinking we were wolves wandering the base at dusk. We had no money, no vehicle, and no idea what to do.

I don't know if you know the formula for figuring how stupid a group of teenage boys is, so let me share it with you. Take the average IQ, which is going to be abnormally low because of hormones, and then begin to divide that by each additional boy present. So basically the more boys in a group, the dumber we become, and let me tell you, we were pretty stupid to begin with. The leader was Joshua, and I thought he was the shit. He had this rat tail that screamed rebellion, along with a set of prepubescent biceps that to an eleven-year-old looked like massive guns. I followed him around like I had a crush on him. And, I was beginning to realize, that wasn't too far off the mark.

Nothing was more sacred on a Marine base than a girl, a Marine's daughter doubly so. If you want to see how dangerous a Marine can be, just look at his daughter. I mean it. Don't flirt or even talk—just glance over at her. I assure you it will be the last thing you ever see before he kills you, most likely with his thumbs. So I never had a chance to interact with the opposite sex, and to be honest I never felt the need to. I grew up around men and liked their company. It wasn't until that summer that I realized how much I liked it. Joshua was my first clue. In my eyes, he could do no wrong. The others laughed off the way I followed him around and called it hero worship, but I think he knew better. He was always grabbing my head and giving me noogies that lasted too long and never seemed to hurt like the ones the other guys gave me did. We spent a lot of time at his parents' place playing video games, sharing a chair that barely fit the two of us.

It was cramped, but we never complained; in fact, we seemed to relish the contact.

My father, realizing that nothing short of sending me stateside would get me away from the guys, gave up trying to convince me to stay away and instead kept as careful a watch as he could on us. That is to say he wasn't able to watch us at all. When my dad was on duty, Joshua and I would go to my place, and we'd sit in front of the television and watch the weird TV shows as long as we could until boredom kicked in. Eventually he'd launch a sneak attack that I had spent all afternoon waiting for and wrestle me to the ground. There was no point in struggling, since he was obviously stronger than I was, but it never seemed to be about who would win but about the contact.

We both spent more time grinding against each other than trying to get free, and on some level we both knew it. At first he spent a long time watching to see if I would protest or say something about it later. When I didn't, the pretense that we were wrestling went away. He'd hold me down as he lay over me, pushing his jeans against mine. I didn't understand what we were doing, but it felt good, and that was enough for me. I guess you can say I fell in love with Joshua that summer, even though I didn't have words for it. He was everything I wanted to be. But what I was feeling was more than that, and it confused the hell out of me. Again I assumed everyone felt this way, but Joshua didn't talk about what we did and pretty much treated me like he always had when we were with the other boys; I figured that was the way older kids handled the subject.

When I spent the night, I would make up a bed on the floor and wait until the lights were out and his parents had forgotten about us before climbing into his bed. Things were different at night under the covers in just our boxers. What was a physical struggle became something else as we held each other, feeling the heat come off our bodies. I had never felt like this, and for the first time since we moved there, I began to find something to like about it. He would whisper to me in the night, secret things that no one else knew, and I loved it. About how much he liked me and was glad we were friends. He seemed to marvel at the fact I was taller than him, and in fact almost as tall as his dad, yet younger then he was. He was also the first person to inform me that everything about my body was larger than normal.

Since my dad and I rarely talked about anything personal, I had never even thought that anything on my body might be above normal. I cursed my height, since it did nothing to benefit me and only served to make my life worse than it was. I couldn't run without tripping, I was always noticed by strangers passing by, and buying clothes was embarrassing, since I could never shop in the kids' section. But there, in the safety of the night, Joshua told me my size was not only good but, when it came to my dick, incredible. It was impossible to hide anything in my boxers normally; when I was hard, I might as well have been naked. He seemed to get great pleasure from rubbing me through the sheer material, and I know I loved it.

I wonder what my life would be like if his dad had never walked in on us that night. Would I have learned to like Germany? Would I have calmed down some and begun to forgive my dad? Would I have realized the crush I had on Joshua wasn't normal and that, therefore, I wasn't normal? Would I have known to keep that information from my dad as long as possible, therefore avoiding the eventual blowup for a while longer?

It didn't matter, because when Joshua's dad walked in on us, my world came crashing down around me again.

Joshua, knowing what we were doing was in no way acceptable, handled the shock better than I did. He jumped back as if waking up, screaming at me to get away from him. I just lay there stunned, my erection throbbing for both of them to see. His dad hauled me out of the bed with one arm. I think we were both a little shocked to find I was almost looking him in the eye when I stood up, but he reacted better than I did. He told me to get dressed, and then he called my dad. It was only at that point I knew how much trouble I was in.

I began to cry while I waited for Dad to show up. Every time I looked at Joshua, he would look somewhere else. His dad paced the living room, glaring every so often at me as he sighed and shook his head. His mother, who, up to this point, I'd thought of as a great lady, just sat on the foot of their stairs and seemed to be trying to push this all away by sheer force of will. I had stopped actually crying and instead just sat there in misery when a knock came at the front door. I felt my chest constrict, and I began to cry again. I looked over to Joshua with pleading eyes as his dad explained to mine what had happened. Joshua's eyes were red too from his own tears, and he looked like he was almost ready to say something when we both heard my dad roar, "*He did what?*"

Joshua looked away, inching another couple of steps toward his room.

I had never felt smaller or more vulnerable than when my dad pushed past Josh's dad and stormed into their living room. I refused to look away as he glared down at me, silently asking me if what he had just heard was true. When I looked down in shame, he knew it was. "Get your ass off that couch. We're going." His voice was almost a growl, and for the first time in my life, I was actually afraid of my father.

He had walked, since the on-base housing was all in the same general area. I walked out of the house with him close on my heels. I noticed my dad couldn't make eye contact with the other dad now, so great was the shame I had brought to us. He was too quiet on the walk back to our house. I thought the silence was ten times worse than any screaming he could have been doing. Dread of what was coming made what was normally a short walk seemingly take forever, which wasn't all bad because I didn't want to know how it ended. The second I crossed the threshold, I ran for my room, but I got maybe three steps before he grabbed the back of my shirt, hauled me back, and tossed me into the living room.

I hit the carpet and scrambled to my feet as he came at me. His voice was like something on high, and it blasted through me when he bellowed. "Did you do what he said you did?" I cringed and backed away from him. "Were you touching him in his sleep?" The loathing in his voice was the worst thing I had experienced in my entire life. I felt a fresh wave of shame sluice over me, and I started to tremble inside. When I didn't answer, his voice became louder. *"Why would you touch another boy like that?"* Another wince from me, and I was pressed up against the back wall, still trying to make myself smaller. *"You know who does that? Perverts. Are you a pervert? Is that what you want to grow up to be? Some creepy guy who touches other boys while they sleep?"*

"He wasn't asleep!" I snapped back in what I can only explain as a moment of temporary insanity. When I saw the disbelief in my dad's eyes, I argued even harder. "He wasn't sleeping!" I took a sobbing breath and said, "He started it!"

That was the first time my dad hit me.

I know it sounds hard to believe, a single military dad who was all about order and discipline never once spanking his son, but my dad never had to. His voice and authority had always been more than enough to keep me in line. I couldn't blame him—that entire summer with me skipping school, hanging out with those boys, smoking, and now this. He was at the end of his rope, and he didn't know what else to do. I justify his actions because he has never hit me again. We were both a little crazy that night, and when he slapped me, it wasn't the physical impact that caused me pain. The gunshot-like crack of flesh on flesh didn't startle me. It was the fact that looking into his eyes, I could tell he didn't know why he had done it either. We were both feeling betrayed, and neither one could fathom where we had gone wrong enough to warrant hitting me.

I held a hand to the reddening welt on my cheek and just shook as he hovered over me with his hand raised for another blow. I don't know if it was the very real fear in my face or the fact he had just lost control that stopped him from continuing. All I knew was that he froze in place for a few seconds, which were enough for me. I dashed around him and made a beeline for my room, slamming and locking my door behind me. This time when I broke down and began to cry, it wasn't from shock, fear, or even pain.

I was crying from disgust.

I didn't know what kind of a person I had become. I liked something as gross as touching another boy, and I knew it wasn't right. *Fag, queer, homo,* and *gay*: these were all well-known insults to a kid my age, and no one ever used them in a good way. I was all those things, which logically meant I was a bad person inside. As I lay there on my floor, blocking my door, I cried myself to sleep, consciously thinking for the first time in my life that I was never going to be a good person.

The next thing I remember was a soft knocking on my door and sunlight streaming through my windows. "Danny?" my dad's voice called from the other side as the doorknob rattled. "Unlock the door." He sounded as tired as I felt. I unlocked the door, and he stood there, looking at me with an expression as unreadable as any I had seen on him before. "Get dressed," he ordered before walking away.

I knew better than to ask where we were going. I simply closed the door and pulled on a pair of jeans and a sweatshirt, knowing last night was not over. He had his keys in his hand, which meant our destination was outside the base. I began to worry as we drove and wondered if I was going to ralph in the car. I wanted to ask where we were going, but he wouldn't even glance at me, and I didn't have the guts to ask without a prompt. We exited the base, and the fear was well on its way to becoming sheer terror as he drove us into town.

When you're a kid, the rules of society are a little fuzzy. Whether or not a parent had the ability to leave a kid on the side of the road without explanation wasn't a black-and-white thing. I had flashbacks to when my mom had died, that feeling I was going to be returned because I was defective. And even though I was pretty sure I knew where babies came from so there wasn't a place you could return them to, I was still terrified that was what he was about to do. I was hungry, tired, the side of my face ached, and I felt on the verge of tears again. We pulled up to what looked like a gymnasium, and I felt lost. He stopped the car and sat for a moment. He looked as if he were weighing a difficult situation and didn't like his choices.

I was sure he was going to sell me off or just ditch me somewhere in the middle of Germany. What could I do? I didn't speak the language. I didn't know how to get back to base. I had no money and no means to make any. I would be dead within a day, wild dogs feeding on my carcass as I huddled behind some trash cans in the middle of the night. Of course I didn't even know if there were wild dogs in Germany, but I'd seen a documentary in the States once, and the thought of something so benign ending up so feral had petrified me. After about a minute, he took the keys out of the car and opened his door. I followed, pretty sure he wasn't going to abandon me in the car. He liked the car.

He spotted an empty bench just to the left of the gym door and sat down and pointed, first at me and then at the bench. I sat next to him. "You have a choice to make," he said, still not looking at me. "I can do two things with you, and I'm going to leave it up to you to decide." I felt the tears welling up again but forced myself to stay steady. "You can go back to the States," he said. "I talked to your Aunt Kelly, and she said you could stay with them if you want." He turned to stare at me. "But if you go, you aren't coming back here. I have another three years in Stuttgart, and other than maybe Christmas, I won't have any way to get back to Texas." I could feel the world falling from underneath me and realized Dad wasn't going to ditch me. He was going to send me off to live with his sister, a woman he described on his best days as a raging bitch. She had three daughters, and each was more self-centered and superficial than the next. I hated their family, and my dad knew it. We barely saw them, and the few times we had, I had literally begged my dad to leave when we were alone, a sentiment he never argued with. The wild dogs and being alone in a strange country sounded better than that.

After a second of letting that soak in, he said, "Or you can change." That brought me up short, since I didn't understand. "You go to school, stop fucking around, clean up your act, and find something else to do with your free time besides be a punk."

"Like what?" I asked, not really knowing what else I could do besides be the loser I had been the past year.

He gestured behind me at the gym. "They have a youth basketball league here. You'd need to be here four days a week, take the bus from the base and back. There is a lot of practice, working out, and learning the game as well as building teamwork skills." I looked back at the building, wondering how such an ugly place had all that inside of it. "You hold down a B average, prove to me you can stick at something, and you can stay." Our eyes locked as I realized this was the moment where I had to choose. "You screw up once, and I'll send you to Kelly's so fast your feet won't even touch the ground before you hit the States. So think about it, because if you don't plan on trying, you might as well as leave now and not waste anyone's time." I knew tears were streaming down my cheeks, but I couldn't stop them. "What's it going to be?"

The emotion became too much, and I buried myself into his side as I really began to bawl. "I'm sorry!" I exclaimed into his shirt as I felt his arm move around me. "I want to stay. Please don't send me away!" And I meant it. I still hated Germany and the base and everything about it, but I loved my dad more, and the thought of living the rest of my life with him so far out of reach was the worst thing I could think of. "I'll do better," I promised as I held on tight to him. "I won't let you down again."

And though I was only a miserable eleven-year-old boy, I meant what I promised with every fiber of my being. I would never again in my life do anything to shame this man who had spent so much of his own life raising me. I had stumbled, but I wasn't down, and I was willing to do anything to make it up to him, and in this case, it meant basketball. The game and my redemption were so closely tied together that basketball was never once a mere game as far as I was concerned. It was a faith, a belief that through it, I would be reborn as a better person. Some people come to that concept through Jesus or through AA, but I came to it through basketball. It was the path I could never stray from lest I lose my dad and his love. It became more than my life; it was my soul.

And has been ever since.

CHAPTER TWO:
CHECKING THE BALL

THE NEXT three years passed by in a blur.

My life became a routine of waking up before the sun had risen, taking a shower, and heading out the door. I'd run around the base before school, sometimes with my dad, more times by myself. I had stolen an old Walkman of his, and though there was precious little on base in the way of cassettes, I learned to get by on my dad's stockpile of eighties music. I'd get home, take another shower, and then eat everything I could find in the house. Then I'd sit in class and do my best to not nod off as I waited until two o'clock in the afternoon when class let out. I'd run to the bus stop and catch the 2:15 to the gym, where my day truly began. We'd change out and do laps around the gym until we started to work up a sweat. Then we started with drills. For those not versed in the fine world of basketball training, allow me to explain.

When you perform a certain skill over and over until it becomes second nature to you, you are doing drills. The key to being a good player isn't being able to do something when you consciously want to. A good player is able to use a skill without deciding to. Passing, dribbling, shooting, you start to learn these individual parts of the game until you find yourself dreaming about them constantly. At first this is all you do—practice a pass, practice dribbling, practice another pass, practice your shooting. When the coach sees something only he can perceive in you, *then* you are allowed to actually play a game against other people.

That's when it gets hard.

Playing against your own teammates is the weirdest thing you will ever do in basketball. Not only are you playing against guys who have watched you learn every move you make, but they have been trained in exactly the same way. The whole focus of learning the game isn't about who wins or loses. It's about how well you play. Make a basket through sheer luck, and you'll get berated. You should always know where the hoop is no matter where you are; sheer luck doesn't mean anything. Steal a ball from a guy, and you'll hear a lecture on the guy's sloppy form and the reassurance that the next guy you try to steal a ball from won't get caught napping. It sounds horrible, and let me assure you, it is.

The funny thing is that you never notice you're getting better.

You're with the same group of guys all the time, and you all evolve at the same rate, so there is never this flash that you know more than anyone else. It wasn't until I had been practicing for about a year and a half and played a pickup game on base that it dawned on me that I knew what I was doing. It was a three-on-three with a few of the older kids, none of them from Joshua's crew, who would never be caught dead engaging in something as lame as exercise. They'd asked me to play because I was a few inches over six feet at the time, not because they thought I had any talent. I was a body to stand on the court and fill in for the guy who hadn't showed up and nothing more. I accepted, because it was a Sunday, and frankly I was bored out of my head looking for something safe to do.

Less than a minute into the game, I realized these guys sucked.

They had no form, no style. They were just running around the court lobbing air balls, praying Michael Jordan would answer and sink one for them. The first time the guy I was guarding had the ball, I took it from him so fast he was still moving forward by the time I was taking the shot. There are few sounds as rewarding as the sound of a ball swooshing into a net. It causes a Pavlovian response in my mind that gives me pleasure no matter where I am. When I turned around to see who was going to throw the ball in, I was surprised to see five other guys looking at me in shock.

The rest of the game went a lot like that.

The guy who was supposed to be my partner was ignored as the three other guys went after me with a vengeance. The game became more challenging, but they couldn't stop me for long. If they'd known what they were doing or had a sense of teamwork, I'd have been fucked, but all they knew was to stand in front of me and wave their arms, hoping that would be enough to stop me. Every time I sank a three-pointer, they realized it wasn't.

They never invited me again, but I didn't care. I walked away from the court with a smile on my face and the knowledge there was something I excelled at. The extra knowledge that I had schooled three guys older than me only made it sweeter. I threw myself even harder into practice after that. I made the actual team my second year, and we ended up winning the local tournament, solidly beating thirteen other teams. The next year I made the equivalent of varsity, and we went up against a whole other class of teams.

We ended up ranking third in league, which was the highest our gym had ever ranked. That was when the coaches talked to my dad. I was oblivious to the conversations, of course, but I found out later that they told him they had taught me all they could. They told him I had a gift, not just my height, and that I had a chance to do something more than just play the game for fun. I always wondered what went through my dad's mind. Did he not believe them? Did he ask them to make sure they had the right dad? Did he wonder if that talent had been wasted on someone like me?

Since I didn't know about the conversation, I didn't know about his thought process, but I do know what happened next. His tour was about up, and that put him at the fourteen-year mark, so we both had a big choice ahead of us. He sat me down to have A Talk, which so far had never been a good experience. The first had brought us to Germany and the second was the threat to send me home, so I didn't have high hopes about the third one. He asked me if I liked Germany and the base, which was more asking me if I had learned to stop hating it. Again, I never found out his thought process, but I'm sure "I love basketball" must have been the answer he was looking for.

He re-upped with a transfer to Texas, a promotion training the security forces on a naval base. I had mixed emotions about leaving Germany that fall. I hated the base because now I hated Joshua and what he had done to me. We'd never talked again, though we saw each other from a distance. Every time I saw him, I had the same strange feeling in my stomach I'd had when we were friends, so I always stayed away, knowing nothing good would ever come from going down that path. On the other hand, I loved basketball in a way I wouldn't have thought possible. I knew there was basketball in the States, but I was afraid at the thought of having to start all over again. Frankly it scared the hell out of me.

I was fifteen, no longer the spoiled brat who had walked off the plane five years earlier. I could look back and see I had never given the place a chance. My own fucked-up little drama had spoiled me for any chance of seeing how nice a country it might have been. No matter how much I may have not enjoyed my time in Stuttgart, though, I had to admit that being in Germany had introduced me to the one great love of my life. The plane took off, and I felt sad as we said good-bye to Germany forever. I didn't know why I felt that way, but I knew subconsciously the place had revealed more about who I really was than I cared to see. On one hand I was sad about all I was leaving; on the other I was relieved about all the things that wouldn't remind me of my past. Now I knew what was inside me. It was my duty to try to keep it under control.

When I fell asleep, we were in Europe. When I woke up, we were in Texas. That was how fast my life changed. We switched concourses and planes in Dallas, and I instantly knew I was back in the States. I had thought I'd known the difference when I was away, but as we walked through the crowded terminal, it was blatantly obvious to me. People were more insular, closed off, lost in their own little world. I understood now how foreigners could see us as rude in comparison. We waited in the USO lounge for our connecting flight, and I could tell my dad was feeling it too.

It's an odd sensation being a stranger in your own country. I noticed there were more than a few good-looking girls walking through the airport. My dad noticed more than a couple had stared at me. "You don't look fifteen," he said once we'd grabbed some food and settled in front of the TV.

I was in midbite of a hot dog and looked over at him. "Is that a bad thing?" I asked, trying to swallow the mouthful whole.

"Depends on who you ask," he said with a smug smile.

"I'm asking you."

He looked back and, though he was obviously having fun with me, as always there was a deadly serious tone in his voice. "Ask the guy who got a girl pregnant at seventeen and had to join the Marines to support her, and he'd say no. Ask the guy who is amazed at the man his son is becoming, and he'd say yes." He took a drink as my mind tried to wrap itself around the compliment. "Ask your father, and he'd say you're too young for sex."

He laughed when I blushed.

We boarded a much smaller plane for the last leg of our flight. Unlike the massive jets used on international flyways, the plane we clambered into was a two-prop baby; I wondered if it could even take off. The flight from Germany had been packed; there were only five people including us on this flight. I was too tired to realize that the plane's size and passenger load were the first warning signs about where we were headed. I adjusted my seat belt and looked over at my dad. "Where are we going again?"

"Corpus Christi. They have a naval base there," he explained.

"Is it a big town?" I asked.

"Define big."

"Like Norfolk?" I offered. He shook his head no. "Like K Bay?" Another no. "Like Jacksonville?" He thought for a moment and then said, "Yeah, like that."

"How big is the base?" I asked as we prepared for takeoff. And then I quickly asked the real question. "How many kids go to school there?"

My dad didn't even look over at me as he replied, "You aren't going to school on base. I enrolled you in a civilian school."

As the plane accelerated, I felt my stomach drop, and it had nothing to do with the motion.

If you've gone to public high school, I'm sure you have no idea where my reaction came from. After all, you were used to walking into a strange school with sometimes thousands of kids who didn't know you. You thought it normal. You were raised to understand how to talk to new kids, get to know them, and then eventually make friends out of some of them. It had always been something of a mystery to me how other kids did it. On base we were all like prisoners of war and had no choice but to know each other. It didn't matter what you wore or how you talked, because in the end we were all stuck there on base until our parents got transferred somewhere else. It made for socializing quickly, but at the same time you didn't make very deep friendships, since we all knew it was just for now anyway. Joshua and his crew were the closest I had ever gotten to friends, and look how that turned out. I was the only base kid who played basketball at the gym, which meant I got to see the rest of the team every practice or game, but after that I headed back to base while they headed back to their homes in Stuttgart.

I had never had friends, and that fact dawned on me while we were making the hop to Corpus Christi.

I know it sounds stupid, but when everyone else you know is in the same boat, you don't think about how deep the water is until you fall overboard. A new school, a new team, a new everything was just about as terrifying a thought as I could imagine. What if I dressed wrong? What if I talked wrong? What if I was a nerd? What if they could tell I'd once fooled around with a guy? As the plane chugged its way toward Corpus, I felt a very real panic start to well up in my body. What was already a small plane became microscopic, and though I was taller than anyone on it, I thought the seats were shrinking under me. This is what Alice must have felt like when she ate the cake, the entire world falling away as she sat completely still.

"You okay?" my dad asked, noticing my hands were now claws holding fast to the armrests. I looked over at him, trying to keep my cool about me, but from the way his eyes got wide, it was pretty obvious I failed at that. "Danny, what's wrong?"

"Nothing," I said in a very small voice.

He continued to stare at me, which made me even more nauseous than the turbulence. My dad was a person who was constructed from different types of strength. If he had a weakness, I'd never seen it. So to me showing any fear in his presence was the equivalent of letting him down. But only a blind man could have missed how I had grown pale and was sitting there shivering in a cold sweat. He put one hand over mine and leaned in. "Are you scared about school?"

My voice actually cracked as I responded with "Who's scared?"

His eyes grew concerned, and I knew I had failed. He could tell I was silently screaming. "Danny, why would you be scared of high school?" I didn't have an answer to that, but after a few seconds he amended it with "Well, no, I can see why, but you have to know you'll be fine, right?" I looked at him as if he had started babbling in Latin. He smiled and explained. "Danny, look at you. You are taller than me, for Christ's sake. You are in fantastic shape. Hell, I had a friend ask me the other day what unit you were with. Trust me when I say that you'll be beating girls off with a stick, and there is no way you don't make the basketball team. And do you know what that means?" I shook my head. "It means that you're a jock, and trust me, jocks do not get picked on."

"I don't feel like a jock," I said honestly, and I didn't. Jocks seemed full of themselves and their abilities in a way I was never comfortable with. Sure, I was good at basketball, but there was always going to be someone better, which meant I needed to try harder. Just because I could dribble a ball didn't mean I was better than anyone. I mean, who the hell would care? No one on base had seemed to, and if anyone was impressed in town, it had never gotten back to me. I suddenly realized I didn't want to be a jock. I didn't want people to like me for the sport I played or how tall I was. If people were going to like me, I wanted them to like me, not my abilities. I wasn't sure if I wanted to beat girls off with a stick, but I do know I didn't want them running toward me just because of basketball.

"Danny, you're a worrier; you always have been." He smiled, and his eyes seemed to focus on something far away. "Your mother was like that. She could get herself worked into a frenzy over almost nothing." He looked back at me. "And I'll tell you the same thing I told her. Things work out the way they want to. We can push and pull and fight every second of our lives, but there will always be things that are out of our hands. All you can do is the best you can and let the chips fall where they fall."

"What did Mom say?" I asked, marveling at even this little bit of information. I tried to stay away from broaching the subject of Mom with him in fear I might open an old wound that would then refuse to close. For him to offer her up as an example was noteworthy in itself.

"She'd say 'fuck off, John,' but she calmed down most of the time."

I burst out laughing. The thought of my mom telling my dad to fuck off made her seem that much more real to me for a moment. We sat there aching for the hole she had left in our lives, both of us happier than words could express that the other one was there with him. "You think it'll be okay?" I asked.

He nodded. "Trust me, you'll be fine."

I didn't believe him, but I did feel better afterward.

When we landed, I found myself more than underwhelmed by the airport.

You have to understand when you move around as much as we did, the only first impression some places got to make was their airport. For example, O'Hare is a city unto itself. There is a mini mall in the center of it with a bookstore and a toy store, which had always entranced me as a kid. Because it's so big, it's ridiculously organized and has about fourteen different ways to get around in. San Diego International has a pace all its own. It's clean, friendly, and overall a pleasure to visit, in my opinion. Even DFW is a nice place with about two dozen different little carts to buy magazines and munchies on the way to each terminal.

Corpus's airport looked like they were still building it.

There was a main terminal that we entered through, and as we walked by to get our luggage, there was another side terminal that seemed to be just tacked on as an afterthought. The walls made the entire place look like a doctor's office, and I found it just completely unappealing. And this came from a guy who grew up thinking military housing was okay. There were no people wandering around, making it look less like an airport and more like a bus stop. I could see by the expression on my dad's face, the "whelm" he was feeling was less than he'd expected.

"Maybe it's an old airport," he said as we watched ten bags come off the flight, six of them belonging to us.

"Maybe we missed the Rapture while we were in the air," I said quietly back.

He let loose a sudden laugh before he realized, in the stark silence of the airport, that he sounded like he was shouting.

We opted to take a taxi to the base instead of calling a military shuttle. We usually did this. It gave us a chance to put some eyes on the town we were never going to see once we were on base. Except things were different this time. I was going to be living there. Actually living there. Going to school, meeting people, making friends? I'd never looked at a city with those criteria in mind, so I sat up and looked out the window in eager anticipation.

I had never been so let down in my life.

The entire town seemed bisected by a main freeway that cut through what looked like a series of small stores on either side. This couldn't be the main part of town. There is just no way *this* constituted the heart of a town. We passed five exits, and then the stores started to become sparser and sparser, until, by the seventh exit, there was nothing.

That was it?

I stared at my dad and tried not to look like I was freaking too much, but he just stared back at me for a few seconds and then shrugged, which was Dad for "Sorry." I sank into the seat, suddenly missing Germany more than ever. There was a special exit for the naval base from the freeway, and as we made the slow turn, the area around the base was revealed, and that was the moment I knew.

I was completely fucked.

There was nothing even close to an actual place I'd want to live in lining the road that connected to the base entrance. It looked worse than you could imagine. There were parts that really looked like they were one strong wind from falling down. This was the part of town that parents would warn their kids about visiting, and the kids would actually listen. Now my dad wouldn't meet my eyes, and it was confirmed.

We were completely fucked.

The base was nice. It was big, with not a lot of buildings around. My dad had explained to me that this was a training facility for pilots, and once upon a time it had been a military hospital. As I looked closer, I could see a lot of the buildings looked closed up, making me wonder exactly what was still working on the base.

The next three days were incredibly boring.

We got moved into base housing, and I was issued a new ID card that would let me on the base and able to shop at the Navy Exchange, or NEX for short. Most of our furniture had been stored when we went to Germany, so seeing our stuff was like buying it new all over again when we unpacked. I began emptying my stuff and ended up reading a ton of old comics I had stored away when my dad came in and bitched at me.

"Seriously?" he said, standing in the doorway wiping the sweat off his forehead. I looked up, and he gestured for me to get off the bed. "It's not 'open a box and then read comics.' It's 'unpack your damn room.'"

"I'm resting," I said, hiding my smile behind the comic.

"You do know I will take you over a knee, taller or not," he threatened.

"Big talk," I said, faking a yawn. "From a short man."

I looked over, and I saw the one eyebrow arch too late. I threw the comic at him as he lunged, both hands beginning to tickle me. Let me tell you, if you ever feel you can talk smack to your dad, make sure you are in no way ticklish. My dad had hands that should have been registered as deadly weapons so any and all kids would know how dangerous he was. You'd think being skinny as a rail would not make me that sensitive, but you'd be so wrong it's sick. My dad would just look at me and make me laugh because I knew what was coming next. It was a humbling moment that made me remember no matter how tall I might get, my dad would always kick my ass.

He had me begging him to stop almost instantly. At the thirty-second mark, I would have told him nuclear secrets if I possessed them. At forty-five seconds, I might have agreed to kill someone if I didn't know them personally. "You going to unpack your room?" he asked with real glee in his voice. I nodded quickly, though at this point, I would have agreed to paint the house and detail his Jeep to get free. "And no fucking around reading comics?" I agreed to that and was pretty sure I would have burned them in the center of my room if he would stop. "Hurry up, because we need to get to the mall to buy you some new clothes for school." Again I agreed, not sure what I was agreeing to until his words penetrated.

"W-what?" I cried, trying not to laugh hysterically.

He stopped. The smile on his face made it clear he was more than satisfied he had this power over me. "You heard me. New clothes if you can get this crap unpacked."

There was an afterimage of me on my bed as I was already running around my room unpacking boxes like The Flash. I didn't even notice he had walked out of the room. I was too busy working. Within twenty minutes the boxes were empty, and my room was... well, it was my room. When I walked out, he was sitting in the living room flipping through the comic I had thrown at him, ignoring me in a pretty bad way. "You ready?" I asked, putting my shoes on.

"Yeah, when I'm done with this," he said holding up the comic.

I saw him laugh when I sighed and sat on the couch waiting.

"Dad!" I complained after an hour, which was probably in actuality two minutes. He put the comic down, and we walked outside.

I had forgotten my dad's Jeep and how much I wanted it when he eventually bought another car. It was a black ragtop that just screamed coolness in a way I will never be able to explain to someone else. I always felt the Jeep was like the brother I never had, because I know we were both fighting for my dad's love.

There were days I'm pretty sure the Jeep won.

We headed past the line of crack houses on the way to the freeway, and again we didn't say a word about them. This was not the place we'd thought it would be, but as with everything that had come before in our lives, we had little choice over it. You have to understand that I was as much under the military's whim as my dad was, and complaining about it did nothing but make me miserable. This was my life. My very first memories were on a military base. I'd never known any other way of living. I knew on the edge of my thoughts that this time our move was more about me than my dad, but that didn't make being stuck here any better.

I wondered idly if my dad resented me for getting us dumped here.

If I was sure this town was not what we were expecting from the freeway, it was solidified when we got to the mall. There's a mall in Waukegan, Illinois that is so big you can fit two normal-sized malls inside it, easy. During Christmas, it's so packed that the population of the mall is larger than most small cities. In San Diego there were three different malls I'd loved to go to when I was a kid even if I wasn't going to get to buy something. From the outside, this mall looked more like two big stores with a couple of smaller stores connecting them. When we got inside, it was exactly what it looked like from the outside.

There were more people than I expected, which was a start.

The stores were a little different, though I saw a Spencer's and a Hot Topic as well, which was cool, I guess. I was so busy taking everything in that I missed the two girls passing by us who checked me out and giggled as I walked by. My dad elbowed me and gestured to them once they were past. I craned my head behind me so quickly that I tripped over my own feet, almost eating it right then and there. The girls laughed again while I blushed and tried not to kill myself walking.

"Yeah, you're a hideous beast," my dad said under his breath. I elbowed him as I tried not to look back again.

When we'd walked into the center of the mall, I looked around, trying to take it all in. It wasn't much, but I had to admit I kind of liked it. There was a carousel in the middle with a few kids crawling over it, which I thought was sort of cool. I saw a bookstore next to an Abercrombie, and I knew everything was going to be okay.

The next day he took me to the school to sign me up for classes. The semester had been in session for a month, so I was already behind the curve a little, but my dad didn't think it was going to affect me. People stared at us as we walked through the halls. It was obvious this was a pretty small town, which meant a lot of these people had known each other for a long time. No doubt that was going to make a difficult situation a thousand times harder. I had opted for faded jeans with a hoodie over a black T-shirt—casual garb, I had thought, but from looking around, I could tell I was overdressed. It wasn't what I was wearing as much as where I had bought them.

I didn't see anyone else decked out in A&F like me, and I wondered if I had made the first mistake of what no doubt would be many to come. My dad was filling out forms when I tugged on his sleeve. "I don't feel well," I whined as another couple of people walked by, staring into the office at me.

My dad saw me dart a look at them and pulled me aside. "Danny, I am going to give you some advice. It was the same advice my gunny gave me the first day I was going to lead us in PT." I leaned in, waiting for my dad to lay some serious wisdom on me, hopefully something that would make this day instantly become better. He grabbed my shoulders, locked eyes with me, and said, "Man up or fake it until you can."

That was it?

"Huh?" I asked, more confused than ever.

"Either get over your fear, or pretend you're over it until you are. This is where you are, and there's no turning back. I know you can do this, so fake it until you realize it yourself."

Fake it? That was his advice? *Hey, Danny let me dump you off into a strange school surrounded by hundreds of other kids who have no idea who you are and might decide you're a total knob and make the next four years a living hell. And how do I suggest you deal with it? Fake it.* Gee, thanks, Dad.

He seemed to find the shock in my eyes funny as he went back to filling out papers. He handed them to the secretary. "Anything else?"

The lady looked them over and shook her head. "No, sir. I think we have it all, Mr. Monroe." She looked up at me, and from the way her eyes widened, she made it pretty clear it was the first time she had noticed me. "You're Daniel?" she asked, unconvinced.

I nodded, wishing I was as small as I felt.

She looked down at the paper and then over to my dad. "And he's fifteen?"

I felt my face grow red as I mentally shrank more.

"He plays basketball," my dad offered, as if playing basketball meant you instantly grew like a mutant.

To my surprise she nodded and smiled. "Oh, okay. Let me find you someone to show you around to your classes."

My dad looked back at me and smiled, which was his way of saying *See? Problem solved.*

I looked back at him with my normal face, which was my way of saying *I hate you.*

He was okay with that.

"You'll be fine. I'll be back at three to pick you up," he informed me, patting my shoulder as he began to walk out. "You have money?" he asked, pausing at the door.

I gave him my best pleading look, silently begging him to let me go with him.

"Okay, so you're good," he said, nodding, completely ignoring me. "Have fun!" he insisted as he walked out of the room.

"Don't see how that'll be possible," I said to myself.

"You Danny?" a voice asked from behind me.

I turned around and saw a cute black-haired guy smiling at me. He looked up at me and exclaimed. "Whoa! Where are you from?"

I looked down in embarrassment. "Um, Germany?"

"You're from Germany?"

"Well, no, but I just moved from there," I answered, still not looking up.

"Oh, oh, you're military!" He snapped his fingers and looked at my hair. I nodded, and he seemed to get it. "Well, welcome to Texas," he said, offering his hand. "I'm Cody."

"Danny," I said, shaking it.

"I know," he said, holding up a folder. "In fact, at this point I know more about you than anyone else in this school." He grinned evilly, and I had to admit he instantly looked three times hotter than I already thought. I shook my head and forced myself to banish those thoughts as quickly as they had entered.

"So tell me about myself," I said as he led me down the hallway.

He opened the folder and began to skim the front page. "You're a freshman, just moved to Corpus. You have grades that make me think military schools have to be easier than high school or that you're a serious nerd. And...." He paused, as if what he was reading had shocked him. He looked over at me. "You play basketball?" I nodded. "You good?" I shrugged, and he looked back to the paper. "Says here you took the regional championship last summer."

"It was a team effort," I said lamely.

He was flipping through the pages now. "Are these stats for real?" he exclaimed, not really asking.

I looked over his shoulder. "I have stats?"

Sure enough, I had stats. There was a page of numbers that had the gym's letterhead printed across the top. There was my name and a list of points, rebounds, three-pointers, everything I had done in each game for the last three years. He kept reading and said under his breath, "Fuck, you're awesome."

I felt a flush move across my face that was in no way unpleasant.

"You're going to try out for the team, right?" he asked me, his voice full of excitement.

"Um, I guess so," I answered, flustered.

"You have to!" he said, grabbing my arm. "Our team sucks! We need someone like you."

"Like me?"

He looked at me in amazement. "Yeah, a fucking giant!" My face must have fallen at the word "giant" because he almost instantly amended it with "No, that's a good thing! Hell, that's the best thing!" I looked up at him hesitantly. "Trust me, man, you are going to be epic!"

I smiled, getting my first taste of what would quickly become law in my new life. Whenever Cody laughed, it was impossible not to smile with him. His emotions were infectious in a way that promised he would be insanely popular even if he wasn't classically good-looking. The fact that he had a kicking body with a damn cute face only made his charm that much more irresistible. I didn't know any of this at the time, but Cody was a weapon of mass destruction seemingly constructed for my own personal demise. Even though I was guarded about my feelings toward guys, in the case of Cody I would have had a better chance of ignoring the sun on a hot summer day.

He showed me around the school, pointing out the different buildings and where my classes were. "Seriously, dude, you're in, like, three honor classes. Is that a typo, or are you like a brainiac?"

I didn't know how to answer that since I didn't really consider myself a smart person. I just knew my grades were part of the formula my dad used to rate my well-being. If I was pulling Cs or Ds, then he'd know I was fucking around again, and that meant no basketball. There were no honor courses on base. You just worked at your own pace at whatever you were working on. There were so few of us that when we got stuck or had a question, we could get one-on-one time with a teacher, but a distinction between this class or that simply wasn't in my vocabulary. I knew kids who were way smarter than I would ever be, so the thought I might be smarter than someone else never once entered my mind. I shrugged again, not sure how to answer. "I don't feel like a brainiac."

"Whatever," he said quickly. "If you get on the team, which you will, you'll probably think about switching to normal classes, because you aren't going to have a lot of time to be studying."

"You're on the team?" I asked, realizing he knew way too much about the team to be just a fan.

He gave me one raised eyebrow and a look that asked if I was ragging on him. After a second he asked, "Yeah, why? You think you have to be from Norway to play?"

"Germany," I corrected him. "And I was born in San Diego."

He waved the explanation off as we kept walking. "Yeah, I made the team this year, and let me tell you, we suck." He talked with no remorse or anger in his voice, just like he would describe the color of paint or what a building was made from. *That wall is brick. That paint is red. Our team sucks.* "The tallest guy we have on the team is not even your height, but if I hadn't seen him changing into shorts, I'd swear he was just two little kids on each other's shoulders, the way he runs. We have no passing game, and I think one of our passing guards is allergic to the ball."

"Allergic?" I asked.

"As in he seems to have a fit every time he touches it," Cody explained. "It's really sad, to be honest."

My excitement at joining the basketball team was diminishing with every step we took.

"So what was Germany like? Could you drink over there? What were the girls like? Were there Nazis walking around? Do you have a gun because your family is military? You ever been in a tank?" he began asking in machine-gun-fire succession. It was like opening a harmless-looking bottle of Coke and having it foam up over the neck

"Um, cool. No. Blond. No. My dad does. And I saw one but never in one," I answered, trying to keep the answers straight in case I answered "I saw one but never in one" about the girls.

"Sweet," he said, nodding. I was unsure if he actually heard my answers or not, but it didn't seem to matter.

He brought me to the gym and led me in, opening both doors in front of him. "Welcome to my house," he said, gesturing for me to enter.

I walked in and could smell the familiar mixture of sweat, wood, and excitement every gym seemed to hold for me. There were two far-court baskets as well as two midcourt ones on either side. They had a digital scoreboard that looked like it belonged on a starship rather than a high school gym. It was just a high school gymnasium, but it seemed so much more to me. I'd never been here before, but as I walked the boards looking up at the baskets, I knew instinctively what I wouldn't vocalize for almost a year.

I was home.

CHAPTER THREE:
HOME COURT ADVANTAGE

CODY HAD been right. I did make it on the team with no problem.

I don't like thinking I'm better at something than someone else is, so when I say I was the best person on the team, that is not a statement of ego. They were good guys, but only three of them had ever played basketball in junior high, and of those three, only one had been a starter. From the first day of practice, it was apparent we had a lot of work to do. The rest of the guys were cold to me, on the border of being jerks. Only Cody was nice to me. I wasn't sure if that made him my friend or not, but I do know if it wasn't for him, I would have quit the first week.

The coach made a huge deal about my experience, and every time he began describing a new technique or strategy, he would look at me and say, "Danny knows what's I'm talking about, right?" After a while I wasn't even listening to what he was saying, just nodding every time I saw him look at me. I could hear the whispers from the other guys every time he did it and inwardly winced, knowing it was another strike against me. The worst part was scrimmage games against each other for practice. No one likes being shown up in front of other guys. Everyone really hated it when I was the one who did it. I'm not sure what the coach was getting at putting a different man against me every day, but I do know it assured that every person had a chance to personally resent me for kicking his ass on the court.

I know I should have loved this. I should have been crowing proudly as I flew past guy after guy. There should have been a sense of accomplishment with every three-pointer I sank. I loved playing, but I was learning to hate winning so much. This went on for two weeks, and it was just getting worse and worse. Dressing out before practice, all I got were angry stares. Bad enough I was taking my clothes off in front of other guys, but to do it while people shot daggers at me just made it unbearable. Even my biggest fan, Cody, was losing his love for my talent as the grumblings grew louder and louder each day.

My dad didn't seem to understand.

He said that guys were always going to resent me for my skills. Just that fact made me sick to my stomach, but he went on past that. He said I had a gift, and that even the people who were going to love me for it would secretly hate me at the same time because they couldn't do the same. It was the first inkling that basketball wasn't just my own personal way to salvation, but that it might be a larger part of the rest of my life. He explained I was lucky that I had no idea how good I was because, without that humility, I'd be insufferable. At the time I didn't understand what he was talking about, but I soon would.

The coach was a largish man who must have been built twenty years ago and then let himself go in a bad way. He had that gut all former jocks seemed to gain after a while. My dad, who was twice my age, was in as good if not better shape than I was, so when I saw someone like this, it just made me grimace. What he lacked in physical stature, he more than made up for in his knowledge of his team. No one had gone to him to complain about me. There wasn't a guy brave enough to bitch loud enough for him to hear, but nonetheless he knew what was going on.

At the start of the third week of practice, two weeks before our first game, he called a team meeting in the locker room before we took the court. Cody explained this was when he named a team captain for the season, usually the most senior player since they had been around the longest. The captain didn't have many duties outside of keeping team morale in check, which was a task all by itself. Now I know this sounds sexist, but I have no idea how someone could handle a team of girl athletes, because I know every team I'd been on so far had been filled with its share of guys who were overly emotional, started fights over every little thing, and were jealous as hell about everything.

In other words, they acted in the same manner I imagined spoiled teenage girls did.

A good team captain knew how to talk to the guys, calm them down, fire them up, and more importantly, knew how to keep certain guys away from each other. Don't let awesome teamwork ever fool you into believing that every person on the court likes each other equally. There were whole currents of fuckery coaches and trainers never even got a whiff of that, if left unattended, could sink a season before one tip-off ever happened.

Cody was only a year ahead of me, so there was no chance he'd get it, and he was the only person on the team who wasn't outright hostile to me behind closed doors. The safe bet was Tommy Grazier, a decent senior who had played this court since he was my age. As it was his last year, he had been a shoo-in as MVP and all-around stud for the team. From what Cody had explained to me, that was all before I showed up. People were talking about me, and not all of it was bad. Though I was oblivious to most of it, Cody kept me apprised of the scuttlebutt the best he could.

What this meant was that the second Tommy was made team captain, my problems were going to just get worse.

Though the coach would call the plays and who did what, once the ball hit the court, it was up to the team to make it happen, and Tommy would make sure as much of it happened without me as possible. It was worse than being benched, because once you're seated you know there's nothing you can do to help the game. On the other hand, out on the court I could do something to help us out, but I wouldn't have the chance because no one would pass me the ball. My head hung low as I stared at a spot between my sneakers, wondering if I should have quit the first week and saved myself this kind of shit. Cody elbowed me, and I looked up quickly.

The coach was looking at me, gesturing for me to come up. I looked over at the team, and I saw a dozen narrowed eyes glaring at me. I started to rise. "Huh?" I asked Cody.

He pushed me forward, whispering, "You're team captain, retard! Go!"

I stumbled forward as the coach slapped me on the back. "Come on, people, make some noise!" he commanded. There were strained sounds of a few people slow clapping that only drove home the point I was the absolute worst choice he could have made. I stood there trying not to openly look fucked, while inside I was screaming my head off like a blond in a horror movie. This was the absolute worst-case scenario. The only thing that would have made this worse is if I realized I had forgotten to put on clothes and was standing up here naked.

What had been smoldering as thinly veiled resentment suddenly burst into a raging hatred as they all drilled holes through me with their eyes. I had less than nothing to say. I just swallowed hard and looked at the coach with panicked eyes.

The coach looked at me and then back to the team, taking in the scene for a moment before nodding at me to sit down. I sat next to Cody, who in no way looked happy at the announcement, since he knew it was about the worst of all possible outcomes. After pacing in silence for almost a minute, the coach began to talk. "You guys make me sick." The words didn't have their normal impact, since his tone was conversational instead of berating. "Show of hands, does anyone think we have a snowball's chance in hell of placing this season?" A few hands went up at first, then a few more. Finally everyone except Cody and I raised their hands.

The coach looked at Cody. "Why do you think that, Mr. Franks?"

Cody refused to look at anyone else as he answered, "Because we suck."

There were a few snorts of laughter from the other guys, along with some grumbling that the coach shut down with a loud "*Shut it!*" Silence echoed through the locker room. "Don't know why you're laughing, because he's right." The smiles fell off everyone's faces as the coach pressed his point. "It's not just that we suck; it's that you guys don't care that we suck." He looked at Tommy. "You haven't done one thing to make this team better, Grazier, not one. All you've done is bitch about Danny over here nonstop since he joined. In fact, if you spent even half the time trying to better this team as you did whining, I'd be naming you captain. You people have had access to someone who knows more about basketball than any three of you put together, and other than Cody here, you won't talk to him. So this is the deal. You want to play basketball because of the letterman jacket and the pussy it will get you, walk the fuck out of my locker room right now." No one even breathed. "If you want to try to win something this year instead of wandering around the court while people laugh at you, then you'll listen to him. Any questions?" He paused for effect and then interjected, "And by questions, I mean last words before I throw you off the team?"

No one said a word.

"Danny, stay. The rest of you start laps," he said, jerking a thumb toward the gym.

The class rose slowly. Tommy asked, "How many laps?"

The coach gave him a hard stare. "Until I say stop or you pass out."

One by one they filed out of the locker room, Cody giving me a shoulder shrug in a way of saying "Sorry, you just got fucked" as he left.

The coach turned around and opened the file cabinet in the corner. "If you want to cry or scream or lose it, now's the time to do it."

"I'm not going to cry," I said coldly.

He stopped what he was doing and looked over at me. After a few seconds he admitted, "No, I don't think you are." He went back to digging through the cabinet as I tried to formulate my next words.

"I don't know if this is going to work," I started with.

"Then make it work," he responded, not even looking up.

"They don't like me," I said, standing.

"So?" He slammed the top drawer and opened the next. "They aren't here to like you. They're here to listen to you."

"But they won't!" I exclaimed.

He pulled out a circular patch that had a capital C on it. "Then make them listen," he said, tossing it at me. "You're captain now, deal with it."

I looked at the patch, never in my life hating something as much as I did that little piece of cloth. The coach walked over to me and put a hand on my shoulder. "Danny, you have a gift. If you don't learn to share it with others, it will do you no good in the long run. God gave you basketball. I'm about to give you leadership. If you are as good at one as you are the other, you have no idea how far you'll go." He continued walking out toward the gym and said over his shoulder, "You have five minutes, then I want you on the court."

And I was alone.

The funny thing was that in no way was this a new feeling for me. I had wandered through most of my life with nothing but my dad's support. I still had that, and this time there was Cody on my side as well. What the rest of the team didn't know was that even though they had all shunned and ignored me, I had already effectively doubled the number of people I cared about in the past three weeks. I wasn't afraid of them not liking me. I was afraid of them not liking me so much we'd lose. Being hated I could handle; being hated and losing I could not.

My first thought was the same thought any male teenager would have in that situation—try to force my dominance on them. Nine-tenths of high school consisted of what my dad had called social evolution. Forcing your own self to *be* yourself in spite of the pressure around you to conform to someone else's version of you constituted evolution. I didn't want to be the stuck-up know-it-all who walked on to the team thinking he was better than everyone else. That guy was the person they thought I was and the person it looked like I needed to be at first glance. The only thing was that I had a voice in the back of my head telling me there was another way to get this done. A way to not only show these guys I was here to help them but to win games as well.

When the five minutes were up, I knew what I had to do.

I walked out into the gym changed. I wasn't going to be hesitant or embarrassed into being timid anymore. The coach had effectively ended that mode of behavior for me. I knew I was going to be hated for acting like a captain and equally reviled if I didn't act like one. I walked over to the coach and said, in the best estimation of my dad's voice I could muster, "I have a few thoughts on the season and how we can win."

His mouth slowly spread into a grin as he grabbed his whistle and blew it twice. "Everyone, line up." The guys stopped jogging and made their way over to the court line. I'm sure they were a little more pissed because I wasn't sweating like them, but I couldn't worry about that crap. "Listen up, your captain has a few words to say."

I saw the eye rolls from most, and Tommy elbowed the guy next to him as he muttered something under his breath. He knew I had seen him and was daring me to say something. He had a long way to go if he was going to actually piss me off. "Okay, let's lay it down," I said, pacing as I tried to formulate my thoughts. "Anyone here think they can outplay me?" No one moved. "One on one, anyone think they can beat me?" I looked at Tommy, who said nothing but glared. No one else dared speak up, so I went on. "Right, so you know I'm the best guy on the team. What we need is for everyone else to know it."

Tommy raised his hand, and I shook my head. "If you got something to add, say it. Don't need my permission."

He lowered his hand as he said, "So let me guess, we're going to build our whole game around you? The rest of us on the court are just going to be the guys who pass to you all game?" I saw almost everyone else nod and agree with him, happy someone else had voiced the sentiment.

"You have a problem with that?" the coach roared, but I held up my hand.

"Actually, Coach, I have a problem with that," I said, cutting him off. I never took my eyes off of Tommy's as I kept talking. "See, that's what we want people to think. We want as many people as possible to think that I'm going to be our secret weapon."

Cody cocked his head and asked, "If it's not you, what is our secret weapon?"

I smiled as I silently thanked him for the setup. "You guys are. See, I don't want the ball at all."

Everyone looked confused except the coach. "You want to force the other team to play to you."

I nodded as I explained. "Look, if I was our secret weapon, it'd take them five minutes to figure out that double- or even triple-teaming me is the key to locking the team down. We don't do that; we use me as a decoy."

"Decoy?" Tommy asked, skeptical.

I nodded. "We force them to go man-to-man with me. No matter how good they are, that's going to leave at least one person unguarded."

"And if they don't take the bait?" he asked.

I shrugged. "Then I blow past my defender, score, and teach them the error of their ways. A couple of those, and they'll put a guy back on me." The guys all just stared at me, not sure if they were truly understanding what I was suggesting. "All we have to do is practice layups that look like we're trying to move me into position to score. What we'll actually be doing is setting the rest of you up for me to pass it off to. Either they watch me and risk you guys scoring or let me go and watch me school them. Which one would you choose?" I asked Tommy.

"Lock you down," he answered instantly, and I saw he was getting it. Once the word got out that I had experience on the court and actually knew what I was doing, any team facing us would gang up on me in seconds. High school basketball isn't big on sacrifice and teamwork. It's a place for guys to hone their talent and get seen by college scouts "Why would you give up points just to pass it off?"

"To win," I said without hesitation. "And if anyone else isn't here to win, I suggest finding another sport, because we're going to win a lot this year." I gave them my best confident smile. "Count on it."

Cody pumped his arm, cheering, and a couple of other guys followed, caught up in the moment. I saw Tommy's expression soften a little. It wasn't a lot, but I was going to take what I could get right now. I glanced at the coach. "We used to practice keep-away drills in Germany…," I began.

He nodded and handed me his playbook. "Way ahead of you"— and with emphasis he added—"Captain." I thumbed through the plays, and all of them were based on the principle I'd just outlined. I looked over at him while the rest of the guys talked among themselves. "Why didn't you just tell me this was your plan?"

He took the book back and put his arm around my shoulder. "Because they needed it to be yours."

That was how the season started.

We built a zone defense principle that became what we jokingly referred to as *zone offensive.* In a sense, we were practicing reverse basketball. Instead of people moving to positions to get the ball to their best player, our team scrambled to get into place for me to ditch the ball to whoever was standing there. At first we sucked at it pretty bad, since we were relearning the way we played the game. It took about three days of constant practice before we stopped looking like we were doing a bad impersonation of the Washington Generals and began to ease into the new rhythm of play. By that weekend we almost looked like we knew what we were doing.

That first week nothing changed with the team at all.

I wasn't sure what I thought was going to happen, but besides the minimum communication needed to run plays, no one said one extra word to me. Cody tried to convince me they'd come around, but I wasn't holding out hope for it. My dad took me out to dinner as congratulations on making captain. When I told him about the guys' reactions, he just nodded and said, "Yeah, that figures." He kept on eating while I stared at him in disbelief. When he saw my reaction, he asked, "What?"

"It figures they hate me?" I asked.

He shook his head as he speared another piece of steak with his fork. "They don't hate you; they just resent your talent." He popped the meat into his mouth. "That or they've seen you dress out and are jealous of something else."

I felt my face burst into flames as I threw a hushed "*Dad*!" at him and he just burst out laughing.

Our first Saturday practice after I was named captain was when things began to thaw. We were three hours into what was sure to be at least an eight-hour day, and we were sitting on the sidelines drenched in sweat as the coach went over the moves with a few of the slower players on their own. Tommy came over and tossed me a towel and sat next to me. "Thanks," I said, wiping my face off and wondering if he had put something on the towel when I wasn't looking.

"This is a good idea," he said, looking across the court as the second squad tried a few layups. I wasn't sure if he was waiting for me to answer, but since we'd never once had a conversation, I just assumed he was talking to talk. "Took a lot of balls to bring up a plan that basically ensures you're probably never going to score." He looked over at me, and we stared at each other for a few seconds. "I don't think I would have thought of that." Before I could respond, he stood up and watched the squad run up and down the court for a moment. "Nice call," he said, walking away, and then added a quieter, "Captain."

Practice ended up lasting over nine hours, and I was almost ready to drop at the end, but I had a smile on my face the entire day.

That next week we began fine-tuning our game as, one by one, guys began asking me questions about specific things they were lagging behind in on the court. At one point I looked over at Cody as I was showing a guy how to pivot on the fly, and he just nodded and smiled. He'd been right; they were coming around.

By the time Friday rolled around, the school was abuzz with excitement.

The coach had a rule of dressing up on game days. Button-up shirt, tie, and khakis made us easily recognizable in the halls, which was a new thing for me. Cody and I walked to class before the bell rang, and more than a few girls smiled at us as we walked by, which made our day. "Dude, we so need to win tonight," he announced after the girls had passed.

"I want to win for more reasons than just girls," I said, trying to ignore how much more attractive Cody got when he smiled.

"Fine, fine," he said, waving me off. "You play for the love of the game, and I'll play for the love of them," he said, nodding to a group of girls who were standing by their lockers watching us walk by.

I rolled my eyes. "You're skeeving me out."

He shot me an evil grin and said, "You have no idea."

I wished my body didn't react to his innuendo, but it did.

During lunch most of the team sat together and talked about the game that night, while we tried not to freak out. To me it was a huge accomplishment just being asked to sit with them, so I tried to stay quiet as Tommy told us about the team that was coming to play and what he knew about the guys who were playing. Everyone was excited to see how our tactic would work tonight. We were all of the same thought that this was going to be really, really good or really, really bad. Tommy was in the middle of describing a game he'd played in last year when a cheerleader walked up to us and looked at me. "Are you Danny?"

My mouth full of sandwich, I looked up and almost choked. Cody leaned over me and said with a huge grin, "He is, but I'm Cody."

"I know who you are, Cody," she replied, rolling her eyes. She handed me a small bundle of something wrapped in cellophane tied with a blue and black ribbon, our school colors. "This is for you," she said shyly. "Good luck tonight."

I nodded thanks to her retreating back; she did a little wave over her shoulder and kept on going. The other guys began to howl and nudge me as I turned redder and redder from the attention. "What did she give you?" Cody asked. I opened the plastic wrap, and I saw about a dozen homemade chocolate-chip cookies. I looked back at her as Cody sneaked a cookie from my hand. "Oh snap. She likes you."

I pushed him back with my elbow and told him to shut up as I began to eat one of the cookies. They were fucking good! "Who was that?" I asked.

"Carol Liventry," Tommy answered, reaching for a cookie. "She's the sister of Susan Liventry." When I gave him a look that indicated I had no idea who that was either, he added, "Head cheerleader? Hottest girl in school?"

I looked at Cody, and he added, "The hot redhead with the huge tits that's in our geography class."

"Oh, her!" I said, nodding as someone else grabbed a cookie. "That's her sister?"

Cody took a second cookie and shook his head. "If she grows up to be half as hot as her sister...."

"She's cute all by herself," I said, looking over the quad at her and the other cheerleaders sitting at their own table. Not as cute as Cody, I thought silently, but cute enough.

That was the day I found out about our boosters.

Boosters were cheerleaders who were assigned a player to... well, obsess over, I suppose. Sometimes they'd decorate our locker. Other times they made these posters for the games, cheering just their player on. Also I found out they rarely gave them gifts like homemade cookies. When I say rarely, I mean once. The guys would not stop giving me shit about it for the rest of the day.

It might have been embarrassing or annoying if I wasn't completely thrilled that the guys were giving me shit. I felt like I'd been accepted as we dressed out that evening, the gym packed for our first game. While we waited for the game to begin, we sat in the locker room, my foot tapping in nervousness as I began to doubt my plan.

Cody sat down next to me. He put a hand on my knee and stopped my foot. "Dude, you need to calm down," he whispered. I tried not to react outwardly to him touching me like that, but inside my mind was awash in thoughts of what the gesture meant. "You're the captain, dude. They take their cues from you. You look like you're about to throw up, and this is *your* plan. How do you think they feel?"

I looked around, and I could see the humming thread of nervousness running through all of us. We were freaked, not just because there were hundreds of people out there in case we failed, but because our entire plan hinged on what might be the worst idea ever suggested. Cody was right, they did need some reassurance, and I supposed it had to come from me. I know I wanted reassurance, but I'm not sure where mine was supposed to come from.

"Thanks," I said, putting my hand over his and squeezing. He cocked his head for a moment and then smiled as he pulled his hand back and joked, "Fag!"

I nudged him back. "You were the one who was feeling me up, Tinker Bell!"

We laughed together as I stood to address the team. I had a feeling he was laughing more than I was.

"Okay, so I guess I should say something," I said, getting everyone's attention. Everyone's eyes fell on me, and it struck me as funny that a week ago I would have internally shrunk away from this attention, and now here I was basking in it. "We're good," I said, not having any idea how to handle an inspirational speech. "I don't say that because I'm on the team. I say that because it's true. If we lose tonight, it's going to be because my plan sucked and no other reason. You guys rock, and I hope we can go out there and show them...."

Tommy stood up, clapping. "Okay, Danny, thanks for that speech. Any more and I think we're going to start crying." The guys laughed as I felt myself blush slightly. He came up and put his arm around my shoulders. "We suck," he said flatly. "But that doesn't mean we can't win. I know for a fact the other team sucks more, and we have something they don't." He grabbed my wrist and raised my arm over my head. "We have this freak!!" he called out, and the other guys cheered with him. "If we win tonight," he said, looking at me, "it's going to be because of you, buddy, so don't kid yourself."

Cody began to softly chant "Danny, Danny, Danny." A few other guys picked up on it and joined in. By the fifth time, everyone was yelling my name, and I felt a rush of emotion as I heard Tommy chanting my name as well. Before I could say something, the coach walked in and called out, "Do you guys plan on forfeiting the damn game because you're not on the court?" We all froze in place. "*Get out there!*" he screamed, and we all moved as one.

I felt someone slap me on the butt as we headed out. "Let's kick some ass, Captain."

The crowd exploded in cheers as we galloped onto the court.

I felt Cody pushing me from behind as I paused at the wall of sound that reverberated in front of me. "Keep moving, Jolly Green!" he screamed behind me. I saw my dad in the stands cheering with everyone else. He was on his feet, and I tried not to feel even more nervous that he was there watching. It was different than in Germany because this wasn't just for fun, this was for a school.

We headed to our side of the court as the coach huddled us together. "Okay, we have this." He looked at me. "I need you to go out there and ham it up." I gave him a confused look, and he explained.

"You're the ringer, Danny. I need you to go out there and sell it." I nodded, and he looked around at the rest of the guys. "Take your cues from him. He is going to have to decide on the fly if he's taking the shot or passing it off. Keep on your toes and be ready for the ball at any time." He put his hand in the middle. "Tigers on three." We put our hands in and counted to three and called out "Tigers" as loud as we could.

When I turned around to the court for tip-off, I ceased being Danny Monroe, nervous and apprehensive teenager, and allowed my instincts to wash over me. As I stood at center court, a part of me realized that I never felt as alive as I did while playing basketball. It felt like the person I was most of the time, stumbling through my life not knowing what came next, was an act. A mask I wore to hide the person I was on the court. The guy from their team walked over to stand across from me, and I smiled. He looked up at me and swallowed hard. I was six three in sneakers, and he wasn't.

"I want a clean game," the ref said, holding the ball between us.

"Take a long look," I said to him as we both crouched. "Last time you're going to see the ball this close for the rest of the night."

His eyes grew wide as the ref blew the whistle and threw the ball up into the air. We both launched ourselves skyward at the same time, but as the ball began to fall back toward us, I was a full five inches over him easy. I batted the ball to Tommy and saw him spin around, trying to lose his shadow. He passed it to Cody, who passed it to me. I turned, looking like I was going for a layup, and saw the guy guarding me bear down to block me. I dodged past him, blew past another guy, and went up for the shot.

By the time my sneakers hit the court, we were two points ahead.

I scored another eight points before the other team called a time-out. We headed over to the coach, who seemed incredibly pleased. "Okay, he's about to tell them to double-team Danny and most likely pulling a guy off of Paul." He looked over at the shortest guy on the team, who seemed deflated by the action. "So, Paul, get ready to teach them the error of their ways." He looked at me. "Paul is it, got it?" I nodded, and he actually laughed in glee. "Okay, this is going to be fun. Our game starts now. Pay attention." We called out "Tigers" and trotted out to the court. Cody was next to me and asked before he moved off to his spot, "You could probably score even with two of these guys on you, couldn't you?" I looked over at him and gave him a sharklike grin that seemed to answer his concerns.

Sure enough, as soon as the ball was in play, the guy who had been guarding Paul moved off to join my guy. I saw Paul station himself over by the basket, and I nodded to Tommy, who shot me a grin. I burst into movement. Their guy was trying to find a guy open to move the ball forward when I came at him. He began to dribble sideways for a moment as he glanced over at the shot clock. He had less than ten seconds to take a shot or lose possession of the ball. So he had ten seconds to either try to take a shot and have me steal it or stand there and do nothing and give it to me anyway.

He decided on the first one and dodged to the left, trying to get past me. I took the ball from him and went to drive forward. My two shadows tried to stop me, and I passed it to the first open guy I saw. I feinted to the left, looking like I was setting myself up for a layup, my two guys on my heels. Tommy had the ball, and I indicated for him to pass. He threw the ball to me and when I turned, looking like I was going to take the shot, I saw another person shift to block me.

I tossed it to Paul, who was literally standing under the basket by himself.

It was the easiest basket I'd ever seen made. Three more like that and the panic began to descend on the other side. Each time they moved back to man-on-man, I would blow past my guy and score. When they grouped to block me, there was always someone else waiting for the ball. By halftime it was obvious we were running the game, and the other team was just struggling to keep up.

In the locker room during the break, we were ecstatic.

We were already celebrating when the coach came back and began to yell at us. "Did they call the game and not tell me?" he asked as everyone grew silent. "Did they decide to cut the game in half and just forget to announce it?" We were silent now as he began to pace. "We haven't won yet, you idiots, so stop celebrating. So far it's working, but I can assure you they are in their locker room right now and their coach is trying to find a way around it." He looked at me. "Am I wrong?" I shook my head, knowing he was right. "So trust me when I say the second half is going to be all uphill. They are going to move to zone defense, which means we need to try working around it. Switch to a ground game, try and keep the passing to a minimum.

Danny, time for some bombs." I nodded, knowing he meant I needed to try for as many three-pointers as I could.

I looked over at Tommy and said, "Your guy is paying too much attention to me." He nodded. "Lose him. Every time I move towards the basket, he ignores you." I could tell he hadn't seen that, but he didn't say anything out loud.

"Okay, we got it?" the coach asked, and we nodded. "You guys are kicking ass. Stay on your toes and do not think you have this yet."

We stood up and surrounded him as we put our hands into the circle. "Tigers kick ass on three," I said, looking at my teammates.

They all stared back, and we shouted "Tigers kick ass."

We beat them easily that night, 56-38. I had never felt like this before, not just part of a team but part of a group of friends. Everyone patted me on the back and congratulated us for a fantastic win. I tried to push through the crowd and look into the stands. I saw my dad when the game ended. He was sitting in the stands, taking to the guy next to him rapidly. He was pointing at me.

It was the first time I saw my dad bragging about me. It was the best feeling I had ever experienced.

CHAPTER FOUR:
PERSONAL FOUL

MY LIFE moved into a pretty sweet groove after that game.

We began winning game after game, and with each win we became more popular in school. That was an odd correlation, since I wasn't really aware all that many people were basketball fans in the first place. Our school was more known for its baseball and football programs; our basketball team had always been an afterthought, as I had understood it. Except for this season.

We began really working as a team, and it showed on the court. Our tactics stopped being gimmicks to fool the other team and began to form into a strategy that was fast becoming unbeatable. Better yet, with our new-found popularity came a whole other level of perks we hadn't been exposed to before.

Namely girls.

Carol had made it clear she'd walk across broken glass to date me, which was flattering, but I was all turned around about girls because of Cody. No, wait, that's not fair. I was turned around about girls way before Cody, but right now, the image of him dressing out was seriously fucking with me. I was fifteen on the edge of sixteen, which meant I spent an inordinate amount of time thinking about sex. I spent more time with my dick hard, pressed into the side of my jeans, than I didn't. My only saving grace was that, with the baggy jeans and boxers I wore, it wasn't blatantly obvious that I was sporting wood, though more than once I saw Cody's stare fall to my crotch, and then he'd look at me with a grin that said he knew. I didn't know if that meant he liked it or not. I simply hadn't spent enough time being friends with other guys to know the protocol for whatever might happen, and I was terrified I'd do the wrong thing.

Carol wasn't the only girl who made a pass at me that first couple of weeks, but I wasn't really sure they were serious or just wanted to chat up the new guy. I knew both Tommy and Cody got new girlfriends by the third game, a fact they liked to crow about every chance they got. My stomach got tied in knots every time I saw Cody with his arm around Tina, a nice-looking sophomore who hadn't given him the time of day before he was a winning jock. Tommy had actually hooked up with Susan, which surprised everyone since she had been dating a baseball player before him. It was a pretty big coup for the basketball team, one of our own stealing the head cheerleader away from the star baseball player. Tommy's success reflected on the rest of us.

I just couldn't find a girl who made me feel like Cody did.

At first I thought I was safe, everyone else too busy with their own squeeze to notice that I was still stag, but that thought was quickly dispelled. We were on a five-game winning streak, and it looked like there was no stopping us when Tommy took me aside after one Saturday practice to talk.

"So lemme ask you," he said casually, completely different from the open hostility we'd shared a month ago. "There a girl you like?" I felt the panic rush through my limbs like some kind of phantom stroke paralyzing me in place. "Because I never see you with anyone, and I know you've had offers."

I felt myself get light-headed as I realized I wasn't breathing. I shook my head and choked out, "No, no girl." I winced mentally because that was a stupid response. Why did I say girl? I should have just said no and leave it at that. With *no girl* it sounds like *yes, I have someone, but it isn't a girl*, which can only mean a guy. I broke out into a cold sweat as I began to panic. Did I just out myself? Am I in? Was that it, was I gay? I felt my hands shaking as I waited for him to respond.

"Awesome, 'cause Susan said Carol is sweet on you, and she wanted me to find out how you felt about her." The smile on his face conveyed much more than his words could. It was the familiar grin all boys had when talking about girls to other boys—part wolf, part shark, all bullshit as we passed along in a not so subtle code that we were in fact talking about fucking. Most of us had never gotten that close to actual sex before. "She's cute, and I know she's dying to see what's under those trunks," he said playfully, swatting at my crotch. I bent my knees away from the blow; it was one of the things I had become accustomed to with these guys.

A massive number of quasisexual gestures seemed to exist among the guys on the team, and they were seriously messing with my head. Slapping ass, flicking at someone's dick, coming up behind someone and pretending to fuck them, one hand grabbing the shirt, other hand slapping back and forth, and then there was the hand kiss. That was when a guy came at you as if to kiss you, pressed his hand over your mouth and then proceeded to make out with his hand. Let me tell you, the first time someone does this to you, the real challenge is not falling backward on your ass in shock. Cody seemed to love this maneuver, catching me when I was not even close to being ready as he'd lay one on me. Everyone thought it was hilarious every time, because the way I reacted was just straight panic, but not for the reasons they thought.

The last time he'd done it was at a party at Paul's house for our fifth victory. We'd all had a couple of beers, provided by Paul's brother home from the military, who thought every age was the right age to drink. Cody was buzzed, and I had to admit, I was too. He was saying something and then turned, slapped his hand over my mouth, and kissed it. As his tongue licked his hand, my mouth opened by instinct, and I licked his palm. His eyes flew open as we stared at each other across his hand. I swirled my tongue around in a circle as I pressed forward. I wasn't sure what was going through my mind as the guys howled, not realizing what was happening. I opted for the most guy thing I could think of and went to flick his crotch....

And felt my finger bounce off his hard cock.

He jerked back, cursing out loud. I saw him wipe his palm on his shorts, but he didn't say anything other than "You fucker!" to me in response. I laughed, finished my beer, and ducked into the bathroom before my hardness was clear to anyone through my own shorts. I locked the door and leaned against it as I pulled my shorts down and began to stroke my cock heavily. I could smell him on me, and the thought he had been hard while "kissing" me made me cum in less than a minute. I shuddered as I felt the warm liquid drip slowly down my hand. I instantly felt embarrassed and ashamed when I caught my reflection in the mirror. I pulled my shorts up and washed my hands thoroughly, making sure there wasn't any evidence on the tile or counter before I walked back out to the party.

All this rushed through my mind as Tommy laughed at making me flinch. "So can I tell her we're going to double date after the game?" I nodded, not sure why I felt absolutely nothing at the idea, but I somehow knew it was the smart choice to make. "Awesome! That new 3-D thing is playing. We can catch the ten o'clock showing and then grab some IHOP. Sound good?"

Again I nodded, not sure what I was agreeing to.

When the rest of the guys were leaving, Cody caught up to me and gestured at Tommy. "What'd he want?"

"Um," I stammered, for some reason not wanting to tell him I had just agreed to go out with someone else. I swallowed the feeling quickly and said, "Carol asked him if I liked her and if I'd go out with her."

He paused for a second and then asked, "What did you say?"

I looked at him for a moment, not sure what his sudden shift in tone meant. "I said yes. I mean, why wouldn't I, right?"

"Sure," he answered, quickly looking away.

"I mean, you're seeing Tina, right?" I asked, already knowing the answer.

"So what if I am?" he shot back, almost angry.

I wasn't sure how to answer that, so I just shrugged and quipped, "So yeah, it's a date."

"Fine," he said in a clipped tone.

"Fine," I shot back, angry myself now.

"Hope you have a blast," he said as he ran toward the parking lot where his mom was waiting for him to finish practice.

"I will!" I screamed after him and marched off toward the bus stop.

I had no idea why I felt this bad, but I knew I was heartbroken.

I had honestly thought there was no deeper confusion I could wade into than the one I was already in, but that night I lay in bed wondering why Cody had been so angry and why I felt this miserable. The next day Carol met me at my locker and threw her arms around my neck, pulling me down into a hug. "Thankyouthankyouthankyou!" she exclaimed as I hugged her back carefully.

"Um, sure," I said, wondering why this made me feel even worse than before.

"Can I sit with you at lunch?" she asked, her eyes pleading with me silently.

I nodded mutely, not sure how else to answer.

Another squeal of pleasure, and she hugged me again. "I'll see you at lunch!" she cried before skipping away with Susan, who looked back and smiled at me. I closed my locker, not sure why everything had become so fucking confusing.

"Looks cozy," Cody snarked, standing off to the side. I glanced over at him, that feeling of guilt washing over me suddenly.

That guilt burned away to anger almost as quickly. "What the fuck do you care?" I shot back.

"I don't!" he snapped, raising his voice.

"Well, awesome," I said, my voice dropping into a deep growl. "Have fun with Tina."

"Oh, I will," he said, scoffing in my face.

"I bet you will," I retorted, ignoring the way it felt like I was about to blow chunks at any second. We glared at each other for a second, and then the bell rang for class. We took off in opposite directions, neither one willing to look back at the other. By noon I had no idea what we were fighting about, but there was no doubt we were fighting. Tina sat on his lap, which was new since most of the time it was just us guys eating lunch together. He looked like he was making a show of having her there with him, ignoring us completely and trying constantly to kiss her. No one said anything, but it was weird nonetheless. Carol leaned over and whispered, "Are you sure it's okay if I sit here?"

I pulled my eyes off of the happy couple and nodded. "No reason you shouldn't be here," I said loudly enough for him to hear. I'm not sure why, but I slipped my hand around her waist and pulled her closer. She didn't resist, in fact she seemed happy about it, though all I did was watch him for a reaction. I caught him looking over at us for a second before going back to making out.

I pulled her closer and seemed ready to kiss her myself when Tommy looked over at Cody and asked, "What the fuck is up with you?" Cody paused and looked over at him. "If you want to make out, take her behind a backstop or to your car, man. No one came to school to see you try to swallow your girl's tongue." Cody blushed, and Tina shrank away, like she suddenly realized where she and Cody were and what they were doing.

Tommy shot a stare over at me. "And if you're about to start… don't." Carol inched away from me slowly as Tommy went on, "I'm not sure what the fuck is going on, but it isn't happening at this table." Tina stood up and said something quietly to Cody before walking off.

"See you after school?" Carol asked me as she stood herself. I nodded absently as she leaned down and pecked my cheek. She walked away, leaving Cody and me staring angrily at each other.

"Look, girls, if you two are going to fight? Just fucking fight and get it over with," Tommy said, going back to his lunch. "But get it over with by Friday, because if you two fuck up the game, I will personally take you both out back and beat you to death." We both looked at him, and he nodded at us. "I will fucking beat you to death. That's a promise."

Cody and I looked at each other and then down at our shoes underneath the table.

"Get out of here and make up," Tommy ordered. We looked at him in shock, and he nodded. "No joke, get lost."

We both stood up slowly, waiting for him to say it was a joke or something, but he was deadly serious. We walked away from the table in confusion, neither one of us knowing what to say. We silently made our way to the gym, which was thankfully empty this time of the day. A ball was jammed between the rim and backboard, and Cody looked up at it and then to me.

"Well, there's no way I can reach it," he said with half a grin.

I jumped up and pulled it down. The sound of it hitting the boards as I bounce-passed it to him echoed around us. He dribbled the ball a few times and then fell back and attempted a three-pointer. The ball bounced off the rim and began to wobble away from the basket before I leapt up and tipped it in. I passed the ball to him, and he checked it back to me as I leaned in and began to press toward the other basket. He instantly saw the seriousness in my face and moved to intercept me with both hands out in defense.

In that moment everything else faded away in our life, and we were caught in the game. I wasn't mad, I wasn't jealous, I wasn't sad. I was playing basketball, so everything was perfect. I surged forward as he moved with me, trying to corral me in. "Don't make me go through you," I said, grinning at him.

"Bring it, son," he answered with a grin of his own.

I faked to the left and then instantly peeled off to the right before he'd realized I was no longer there. I pumped three more steps, setting up for my jump… and suddenly Cody was there in front of me before I could check my forward momentum. We collapsed into each other instantly, his arms moving around me as the ball went flying away from us. We landed with an audible thud as gravity took hold of us, yanked us out of the sky, and we hit the floor solidly. We skidded a couple of inches and burst out laughing. I was very aware I was lying on top of him, and that his arms were still around my waist. I looked down at him and felt the smile slipping off my lips.

"I'm sorry," I said quietly, not sure what I was apologizing for, but I did know I was indeed apologetic.

"Me too," he murmured as my face moved down to his.

"Come over after your date?" he asked against my lips.

I nodded as I eased my tongue slowly between his lips. I was amazed to feel his tongue slip past mine.

It was a quick kiss, but what it lacked in length, it made up for in passion. He stared up at me with a huge smile. "Fag."

I ground my crotch against his. It was blatantly obvious we were both hard. "Queer."

We both laughed again as I carefully lifted myself off him. I held my hand out and pulled him to his feet. "Can you spend the night?" he asked as we brushed ourselves off, willing our erections to go down.

"I can ask my dad," I answered.

"Sweet," he said, flashing me a grin that in no way helped me become unaroused.

I patted my hair down as he grabbed the ball and tossed it at me. His eyes glanced at the hoop and then back to me. I took three steps and flew at the basket, wedging the ball back where we had found it. "That is so hot," he said as I landed.

I felt a blush rise to my cheeks as we walked out of the gym.

If anything of importance passed between that moment and Friday, I have no idea. I was lost in a haze of emotions and hormones that made me as close to drunk as I'd ever been without drinking. Every day Cody and I joked and roughhoused, looking to the world like a pair of normal, all-American jocks. At night I would furiously masturbate to the thought of us kissing before I went to bed.

I, of course, said nothing to my dad about any of this. I told him I had a date after the game with a girl and then was going to spend the night at Cody's and nothing more. If he had any doubts that the main point of the night was me getting to Cody's house as quickly as possible, he didn't give a hint of it. Again, from his point of view it must have been the most normal thing in the world for his son to do. Play a basketball game, go out with a girl, and then spend the night with a friend afterward. Just seeing it in plain English, it looks completely straight to me. After all, we were both seeing girls, were best friends, and played on the same sports team.

What could possibly be gay about that?

This time it seemed different to me than what had happened with Joshua. I was completely unconfused by the way I felt about Cody. The darkened shame I had always felt with Joshua didn't raise its ugly head. This being with Cody felt exactly like what every guy described having a crush on a girl. Every thought I had was about Cody; every image I saw when I closed my eyes centered on him. Even though I had more than enough sexual thoughts about him to fill my life, this felt purer somehow. It wasn't lust, though I lusted after him, and not infatuation, even though I was infatuated with him. There was only one word that encompassed everything I was feeling at that moment, only one single concept that covered all of this to my teenage mind.

I was in love with Cody Franks.

It sounded insane, but it was how I felt. I was walking ten feet off the ground all the way up to the night of the game. I was on the court in a huddle when Tommy snapped his fingers in front of my face. "Hey, retard, is our basketball game interrupting your night?"

I looked around, and I focused my thoughts back to the game.

We were behind by eight points with less than twenty-four seconds on the clock. The opposing team had a pretty devastating offense and had learned the only way to keep us out of the game was to outscore us. I had been floating through the game not even paying attention to what I was supposed to be doing. I nodded at him, trying to put my game face on, but he just shook his head and rolled his eyes. "Okay look, we have to push these fuckers hard. We can tie this up if we're lucky, but if they score again, we're hosed."

"I got it," I said quickly, making sure not to look anyone in the eyes. I knew if I looked at Tommy or Cody, I'd lose it because one would make me feel like shit and the other would make me smile. "Just get me the ball."

No one said anything for a few seconds, and the ref blew the whistle calling us back. "Okay, Danny's got the ball. Everyone else back him up."

We broke on "Tigers," and I saw Cody holding the ball, waiting to throw it in. He nodded once at me and then looked away at the other side of the court. I moved the opposite way, and he tossed me the ball without ever looking back at me. The guy guarding him was too busy watching his face and ignored his hands. The ball bounced right into my palms. Without a second's hesitation, I popped up and tossed it in for three.

The crowd exploded as we scrambled into position and the other team threw it in. I moved next to the guy they were most likely going to pass it to and waited. I said under my breath just loud enough for the guy to hear, "Touch the ball and I'll end you."

He looked over his shoulder and saw my chest and then looked up to my face.

Which was when I darted in front of him and took the ball. Another shot and we were only three points behind. The other team began to wake up, now realizing I hadn't been even close to playing the entire night. They tightened up their defense as they looked to throw the ball back into play. I glanced over at Tommy and nodded, and he returned it with a grin. This time they passed it to the closest guy, not daring for a longer throw. I hovered around the ball holder. A five-year-old would have seen he was looking for an open man. He waited for a man to move beside him and passed it laterally, which was when I made a clumsy attempt at the ball.

The other guy tossed the ball in the other direction as I stumbled past him... and found Tommy waiting to cut him off. Once he had the ball he moved to the right, losing the guy who had lunged at him to block, and went up for his shot. The ball seemed to move in slow motion as it sailed over our head toward the hoop in a perfect arc. Everyone stopped as they watched the sphere move closer and closer to deciding the game's fate.

Now I don't know a thing about geometry. I am dumb as a rock when it comes to math and calculating radiuses and circumferences and all that garbage. I squeaked by in anything that dealt with numbers, but there was a thing I knew better than anyone else, and it was basketball. I knew just by looking at a ball, based on the speed and angle of the shot, if it would go in or not. I knew if it would hit the rim and bounce off. I knew if it was going to tap off the backboard and roll off. I just knew. It was like I could see everywhere the ball should go to make a basket and then compare it to where it was headed.

Tommy was about to blow that shot.

It looked perfect. I could tell everyone else thought it was a done deal, and he had just tied up the game. Because of that, I was the only one moving toward the basket instead of looking. The ball hit the rim and its forward spin pushed it against the backboard. Along the same curve it had used coming in, it started flying back to the court. Everyone else began to move at once, but I was already airborne.

The crowd went wild as I rebounded the ball and sank the basket.

As soon as my sneakers hit the boards, I turned around and formed a T with my hands. The ref called the time out as I looked up at the clock. We were one point down and had less than four seconds left, and they had the ball. We moved over to the sidelines and huddled around the coach. "Any thoughts besides hope we get the ball?" he asked.

No one looked up as we tried to catch our breath for a moment.

There was no time to try to steal the ball away. Four seconds would be over before the guy even pivoted with the ball. We were screwed, and it was my fault. I felt like shit as I saw the rest of my teammates look down dejectedly. I glanced out across the court to the other team's bench and saw the guy I had whispered to before glaring back over at me. He was pissed I'd gotten in his head and wanted a little payback, it seemed.

"Cody, guard seventeen," I said, coming back to the huddle. Everyone looked at me as I explained. "Trash talk him a little. He's already wound up some."

"How does that get us the ball?" Tommy asked.

The coach seemed to get it but didn't look thrilled. "Franks, you can piss anyone off. Use that power for good."

Cody grinned and looked over at the guy and nodded. "I can do that," he said.

"What do we do?" Tommy asked, his voice a little pissed.

"Hope that guy thinks Cody is as annoying as we do," I said, smiling as I put my hand in. "Tigers on three."

We broke, and Cody moved over toward the guy.

I would have paid cash money to hear what he said to him, but within seconds he had spun around and pushed Cody as hard he could. Cody slammed to the floor and slid back a few inches, the grin on his face never wavering.

The ref blew his whistle twice and called a foul against the guy. Cody had two free throws now with the clock stopped. You could see the life drain out of the other team when they realized what had just happened and how close they had just come to beating us. We lined up while Cody bounced the ball a couple of times and made the first shot. We were tied now. Even if he missed this shot we'd go into overtime and have four minutes to make up for a miserable showing so far.

He bounced the ball twice and then held it in his hands. His eyes glanced over to me, and I smiled back at him. The corner of his mouth curled up as he looked back at the basket and tossed the ball in what was easily the sexiest free throw I had ever witnessed. The crowd erupted into cheers as I ran at him and hugged him tightly. He hugged me back and tensed for a moment, and I picked him up and twirled him around as the rest of the team engulfed us. From the outside it looked like a team celebrating a close win, but inside our arms it was so much more.

We were screaming for our victory in the locker room when the coach came in and shouted at us to shut up. "You're happy about that shit?" We froze in place as the cheers deflated on our lips. "You are seriously going to celebrate that fucktard of a win?"

Cody was behind me and called out, "Hell yeah!"

The rest of us joined him in laughter and glee. The coach just shook his head and said, "Sunday practice, 9:00 am! No excuses." Normally such a pronouncement would have caused a cacophony of jeers, but at that moment, Sunday was a million miles away.

As we changed out, Cody leaned in toward me and nudged me. "Thanks for that."

I nudged him back. "For what? You have the biggest mouth on the team," I said, grinning widely at him. "Who else would I have picked?"

Cody jumped at me, tackling me to the ground as we burst out laughing. "Who has the big mouth now?" he crowed as he tickled me. I cried for mercy as the celebration exploded around us. You could hear the guys in the shower badly singing a rap song as two others guys stood in just their trunks bumping chests. As I wrestled with Cody, Tommy walked over and stood above us.

"If you two girls are done making out, we do have plans."

We looked up and saw him standing in just a towel, his hair still wet from the shower. Cody glanced down at me and smiled evilly as he yanked the towel free. Tommy cursed, covered his junk, and backed away. We both howled with hysterical laughter and tossed the towel to the side and retreated. Our abs ached from laughing. We got into the shower and quickly rinsed the game off us. Tommy was already in jeans when I got back to my locker. Cody dried off next to me and asked in a low voice, "So give me a call when you get home?" I nodded and pulled my boxers on. "I can swing by and pick you up since Tommy ain't gonna drop you off at my house."

"I can just wait wherever we're eating," I offered as I slipped on my jeans. "Easier than you trying to get on base."

Cody leaned forward and asked Tommy, "Hey, where you guys going to eat after the movie?"

Tommy looked over at us, and his eyes narrowed for a couple of seconds. "IHOP, probably. Why?"

"I'm crashing at his house tonight," I said, pulling on a fresh shirt.

Tommy didn't say anything until he finished combing his hair. "IHOP, unless the girls want something else," he said stiffly.

I looked at Cody questioningly, and he shrugged silently back at me. "Okay, I'll just wait at IHOP and give you a call when we're done."

"Sweet," Cody replied with a grin. He looked away quickly, but I saw the blush on his cheeks. When I leaned over to tie my shoes, I fought to suppress my grin as well.

The air had turned colder than I expected, and I wrapped my arms around myself while Tommy and I walked to his car. I shivered as we got into his Mustang. "Jesus! Colder than a witch's tit," I complained as Tommy warmed up the car. He didn't say anything in response, but he looked upset. "You okay?" I asked, not sure what he'd be upset about.

For a few seconds he continued to stare down at the pedals, and I had a feeling I needed to repeat the question. However, slowly, he started to talk. "Look, Danny, you're a great guy, and personally I don't care what you do in your free time." He paused just in front of the obvious "but" in the next sentence. "But Carol is a nice girl, and I really like Susan, so I don't want to see her hurt."

"I don't understand," I said hesitantly, not sure what he was going on about. "Why would I hurt Carol—"

"I saw you and Cody in the gym the other day," he interrupted.

I felt the seat drop out from beneath me, and my mind began to spin. I wondered if Tommy'd be upset if I blew chunks in his car.

"I don't care what you guys do in your own time...," he said and then stopped. "Look, you're a badass player, and this is easily going to be the best season we've ever had, so we owe you." Then he looked straight at me. "But there is no way the guys are going to accept you and him together. Period." I felt like the world beyond the car was spinning, dragging the car with it. From someplace beyond my head, I heard him talking. "If you guys are going to do... whatever you're doing, you need to be more careful." As an afterthought he added, "And I don't want Carol going out with you and then finding out you're...."

"I got it." I choked as I struggled to get a full breath of air. It was too hot, almost stifling in the car suddenly as I rested a hand against the door. "I won't... I'm not...." But I couldn't find the words.

"Hey, dude, I'm not threatening you," he explained quickly. "My brother is gay, so I'm okay with you. I just don't want her to—"

"I'm not gay!" I half said, half cried, opening the door and falling out of the car. The cold brought some of my senses back to me, and I heard him call out behind me and realized I was on my feet, somehow.... I stumbled across the parking lot, no idea where I was running to.

But I sure knew what I was running away from.

CHAPTER FIVE:
GAME FACE

WE CAME in third place that season, no thanks to the other teams.

Our cohesion came apart at the seams the very next game and was mostly my fault. I never called Cody that night, and in fact didn't say one word to him until the next Monday. When he approached me and tried to ask me what had happened, I just made an excuse and headed to the office. I changed most of my schedule around so I didn't have four classes with him anymore. That lunch I didn't bother to show up at the table, instead eating in an empty classroom as I dodged the inevitable.

It came in the locker room as we changed for practice. The look of hurt and confusion on his face was like razor blades moving up my arm. I just ignored him as I tied my shoes and tried to slip away from him before everyone else walked out. As I turned away from him, I saw we were alone, and I cursed under my breath as he grabbed the back of my jersey.

"Hey, what's wrong?" he asked, his voice laced with emotion.

I sighed and refused to turn around. "Someone saw us in the gym, dude." His hand dropped away. "We need to stay away from each other." I waited a five count; when he didn't say anything, I walked out to the court. It was the last time we ever talked alone again. The coach tried to whip us back into line, but the magic was gone. I'm not sure how much the rest of the team knew; almost nothing, probably, since we weren't openly mocked or ridiculed as being fags. Tommy was good to his word. I never heard one rumor about me or Cody, which was a good thing. I spent the rest of the season and then the school year in quiet misery.

My dad never asked specifically what had happened, but I think he might have guessed what was wrong. The third week into me coming home from practice and just lying quietly in my room, he came in and asked me the only question he ever asked on the subject.

"You okay?" he asked, sitting on the edge of my bed. I nodded but said nothing. "You ever go out with that girl?" I shook my head no and forced my face to remain completely inexpressive. We sat in silence for a few moments, the room dark as I listened to him breathing. "What happened to that boy you were friends with?" I refused to look at him as I said nothing. He sighed as he got up and shook his head. "Life sucks, Danny," he announced out of nowhere. "It sucks even more without friends... or happiness."

I no longer had any idea what happiness felt like.

The school year crawled to an end, and the team drifted even further apart as Tommy and the seniors prepared to graduate. It was a few days before the end of the year when Tommy walked up to my locker as I was stashing my books. "Got a second?" he asked. I nodded, though my stomach quietly began to turn itself into knots. We walked into an empty classroom, and he closed the door behind him. "Look, man...." He ran a hand through his hair as he seemed to struggle for the right words. "I don't know what went down between Cody and you, but I know I had something to do with that, and I'm sorry."

My face could have been etched out of marble. Blinking felt like too much expression.

"But I don't want to be the cause of you guys never talking again." I didn't say anything, and he gave me a look. "Seriously, man, if you don't talk to him again, you'll never forgive yourself."

I sighed and held up a hand to cut him off. "Fine, Tommy, I promise to talk to him over the summer, okay?"

I saw the look of confusion on Tommy's face, and he saw the lack of understanding on mine. "Dude, his family is moving. Today is his last day here."

I'm not sure if I pushed him aside in my rush to get out the door, but I wouldn't be surprised if I had. His locker stood empty, the door hanging open, and I took off for the front parking circle. By the time I got out front of the school, I saw his mom's car just starting to pull away. I saw Cody in the backseat look at me through the rear window, and I raised my right hand, waved—I think—and, when the car kept going, lowered my arm.

If I hadn't been in front of the school and dozens of people, I would have broken down and begun to cry. I have no idea how long I stood there watching the car drive away. I knew there was almost no one around by the time I got to the bus stop, which meant it was sometime after school. I sat and tried not to break down on the bus as I listened to music on my iPod. I didn't know what felt worse: the fact we had been caught by Tommy, the fact I had blown Cody off for the rest of the year, or the fact I was never going to see him again.

When I got home, I flew into the door with the intention of calling Cody's house and saying something. My hand hovered over the phone for almost a minute, while both sides of my brain argued about what I could say. I didn't know if I should apologize or just beg for forgiveness. All I knew was that I felt abjectly miserable and guilty and stupid. I looked up when I passed the living room, and I saw my dad, talking to a stranger.

"Danny?" my dad called out. "Can you come in here, please?"

I felt my mouth go dry as I backtracked a couple of steps and bought myself a second to think as I closed the front door tight. My mind scrambled through every movement I'd ever made. Ever, starting from where I was standing and telescoping back as far as Germany. I searched frantically for something I had done wrong enough that a visit from a strange adult might be warranted. I couldn't find anything besides Joshua that was that bad. I sat down on the free chair and tried not to feel like I was a six-year-old waiting for a spanking.

My dad turned toward me and looked me directly in the eyes, effectively shutting out the other man. "I want you to answer his question as honestly as possible." I nodded, though my eyes flicked toward the stranger and then back to my dad. "Are you serious about basketball?" I instantly began to nod again, but he held a hand up to stop me. "I don't mean for just playing and having fun. I mean for real." That caused me to pause. "Is this something you possibly want to do for the rest of your life, or is it just a hobby that you're enjoying for the time being?"

I didn't understand the full complexity of the question, but I could sense how earnest he was and how important my answer would be.

I didn't have the proper words to tell anyone how much basketball meant to me, but just as I always had every other time in my life I'd been asked that question, my heart knew all the words.

I had spent most of my life so far sailing somewhere between two coasts, the one who I was and the other who I was supposed to be, and the journey was driving me slowly insane. More times than not, I had spent endless stretches of time stranded on those still waters, slowly drifting, with no clear direction to pick. I was waiting for a great gust of wind to choose for me once and for all and push me in the direction I needed to go. But the older I grew, the more it dawned on me that the decision was going to be up to me. Which way? How to get there? Where *is* "there"?

The only time I never felt like that was when I was playing basketball.

The very moment my fingers touched that ball, I was both who I am and who I was supposed to be, and there was never a doubt in my mind about that as long as I was on the court.

If someone were to take basketball away from me, I had no idea what I'd end up doing. More accurately, I had no idea who I'd end up becoming. Which pretty much answered the question for me.

"It's my life," I answered, not realizing at the time the dual meaning behind my words.

My dad didn't blink as he scrutinized my face and thought over my words more thoroughly than I could ever remember him doing. "Fair enough," he said, leaning back in his chair. "This is Mr. O'Keefe from Nike, and he has an offer for you."

"Nike?" I repeated, confused.

He smiled and nodded. "Hi, Danny. It's a pleasure to finally meet you. Call me Jim. I've seen six of your games this season, and I have to admit I was pretty impressed."

"You saw us play?" I asked, completely floored that anyone outside of my school and our competitors had seen us play.

He nodded and flipped open a folder he had on his lap and began to skim it. "Decent scoring, impressive rebounds, but what really got my attention was your assists." He looked up at me and asked, "Do you know what the percentage of points scored this season by your team was directly attributed to an assist from you?" I shook my head. I didn't know anyone even kept track of stats like that. "I didn't think so. Suffice it to say the number the Tigers make drops drastically every time you walk off the court." He put the folder back down on the table and leaned in toward me. "We'd like to invite you to join us this summer at our skills camp."

I blinked a few times. "Join who?"

He chuckled. "Nike sponsors a skills camp every year for high school players we think have potential to be a lot more, to go further than the average player. It's by invitation only, and trust me when I say not a lot of freshmen get invited."

I thought he was going to say more, but he was waiting for me to say something. After a few seconds I asked, "How many?"

He looked confused now. "How many what?"

"How many freshmen were invited this year?"

"Including you?" I nodded. "One." His smile said it all.

I looked at my dad, whose face was as unreadable as a bar of soap. I looked back to the guy. "How much does it cost?"

"We can afford it," my dad stated. I looked at him because the tone of his voice was sterner than normal. "*If* you're serious about it."

"I am," I answered quickly. And all of a sudden, I was babbling. "I really am. I was already worried how I was going to stay in shape this summer. I don't know anyone who plays so I was just going to try to find pickup games." His expression didn't waver. "Please, Dad! I want to do this." Nothing. "I need to do this." More nothing.

"We do need to know quickly," the man said, gathering up his stuff. "The spots are extremely limited."

My eyes widened as I silently begged my dad.

My dad stood with the man. "He's in."

I tried not to jump up and cheer as they shook hands. "Excellent!" Mr. O'Keefe said as he dug in his briefcase and handed my dad a large envelope. "Here is the admission packet. Send it in by the end of the week, and you'll receive a registration packet in the mail." The man looked at me and then looked up higher to meet my gaze. "You have a gift, Danny." He held out his hand. "We look forward to helping it flourish."

I probably almost squeezed his hand off as I pumped his arm up and down and gushed, "Thank you *so* much, Mr. O'Keefe! This is a dream come true! I won't let you guys down!"

He laughed as he extracted his hand and rubbed the blood back into his white fingers. "Trust me, son, just show up and play as well as I saw you this season, and you won't let anyone down." He tried to get around me, but I didn't register it. I was much too busy gushing and babbling mentally.

"Danny," my dad said in a low voice, "let the man out. You're blocking the door." I scrambled out of the way, and they both smiled at me. "Thank you, sir." I followed them the few steps to the front door because I didn't have a clue what else to do.

The man shook his head as my dad opened the door. "No, Danny. Thank you."

I had never been so damn happy in my entire life. Dad stepped out of the house to have a few words with Mr. O'Keefe, while I stood in the entry, smiling and then really smiling. When Dad came back inside, he slipped by me and headed to the kitchen, no doubt wanting to be safe when everything that had just happened sank in.

I finally exploded in exhilaration, letting off several whoops of absolute joy as I danced around the living room like a maniac. My dad sat at the kitchen table thumbing through the papers, no doubt learning all he could about it before he put a pen to paper. I stopped midleap and looked over at him. "Where is it?"

"Florida," he answered, not looking up from his reading.

"I'm going to Florida to learn basketball?" I asked myself out loud, completely blown away by just the thought.

"Looks that way," he said, turning one paper over and examining the fine print on it in detail.

I instantly went back to dancing. "I'm going to Florida! I'm going to Florida!"

This went on for some time. Possibly two days.

Over an hour later, I had settled down and was sitting across from my dad, looking at the paperwork as well, as we waited for the pizza to arrive. I was scanning over the pictures of the guys who were pictured playing the game in years past when my dad put the papers down and looked over at me. I glanced back over the paper I was browsing and waited for him to say we needed to talk. "So we need to talk."

I tried not to smile as I put the paper down.

"I am not accusing you of anything, and I don't want you to think you're in trouble." And that feeling of sitting in the seat of shame returned. "But this is a big thing." I nodded, knowing he was nowhere near the point he wanted to make. "Places like this are where you start making a name for yourself; the people who are in charge and who'll be teaching you are professionals in basketball." Another nod, because we were getting closer but not quite there. "That means when you go there, you're going to have to be on your best behavior." Slower nod. "That also includes anything someone else might find offensive or inappropriate." I felt a chill move through me as it began to dawn on me what he was talking about. "I'm not saying whatever happened with this boy on the team was like it was with Joshua, but nonetheless, there was something odd about it." I strained to hear him over the pounding of my heart as it struggled to burst free from my chest. "That's all well and good, but if something like that was to happen at a place like that and it was to get out...."

"I get it," I said, my voice sounding to me as if it were from very far away. "It won't happen again, sir." The "sir" was a throwback to when I was far younger and still practiced the rule that politeness trumped everything.

"I'm not implying anything, Danny. I'm just.... If that boy ended up saying something...."

The fact Cody had left hit me again, and the elation of the past few hours disappeared completely. "He's gone," I mumbled just as our doorbell rang. "He moved away."

My dad got up, pulling his wallet out. "Well, it's for the best, right?"

I didn't answer. Instead I stood up and stumbled off to my room like a zombie while my dad paid for the pizza. I heard the front door close, and he called my name. I fell down on my bed face-first, wanting more than I ever had in my entire life for the world to swallow me up. He knocked on my door and cracked it open. "The pizza is here."

"I'm not hungry," I said, my voice muffled in my pillow.

He was silent for a long time. I wasn't sure if he was still there or not and at that moment I didn't care. I had honestly thought we'd moved past this point in our life where he assumed I was going to grope random strangers while they slept. I really never imagined us ever coming back to this impasse in our relationship, but here we were. Him judging me and me feeling like absolute shit about it.

I knew I was crying again but I refused to let anyone else see my tears. It has been one of the few promises I've made to myself I've kept.

The next few days passed in a blur. My sadness seemed to bottom out and became a constant state of background misery that began to morph into numbness. The school year ended not with a bang but with a whimper. I told no one about my invitation to the camp, partly because it would have sounded like bragging but more because I didn't have anyone to tell the news to anymore. Tommy invited me to his graduation party, but I refused, not sure what I'd do at a party full of guys who were three years older than me and heading off to college.

I even felt guilty for being so excited when the registration came in the mail and the dance of joy began anew, this time in the kitchen.

However, from that moment on I didn't have time to be sad. From the second I filled out the top line of the first form to the moment I stepped off the plane in Florida, it was as if only a few hours had passed instead of a week and a half. My dad took me to get new clothes, since I had already outgrown the ones I started school with. I bought new sneakers, an actual gym bag since I usually carried my stuff in a backpack, and to my surprise a brand-new electric razor of my own. My dad seemed to get a little weird about this, saying as the lady ran his credit card, "I still remember buying diapers for you."

I was two inches taller than him by then. Patting him on the shoulder, I said, in as reassuring a voice as I could, "And one day I'll be buying them for you."

He elbowed me in the gut when I burst out laughing.

We sat at the airport terminal waiting for my plane to board, neither one of us knowing what to say. "So you have money, right?" Dad asked, breaking the silence. I nodded. "And you brought your cell charger?" Another nod. "Remember, no matter how much someone may rag you on the court, do not lose your temper with—"

"Dad," I said, cutting him off. "I'll be okay, I promise."

He shook his head when he realized he was rambling. "This is the first time we've ever been apart. Give me a break, Danny."

I saw the worry in his expression and realized in shock that I wasn't worried at all.

I reached over and hugged him tight. "I'll be fine, Dad." He hugged me back, and I could sense he didn't want to stop. Thankfully they called my flight, and we had to let go.

I didn't feel worried until I turned around at the gate and waved good-bye to him. The reality hit me then. Dad wasn't going to be five minutes away in case something went wrong. This was going to be the first time I had ever flown without an adult. I knew rationally that Dad was just thirty-two, but for some reason he looked older to me. Out of nowhere, I felt the little kid in me completely freak. I dropped my bag and raced over to him. This time I was the one who didn't want to let go until he said quietly to me, "I'm proud of you, Danny. You're going to be fine."

I really had believed I was going to get out of the state without crying.

I sat on the plane and looked out the window and imagined I could see my dad looking out of the terminal at me, and it made me feel better. By the time we took off, I was okay again. This was an opportunity of a lifetime, and I wasn't going to let being all weepy because I was a daddy's boy screw it up.

I fell asleep as I usually did during a flight and woke up in another stage of my life.

It was the first time I was met at the gate by a guy holding up a card with my name on it. I felt instantly more important. The man led me to a small pizza place in the middle of the airport, where he told me I'd be waiting for the rest of the people showing up today to arrive. There were already four other giant people sitting at a table; one was watching the TV as the other three fiddled with their cell phones. "We have forty-five minutes before our last person arrives. Try not to wander off," the man informed me just before he walked off.

I was unsure if I should go and sit with the other guys or order pizza first, but, as it did most of the time, food won out. I ordered two slices of pizza, each one as big as my head, and a bottle of water before I joined the other guys at the table. Four pairs of eyes looked over at me, three guys went back to their phones, and the fourth smiled and held out his hand. "You have to be one of us," he stated as I put my food down.

I smiled back instantly. I'd never been one of anyone before.

"Depends," I said, shaking back. "Is this the table for ridiculously good-looking guys?" I tried my best *Zoolander* impression and earned a half glare from the cell phone guys plus a barking laugh from the nice one.

"Classic movie!" he said, slapping his leg.

"Right?" I said, sitting down. "I'm Danny."

He nodded and began pointing at the other guys. "That's John, Levon, Ricky, and I'm Nathan."

"What high school you guys go to?" I asked before taking a bite.

You could hear a record scratching somewhere in the background.

After a few seconds of silence, Nate asked, *"You're* in high school?"

I nodded around the bite.

"What year?" Levon called over, putting his cell phone down for the first time.

"Um, just finished freshman year," I replied, now completely self-aware, since the entire crew of guys was looking at me.

The other two guys stopped texting.

Nathan's eyes were wide as he exclaimed, "Wait, you're a fucking freshman?" I nodded again, trying to swallow. He burst out laughing and announced to Levon, "He's on *my* team!" When the rest of them began laughing as well, I realized they were laughing with me, not at me.

It was the coolest feeling of my life.

We spent the next hour shooting the shit, talking about basketball in a way I'd never talked about it before. They were easily as in love with the game as I was, so the level of discussion was intense. I learned that Ricky and Nathan were both starting college in Texas, which was incredible to me since I hadn't quite grasped how big Texas really was. Levon played for Kansas State, and this was his second invitation to the camp, which made him kind of a celebrity since being asked only once was a feat in itself.

The fifth guy was a high school senior who had committed to ASU, and it was obvious he was one of the younger guys who had been invited to the camp. Nate took great pride in telling him I was a high school freshman and that I was from Texas also. I didn't have the heart to tell him I wasn't from Texas; it just felt awesome to be part of a group for once.

We all piled into a stretch minivan just barely big enough to hold us all. I felt slightly out of place since the rest of the guys were dressed in training sweats in their school colors with zippers up the legs, making them look like they were ready to step onto the court and play at any second. I was in jeans with a pullover that made me feel like I had showed up for a formal party way underdressed.

As soon as we left the airport, the other guys slipped their iPods on, obviously trying to seem like this was old game to them. I, on the other hand, looked around like a seven-year-old on the way to Disneyland. Nathan, who had sat next to me, elbowed me and whispered, "We seem to be the only ones who thinks this is badass."

"I know!" I hissed back, obviously talking way too loudly to be whispering. Levon sent us a withering glare and then went back to his cool game. We both burst out laughing. I knew I was going to enjoy myself immensely this summer.

We were assigned rooms once we got to the complex. Nathan and I were given different rooms, but we quickly found our respective roommates and switched things around so we could share a room. Once we found our floor, we raced to the room after he called out from the elevator that the last one there had to sleep on the floor. We pounded down the hallway. He was taller than me by a few inches, but it was obvious he was as unsteady with his legs as I was. I don't know how it is for normal people, but let me give you some wisdom from those of us whose legs are too long for their own good. The human body can balance well enough when everything is the right size, but when you make legs as long as we had, they become ungainly over long distances. Short bursts across a court, piece of cake; down a hall as fast as you can, train wreck. We tripped over each other as we stumbled to the door. We both hit it at the same time, laughing like loons as we fought to shove our key cards into the slot.

The door next to us opened up and an older boy stuck his head out. He shot us an angry look. "Will you two fools keep it down?"

Nate and I tried to swallow our laughs like two kids getting caught by their grumpy father. Both of us were about to explode when Nathan finally got the key card to work. He opened the door, and we fell inside. Once the door was closed, we let out roaring bursts of laughter as we threw our bags on the two beds assigned us. We found the outraged neighbor so funny, it took us minutes to compose ourselves and take stock of the room.

The room was completely epic.

The beds were huge, which we appreciated given the fact that each of us was tall enough to have altitude instead of height. Mounted against the far wall was a wide-screen TV that scrolled information for the hotel and basketball camp. It was bigger than any three TVs my dad had ever owned and probably had better resolution than all of them combined as well. Nike had obviously spared no expense for the room, which made me wonder again how much my dad had paid for me to have this privilege.

"You hungry?" Nate asked, looking over the room service menu.

"I am never not hungry," I informed him as I peeked over his shoulder.

"Burgers?" he asked, picking up the phone.

"Hell yeah!" I answered, looking for the remote.

"Man after my own heart," he said as he waited for them to pick up.

I felt something inside me react, and it was instantly followed by a mental voice that sounded a lot like my dad screaming, *Do not start to have feelings for Nathan!*

I'd given myself a mental face full of cold water, and all the mirth and enjoyment I had just been feeling drained away slowly. I found the remote and fell back onto my bed, quietly looking through the channels to see what sports channels they had. Nate ordered us dinner and pushed his bag off his bed to lie down also. "They have ESPN4?" he asked, marveling.

"I didn't even know ESPN *had* a 4," I said, switching over to see what was on.

I stayed distant for the rest of the night.

Nate said he went to high school in Houston and had just signed to A&M after being named MVP two years in a row on his high school team. He said he had been approached by schools in Tennessee, Florida, and Kansas before settling on A&M. I asked him why, and he just grinned as he answered, "Because they're the best school in the nation."

I didn't know it at the time, but he had just delivered the best pitch for the school anyone would say to me.

We went to bed and woke up hip deep in work. The camp wasn't a course in how to play basketball—the assumption was that everyone already knew that. Basketball camp was focused on playing basketball well. A series of drills was set up, at first to gauge each person's level of expertise and then to refine it. Those first two days were the hardest days of my life. My dad had fed me horror stories about boot camp and each night as I fell into bed, almost unable to walk myself into the shower, I wondered if he had felt anything like this. The only saving grace was that Nate was as beat as I was, and he had been playing four years of high school ball already.

I was the youngest person at the camp, and that put me in a difficult position.

On one hand, I knew the least about playing of anyone else there. I had accumulated the shortest amount of time on court, which meant I had the most to learn. Yet, since I was on the verge of sixteen, it meant the professionals expected me to do something amazing to justify my being there. I don't know what that was, but I do know the first week or so, I didn't produce. I got yelled at constantly by the coaches, by the trainers, and by the other players. I was so tripped up that I literally fell one day trying to follow the directions of two different people. The entire time I refused to let it get to me. Gone were the days of getting frustrated and throwing a fit. I couldn't afford to cry and beat my fists on the boards. Instead I kept my game face on, making sure no emotion slipped through while on the court.

As we became adjusted to the grueling workload, we began to have more and more conscious time at night, which meant socializing. I had never been good at the socializing game. Again I found myself surrounded by a pack of guys who were so obviously alpha males, it was comical. The lengths they went through to show their dominance over each other in one form or another was at best hilarious and at worst daunting. The more I watched, the more I became aware I wasn't like them. Don't get me wrong, I wasn't girly or anything. I just didn't feel the need to prove myself outside of a basketball court.

I'm not sure if it was my age or the fact I had no experience playing college ball, but I was quickly singled out as different and the guy who needed to prove the most to the rest of them. I was a month away from sixteen, six three, and had no social skills to speak of. I felt like I was everything that was Not Cool all bottled up in one person, and I thought everyone could see it. The one-up contests started with arm wrestling, a game I had never played before and lost at rather quickly and spectacularly. We then moved on to sports stats and, after that, to girls. I'm not sure how that ranked in their hierarchy—physical strength, sports knowledge, and then female conquests—but it seemed to matter to them.

I thought there was nothing to be ashamed of about saying I was a virgin. After all, I didn't know any other freshman who had actually done it with a girl yet. I mean, sure, there was talk, but guys knew when most guys talked, it was bullshit. The Unspoken Guy Code said we never called a guy on it unless his claims were just too much. For some reason, though, me admitting I'd never had sex was the funniest thing nearly everyone in the lounge had heard. The laughter was obviously at me this time, and it hurt. The only person not laughing was Nate, and for that I was grateful. I wanted to just bolt upstairs and lock myself in the room, but I knew instinctively to run was to admit defeat. Like a pack of wolves, they would simply pounce on me from behind, and the rest of my time here would be spent being the butt of many, many jokes.

I didn't know what to say, and I suppose my embarrassment was all over my face, because Nathan spoke up for me. "You guys do know he's only fifteen." Which didn't seem to matter much to them since they didn't stop laughing at all.

Levon shot back. "And? I was getting busy at thirteen, man!" He got a high-five from a friend of his, which seemed to be the proper way to reply.

"Maybe that's why it took you four more years to get invited here, then," Nate said over the noise. "Too busy fucking and not enough playing."

I looked at him in shock. What the hell? The laughter transformed itself into ominous calls of "Ooohhh!" and "*Snap!*" and Levon's eyes narrowed in anger. "Got here before you did, didn't I?" he said, poking at Nathan's chest.

"Yeah, but we aren't talking about me. You were too busy picking on a high school kid, remember?"

A guy in the back called out. "Yeah, leave the kid alone, Lev!" which got a few votes of agreement from the others.

Knowing he was losing the crowd, he ignored Nathan and pointed at me. "You think you're better than me, punk?"

I looked back in confusion as I pointed to myself too. "Me? I didn't say that!"

"He's going to be better than all of us, Lev, and you fucking know it. So back off him and pick on someone who knows how to fight back." I'd been sharing a room for a week with Nathan and thought I knew him pretty well, but this was all new. I felt the glow of appreciation in my chest as he stuck up for me and locked it down just as fast.

"You got a big mouth there, Walker!" Levon said, standing up.

Nathan said nothing as he stood up with him.

"You wanna settle this on the court?" Levon asked, looking back at his friend. "A little two-on-two against you and your boy?"

I was his boy?

"He ain't ready yet, jackass," Nathan said, somehow growing angrier. "We're all here to learn, not measure each other's dicks, so why don't you either chill out or get lost." Now the sounds of agreement were much louder. The guys in the lounge were obviously tiring of Levon's game and ready to move on to something else.

He glared at me and then back to Nathan. "Don't matter. We'll kick your ass next season anyways." He stormed off, the crew of guys he hung out with following in his wake.

A couple of guys clapped as Nathan sat down again, taking a mock bow before he did. I didn't know what to say; no one in my life had ever done that before. The sense of indebtedness and affection I had for him tripled instantly. "Thanks," I said once everyone had gone back to their own conversations.

He flashed me a smile and brushed it off. "He's an asshole. You should hear him talk on the court."

"You didn't have to do that," I said, trying not to gush.

His smile only brightened as he replied, "Dude, I always wanted a little brother. Just had no idea he'd be taller than me."

I felt my heart skip a beat as his words moved through me. It was the very moment I fell in love with Nathan Walker.

CHAPTER SIX:
HEAD TO HEAD

I HEADED home from Florida with two very real things that summer.

One was the knowledge I could play basketball competitively as well as other players. I know that sounds like a stupid statement, but at the time I had no earthly idea basketball could give me anything more than it already had. I was happy with stability, focus of mind, and a way to impress my father with the person I was. It also seemed like it could get me into college. From the way the other guys talked, they had built their life around basketball. College picks, going pro, eventual shoe and endorsement deals. I had never once put myself in that bracket, as I'd simply assumed I was just a kid playing a game and nothing more.

The camp taught me I was a little more than that.

It also got me Nathan's contact numbers. We had become close friends, at least in my mind, and even though I was sure he had none of the feelings I had for him, he still insisted we stay in touch once we got home. I had agreed for more than the fact I felt an insane amount of affection for him. Nate was the first actual friend I felt I'd made on my own. The one time I asked him if he really thought I'd be better than all of them, like he'd said to Levon, he just smiled and said, "That's something you need to figure out on your own."

When I got home, I was ready to start the season right then and there. I chomped at the bit, eager for summer to end so school could start up. My birthday had passed when I was in Florida, a celebration that consisted of Nate and me sharing a dozen cupcakes in our room and watching *Hangover* three times in a row. My dad, in lieu of a party, instead took me to the outskirts of the base and turned off his Jeep.

I'd never explored this base as I had my other homes, since most of my time had been consumed with practice. We had pulled up on a series of old airstrips that they never used anymore, which pretty much ensured privacy. I didn't know what we were doing out there, but I no longer had that guilt-ridden feeling every time he took me aside. I had received exemplary marks from the instructors and actually taken home an award that I didn't feel I deserved. So I knew I wasn't in trouble, which meant this was my dad's way of trying to say something important.

"Before you left…," he began, and I got nervous, wondering if somehow he could tell my feelings for Nathan.

"Dad, it's okay…," I started, but he waved me off.

"No, it's not," he said firmly, still looking out over the deserted airstrip. "I don't know…." And he stopped. "I mean, if you…." And again he faltered.

"Dad," I said, trying to grab his attention.

He looked over at me, and I was stunned to see tears in his eyes.

"I don't want to chase you away, Danny. I just want you to be the best man you can be." His voice was wracked with guilt and pain, and I felt my own emotions well up as well.

"I'm still here, Dad," I said, reaching over and hugging him. "I'm not going anywhere."

He hugged me back, and I heard him say, "Yeah, you are. Trust me, son, you're going far."

I didn't know how to answer that, so I just kept hugging him, hoping this sadness would pass.

"Anyway," he said, pulling back and wiping the tears away. "Before you left I was unfair, and that was not fair to you. So I'm going to make it right."

I laughed as I dried my own eyes. "Dad, you sent me to Florida! That was more than enough." And it was. Of course, he had no way of knowing how much it meant, and I had no way of explaining it to him, but I think there was an understanding—at least I hoped there was one.

"No, you sent yourself to Florida. I just paid for it. This is for you being a better kid than I ever get around to telling you." And he handed me his keys.

I took them, confused. "You want me to drive us back?"

He stared at me for a few seconds, wondering if I was that clueless, which I have to admit I was. When he realized I wasn't yanking his chain, he clarified. "Those," he said, gesturing to the keys, "are for you."

My face lit up. "You mean I get a set of keys to your Jeep?" This was monumental! I mean, I felt lucky to ride in the actual car sometimes, the way he babied this thing. To actually have my own set of keys was just… well, unprecedented in our family.

Again with that look, and he shook his head and just laughed. "Man, you really just don't have a greedy bone in your body, do you?"

I cocked my head, not understanding the reference at all.

He put his hands over mine and squeezed them around the keys. "Those are yours." I nodded slowly. "So you can drive your car." I nodded. He waited for me to get it. "Danny, it's your car." I nodded one more time.

And then it hit.

"*What!*" I screamed and he pulled back and covered his ears.

You have to understand, he had just handed me the keys to the Batmobile.

He began to laugh as I jumped out of the Jeep and began to celebrate madly on the airstrip. He got out of the driver's side and waited for me to compose myself so he could show me the ropes on his precious baby.

He waited for at least five more minutes, maybe longer.

When I was finally able to regain my shit and make my way to the driver's side, I felt like I had just won the lottery. I eased myself into the driver's seat, worried that either I was going to scratch something and he was going to change his mind, or that I was going to scratch something and he was just going to shoot me.

He really loved this car.

It felt like I was sitting in a space shuttle or in the cockpit of a jet fighter, except it was mine. I slipped the key into the ignition. I have to admit a little shiver went up my spine when it clicked into place. I pulled the seat belt on and glanced over at him to be double-sure he was okay with this. He nodded as he strapped in himself. I grasped the key and held my breath as I turned it.

The car jerked forward quickly, causing me to bark out in shock, and then it died.

Oh my God, I had killed his Jeep. This was it, I was going to turn to face him, and he would either have a huge gun pointed at me or maybe a pair of Freddy Krueger claws. This would be the end of my life and no one would blame him. After all, I had just killed his favorite son. I refused to look at him and turned the key again. Once more the car exploded forward and then died one more time.

Oh God, I killed it twice!

"Danny."

I closed my eyes, waiting for the bullet.

"Danny, look at me."

I shook my head; just kill me already.

"Daniel Devon Monroe, look at me."

Ah fuck. I glanced over at him and saw no gun, no claws, no fangs dripping blood, which was a new thing I just thought of.

"Have you ever driven a stick shift before? Maybe in that driver's ed course?"

I shook my head slowly.

And he laughed out loud.

Do dads laugh before they kill you? Was that fair?

"Okay, then," he said when he could actually talk again. "So we teach you to drive a stick and *then* you get the Jeep."

"You're not going to kill me?" I asked in a low voice.

"If you ruin my Jeep? Yes, I will kill you," he said seriously. "But until you learn a stick, you get a pass."

The rest of my summer was a mixture of insane delight and towering frustration. I passed my driver's ed class and got my learner's permit the same afternoon. I knew the laws of the road and could drive any car with an automatic transmission, which was also a plus.

But driving the Jeep was something else altogether. My dad was a great teacher, never short, never pissed off. He worked all day and then took me out to the airfields to practice driving for hours before dinner and never once complained. So that was awesome. The bad part was that the towering beanpoles that passed as my legs refused to understand the system. I could dribble a ball and sprint up and down a basketball court with no problem whatsoever, but figuring out a clutch seemed beyond me. I was pretty sure I was going to have to replace the transmission by the time I was able to drive it, but my dad said it always took time.

After a month he stopped saying that.

I thought the Jeep was too small for me. He thought I was too big for the Jeep. Either way, things were really not working out. The harder I'd try, the worse it would get, and the worse it got, the less patience he had. Every time the car made that horrible grinding sound, I felt my entire body tense up because it felt like I was stabbing a family member. From the look on my dad's face, I could tell he was thinking just about the same thing.

Five weeks in and a week away from school starting, the only thing I had learned was that my dad had three faces for when I was driving. The first was a strained smile that passed as rest or relaxed for him but looked more like he was concerned about how badly I was going to hurt his baby this time around. The second face only came out in brief spurts, mostly when the Jeep made a strange sound, which wasn't so strange when I was behind the wheel. It was what I imagined my dad would look like if someone stabbed him in the butt with a rusty knife. I wasn't sure why a rusty knife would cause more pain than just an everyday, normal knife, but the pain that was expressed in those few seconds just seemed more than a normal knife could convey, hence the rust.

And then there was the third face. It was easily the worst.

The third face was the one he pulled out when he had suffered enough. It was a silent acceptance of yet another failure on my part mixed with the attempt to not to show how disappointed in me he was. It was the same look he had given me in Germany, and every time I saw it, I died a little more inside. Of course, the more I thought about the look, the worse my driving became, until he would finally tell me we were done for the day. What had started as an incredible gesture had somehow been turned into slow, arduous torture. A week before school began, he stopped me about twenty minutes into the session, signaling me to turn the engine off.

"We're done?" I asked, not sure if I should be relieved or disappointed.

He shook his head as he leaned back in the seat. "Danny. You know I love you, right?" I nodded mutely but couldn't help but feel the familiar tingle of fear begin to creep up my spine. "And you know I am going to be proud no matter what you do." I nodded, even though I knew that was a lie. I had already done things he wasn't proud of, and I knew deep down if he knew everything, he'd end up hating me. "Look," he said after a few seconds of thought, "you're trying too hard. Driving a stick isn't that big a deal." If the words were meant to be reassuring, they failed in just about every way possible. Not only did I suck, but I sucked at something that was relatively easy. "I think you're so wound up about what I might say or feel that you aren't concentrating on the actual driving."

He was right, of course. I mean, as long he had owned this Jeep, I had been taught it was more than just an average, everyday vehicle. This Jeep was his pride and joy, and whatever brain aneurism he'd suffered that made him think giving it to me was appropriate was all fine and good, but it didn't change the fact that there were days he liked it more than me. It was like eating on your best china or wearing your best clothes: you just knew if you screwed them up, there was a whole new level of punishment waiting for you.

"Driving a clutch is like…," he began, mentally searching for an appropriate metaphor. After about thirty seconds he snapped his fingers and announced, "Driving a clutch is like being with a girl." I looked at him like he'd grown a second head, but he seemed oblivious to my reaction. "Girls are delicate, no matter how tough or independent they seem on the outside. The plain and simple fact is that physically they just can't take the same amount of punishment a guy can. Now, the worst thing you can do is to treat them with kid gloves, because trust me, they hate that. Then they'll try to roughhouse or play around like one of the guys. But deep down you know you can't treat them the same as a guy, no matter how they act. So there's this line…." Again he paused as he tried to summon up the correct words. This was the most my dad had said about anything except sports in a long, long time. We just didn't have conversations like this normally. I was seeing a whole new side of him.

"There's this balance you have to find," he started again, "where you aren't walking on eggshells around them, but you're still respectful of their space." He looked at me, but I was more confused than when we started. "I'm saying that there is a level of physicality you can have with a girl, but you have to be aware of your own strength at all times." The blank look on my face must have told him his words were completely lost on me. He sighed and gazed down for a moment as he tried to mentally regroup. "It's a Jeep; it's not going to break. But that doesn't mean you can just jam it into gear. You have to give a little with the clutch while putting just a little gas into it. Balance," he said, holding his hands out like scales. "Do you understand?" I answered truthfully by shaking my head. "Look, Danny, you're a big guy. No matter who you end up with, you're going to have to be careful."

I froze as my heart skipped a beat.

"You're going to need to find that line between strength and control eventually," he added. "This is a good first start."

I sat there gripping the steering wheel for almost a minute, trying to calm myself down enough to talk. No matter who I ended up with? Was that a crack about a guy instead of a girl? Did he think I wasn't getting it because he was using a girl as an example? Was that what my dad thought of me? Was I so queer to him that I couldn't relate to a girl even when one was used as a simile?

He finally noticed something was wrong. He put a hand on my shoulder and asked, "Hey, are you okay?"

I pulled away from him with a jerk of my arm. He seemed shocked by the outburst but didn't say anything.

"Can we just do this?" I asked, obviously upset.

"What did I say?"

I refused to look at him as I shook my head. "Let's just drive." I could tell he wanted to say more, but I ignored him, and I turned the key. Was this how Dad and I were going to be for the rest of my life? Was he always going to question my sexuality? Worse, should he? I had no idea what I was, but I knew it was still unknown and every time he opened his mouth, he made it sound like it was a sure thing, and I hated that. He talked as if he had closed the book on what I was, and there was no way for me to change. Would he always be disappointed in me? Was he more disappointed than I was in myself?

"Danny."

I ignored him.

"Danny."

I forced myself not to look at him.

"Danny!"

I snapped and looked over at him. "What?"

He pointed at the road. "You're driving."

And so I was. I had been so upset and lost in thought about what he had said that I had just zoned out about the mechanics of what I was doing. I almost freaked and slammed on the brakes, but I stopped myself as I realized I had found the balance he had been talking about between the clutch and gas. I smiled despite being upset as I shifted into fourth gear without a hitch.

"See?" he said, slapping my shoulder in congratulations. "I'm glad my talk helped you."

As we drove across the airstrip, I had an epiphany about what I had to do next. There was only one way I was going to be able to change my dad's opinion of me and make him proud of me once and for all. An action that would redeem me in his eyes and end my own internal questions in one fell swoop.

I needed to find myself a girlfriend.

I spent the next week making a game plan. I had screwed things up pretty bad with Carol, so she was out of the question, but it couldn't be that hard to find a girl to go out with. After all, there were always girls hanging around after parties trying to get our notice. Some of the guys took advantage of the readily available attention, which just added to the allure of landing one of us in an actual relationship. Susan dating Tommy was a fluke: no one had expected them to last very long. They were the exception and very much not the rule. Most of the guys played the field in a way that bordered on hedonism, but no one complained. It was an equitable deal; the guys got laid, and the girls got one step closer to getting them to commit.

I was guessing at most of what I just said, of course. The closest I'd been to going out with a girl was Carol, and that had ended *so* well. From what I could tell from the outside, dating looked like a game with very liberal rules and more than a few emotional elbows thrown as it came down to the wire. Guys cheating on their girls, girls playing mind games with the guys—they just seemed to circle around each other in what looked to me like a dizzying display of give-and-take.

As the week dwindled away and the first day of school got closer and closer, I vowed that this year would be different. I was going to socialize more, be normal, and find a girl like every other guy did. No more guy shit, no more being gay. This was my chance to flip the script once and for all.

The night before the first day of school, I lay in bed and tried to will myself to sleep with no success. All I could think of was what a difference a year made. Last year I was scared shitless that I wouldn't be able to handle public high school, and that I might not be able to handle playing basketball. Now, after Florida, I knew I had real talent, I knew the school well, and I was ready for more. Cody was gone, Tommy had graduated, and what I did was all up to me.

At some point I dozed off, because my alarm clock going off scared the crap out of me.

I threw on some of the new clothes my dad had bought me last weekend; most of everything we had bought last year was already too small before basketball camp. I took a good look at myself as I brushed my teeth. I still looked like a goofball to me. My ears were too big, and my face still looked like a little kid's, even though I was already taller than most adults I had seen. I was skinny as a rail in my opinion, but in my sweatshirt I looked like I had some kind of a body underneath. I wasn't ugly by any means, but I wasn't sure what would draw someone's attention enough to be attracted to me. Cody had been way better-looking than I was. Even Tommy had more chiseled looks than I had. My dad said I was still growing into my looks, but at six five, I wasn't sure how much more growing I could handle.

"You're going to be late if you just keep staring at yourself," my dad said, coming around the corner of the bathroom. I looked away quickly, but from the way I was blushing, it was obvious he had busted me. "You nervous?" he asked as I rinsed my mouth out. I shrugged as I turned off the water.

"Yes and no," I answered honestly.

He came up and stood next to me. Even though I was inches taller than him, he was still way more impressive in his BDUs. You could tell I was his son; we had the same general features, except for the eyes. I had seen pictures of Mom, and it was obvious I had inherited not only her eyes but eye color. Where my dad's eyes were dark brown, mine were a bright blue that just ended up making me look younger in my opinion. Where my dad had ruggedly good looks—that whole square jaw, tough as hell Marine type of face—mine was softer, and I hated it.

"You're lucky," he informed me soberly after a few seconds.

"Why?" I asked, still examining the differences in our faces.

"You have those cute, lost puppy dog eyes," he said with a wry grin. "Girls go crazy for that shit." I elbowed him, but he pushed back. "I'm serious. By your age I was already shaving every day and looked like a goon. Why your mom ever went out with me, I will never figure out."

"I look like a baby!" I complained.

He grabbed my chin and shook my face. "But you're such a cute wittle baby!"

I tried to jerk away, but he just laughed. "Seriously, Danny, you're a kid. Enjoy it while you can."

"I'll try," I said, suddenly feeling emotional about how fast time seemed to be passing.

"I hate to tell you this," he said in a deadly serious tone. I paused, dreading what his next words would be. "You're going to be late for school."

I looked at the time and realized he was right.

I ran out of the door and threw my backpack into the back of the Jeep. I paused and smiled as I realized it was indeed my Jeep and not my dad's. I felt like a completely different person pulling into the school parking lot, and, in a lot of ways, I was. I found a space in the student lot and jumped out as the first bell rang. I barely made it to my first class on time; the tardy bell literally rang as I walked in.

The teacher looked over at me with one eyebrow arched. "Perfect timing as always, Mr. Monroe." A small eruption of laughter from the class greeted his words, and I looked around to find a place to sit. There was only one seat left, and as my eyes fell on it, I knew that fate had conspired to help me out with my plans.

I slid into the seat and, with a small smile, looked over to my right.

"Hi, Carol," I said under the cover of the teacher's voice.

"I'm still mad at you." she sniffed, trying to keep her face serious but failing pretty badly.

"Fair enough," I said, nodding solemnly. "Too mad for me to try to make up?"

She turned her head toward me almost imperceptibly. "What kind of making up?" she inquired.

"Lunch and a lot of apologizing?" I offered.

She looked away and went back to concentrating on the front board. "We'll see," she whispered with a smile.

I tried to hide my own grin as I shifted back toward the front. Though I didn't like to celebrate before the game was over, I had a feeling that would not go away.

I knew this was going to be my year.

CHAPTER SEVEN:
FLOOR VIOLATION

WE SAT in the huddle and pondered on what to do next.

We were in the fifth game of the regional playoffs and were down by six points. With less than twenty seconds on the clock, six points might as well have been a hundred. I looked over at the other team and saw their point guard glancing over at me as well. He had a small grin on his face that told me he was well aware of the fact he had been shutting me down all night like I had never played the game before. I would be furious if the guy wasn't pushing every one of my buttons when it came to being attractive. He was as tall as me, which was a turn-on, since I loomed over just about everyone my age in my school. He had dark blond hair that was cut short, with a pair of dark eyes I had been staring into all night.

I had been playing most of this game with my downstairs head, and it turns out it wasn't all that skilled at hoops.

"You still with us?" the coach asked me.

I looked back and nodded quickly as I tried to ignore the rest of the team staring at me like I had a rabbit hidden somewhere on my body. We had played an incredible season up to this point, and if you had asked us last week if we'd be down three games to two with our lives hanging on this game, we'd have laughed in your face. We had been so sure we were headed for our school's first state championship that we could taste it. We had started the season by the coach putting it to the team who they wanted as captain for the year, instead of him choosing it arbitrarily. I won unanimously, which only solidified my belief that this was my year.

Carol had forgiven me, and we were going out pretty strong now. Unlike her sister, she was far more reserved when it came to physical intimacy, which suited me just fine. I had hoped having a girlfriend would somehow make me like girls more. Like there was some form of social osmosis that would imbue me with heterosexual feelings. All I needed to do was stand next to a girl to make me straight, or that was what I told myself. It had been five months now, and after countless hours of making out and one halfhearted attempt at a hand job after our first game, I was no closer to straight than she was to being a koala bear. She took my reluctance to paw all over her as me being a gentleman, a misconception I didn't dissuade her of. We made a great couple and everyone seemed to accept it, which worked for both of us on different levels, I assumed.

I tried to convince myself that Carol liked me because I was on the basketball team and gaining in popularity, which of course reflected well on her. I tried to, but to be honest, she was a really nice girl. The thought of using me for popularity would never cross her mind, and I knew it. I was using her, and it was killing me inside. Not enough to do something about it, but killing me nonetheless. I had never had a group of friends before that I was trying to impress, and having a cute girlfriend helped me in that department immensely. According to a few guys on the team, if I wasn't taken, there were more than a few girls who would have asked me out, which only cemented the value of having a girl on my arm.

With my personal life squared away, I was able to concentrate on basketball in a way I hadn't been able to before. With no Cody or Tommy to distract me, I focused on the game and getting us to the state championship. I initiated a before-school jog for the team, which then led to an early morning workout session to get us into playing shape. At first they were resistant; no one liked getting up that early to do anything, much less run, but the coach backed my decision and made it mandatory. It didn't make me popular with the guys, but after a few days, they got into the rhythm and stopped bitching so loud. After a month we started seeing results, and our results started getting compliments from the school.

There is nothing that inspires a teenage boy more than a teenage girl asking if he'd been working out.

With our workout out of the way by first period, it left us our entire practice session to work on our game. The coach began to separate us into smaller teams to work on specific skill sets. Slowly but surely we stopped being a group of teenage guys trying to play basketball and began to turn into an actual team. Seeing the guys around me picking up their level of ability took the pressure off my shoulders as we all began to realize this season wasn't going to be just about me. Our strategy wasn't going to be four periods of trying to trick the opposing team to either look or not look at me. I was still the best player we had, but I was no longer the only player.

Yet here we were, twenty seconds away from washing out of the finals, and there was nothing I could think of to stop it.

"So what's the plan?" someone asked me when it was obvious I had nothing to add by the way of an answer. I looked over and saw it was Frank who asked; he was one of the seniors who had been on the team since he was a freshman.

Before I could even think about it, I heard myself snap at him. "Wow, Frank four years and you *just* woke up! Nice of you to join us." He blinked a few times in confusion at me as a couple of the other guys looked down and stared at the ground. "That guy is on me like I owe him money. If I can't shake him, we're sunk."

Scott, another useless senior, opened his mouth as if to say something, but the second I glared at him, he closed it and looked away. I was pissed, and I couldn't tell you where it was directed at specifically. I glanced up and saw our time out was almost over. This was it, this was how our season ended, and I was helpless to change it.

"Just get that asshole off of me and get me the ball," I said, ducking out of the huddle before anyone could respond.

The fact that no one said anything to me was an indication that this was not new behavior for me. As we grew more competent as a team, the harder I seemed to push them. I suppose it was a vicious circle that the closer we got to the playoffs, the more I wanted to go to state, which then made me drive the team harder, which then made us play worse and worse. Everything I tried to tell them seemed to fall on deaf ears, which just made me talk louder and louder.

After a while I was just screaming.

I think it was because I had never had to deal with a real social environment before that made me oblivious to the fact I was becoming less and less liked by just about everyone around me. I assumed the coach would pull me aside if I was doing something wrong, but he never said a word as I tore into the team week after week, no matter if we won or lost. I knew we were far from being able to take the title, and if we didn't get better, then this would be for shit. A waste of a season, busting our ass just so we could see another group of jackasses walk away with our trophy.

And here we were two months later, exactly where I was afraid we'd be.

I went out to center court as Scott sat on the line, waiting to throw the ball back into play. My shadow was right behind me. I could almost feel him breathing on my back, even if I didn't turn around. I saw a couple of guys scrambling around in front of me as we moved into position.

"So I hear you're the guy to see after the game to get blown," a voice behind me said, the sneer audible in the guy's tone alone.

My blood felt like ice as every single hair on my neck stood on end. I spun around and found myself face-to-face with the very sneer I had imagined from his words. I saw his eyes widen as he realized his words had gotten to me, and he pantomimed a kiss at me in response. Something hit the small of my back, but I ignored it as my fist connected with his face. It was obvious he wasn't expecting it from the way he went down, like I had just punched a little kid instead of a high school senior. Someone tackled me from my left side, which brought the rest of our team off the bench like it was a hockey game instead of basketball.

Two of their team landed on top of me, and I curled up into a ball to protect my head and junk. I could hear fights all around me as the referees, coaches, and more than a few parents tried to break us up. It took more than twenty minutes before we were all sorted out. Most of us had bloodied noses, others blackened eyes. I saw at least one guy cradling his arm in a way that made me sick to my stomach. I was kicked out of the game, and the other side was given two free throws, which gave them an eight-point lead. Twenty seconds later they had won the game.

The cheers from the court echoed to the locker room, and I felt an ache in my body that had nothing to do with my wounds.

After a couple of minutes, the rest of the team walked into the locker room. No one said a word, but trust me, the silence was deafening. A couple of guys sat on the bench staring into their lockers; a couple of others glanced over at me with a ferocity that made me wonder how I didn't burst into flames. Five minutes into this, the coach walked in. He was as quiet as everyone else. I just kept looking down at my sneakers; I was too pissed to risk actually trying to talk right then. He stared at us for a few seconds and then, in a low voice, said, "Shower up and head home. We're done."

Most of us looked up at him as he walked into his office and slammed his door.

We showered like zombies. This day had started with such promise, slapping each other's backs and saying words of encouragement. Now we couldn't even look at each other. I was the last in, since I had no desire to strip down and stand there naked with a group of guys who were pissed at me. When I got out, the locker room was empty; everyone else had already left. As I slipped on my jeans, the coach walked out of his office. He had a glass of something in his hand that didn't look like it was a soda.

"Why are you still here?" he asked sharply.

"Just dressing out," I answered, grabbing a shirt, wanting to get the hell out of there.

He came in and sat down on one of the other benches. "You do know you really fucked up the game, right?" I looked over at him in shock as he kept talking. "I mean, when you joined the team last year, I really thought you'd turn us around, but after tonight—" He finished the drink and hissed as it went down his throat. "—well, I sure got that wrong, didn't I?"

Normally I wouldn't have said a word back. The coach wasn't someone people tended to argue with. He was just too serious a guy for anyone with half a brain to consider giving lip to.

If you haven't noticed, I am about nine yards short of having half a brain.

"How was that my fault?" I asked in a far harsher tone than I intended. He raised one eyebrow in response but didn't say a word. Of course, I just went on talking. "I was your top scorer, led the season in rebounds, and was personally responsible for winning at least four of our games. So tell me how I screwed up my season?"

He came off the bench like he was on springs. "*It wasn't your fucking season!*" he screamed in my face, the smell of bourbon almost overwhelming. "That's why we lost," he added, lowering his voice. "Because you went out there and thought this was your team and your season to win or lose." We glared at each other for a few seconds. His words caused the blood to drain from my face, and I wondered if he was right or not.

"Last year you were all about the team, ready to do anything to get the team even a half step forward. I thought that kid was the best player I'd seen in a long time." I thought he was going to hit me for a moment, but he turned away and made his way back to his office. "If that kid shows up next season, he's on the team." He paused at the doorway and leveled a look at me. "If it's you who shows up, don't even think you have a chance. I'll suit up a group of monkeys and gladly lose every game before I let you make this team feel this bad about themselves again."

He slammed his door shut without another word.

I sat back down on the bench and tried to figure out how he was wrong. I tried, but I couldn't.

I was supposed to go out with Carol after the game, but I blew it off because I needed to be alone. I got into my Jeep and just drove as far as I could. I was mad. Mad at myself, at the coach, at the team, at life in general. In one season, I had somehow become an alien version of myself. Looking into a metaphorical mirror, I could not recognize the guy staring back at me. I'd started this year with so much hope, and now all I had were ashes.

The road that twisted its way between the ocean and Corpus was pretty dead this late at night. I was pushing seventy as I raced toward the back entrance to the base. I felt like I was in a horror movie, a maniac with a chainsaw right on my heels. Basketball was the only part of my life that was pure, untouched by the darkness I knew crouched just out of sight in my head. It was my public face, the one people were supposed to like and love, and I was screwing it up.

I had no idea how to fix what was happening.

The last thing I remember were headlights in front of me and slamming on my brakes.

INTERLUDE:
TIME OUT

LIFE HAS a different feeling when you're on pain meds.

There are no real days, just one endless stream of images that never seem to connect to each other. You're aware that time is passing, but it doesn't mean anything since there is just blackness between the brief moments you're awake. I knew I was in the hospital, but I was unable to generate any concern since my brain was wrapped in a nice little pillow of narcotic bliss. I remember moments of seeing people I assume were doctors and nurses and once my dad.

It might have been hours, might have been weeks, but I lay there for an indeterminate amount of time in a haze, not sure of anything at all.

Whenever I opened my eyes, it was dark, giving me the feeling that either I had been out for one long night or several days in a row, always waking up at the same time. So there was no way for me to know how long I had lain there in a drug-induced slumber when I finally regained consciousness. The room was dark, but even so I could tell I was in a hospital room. I had no clue how I had arrived here, but the second I tried to sit up, one thing became blatantly obvious.

My leg was broken.

There was a cast from just under my knee to my heel, and it was resting on a pillow tucked under my calf. I could tell my leg was screaming in agony, but it was as if it was connected to someone else. I was in a hospital gown, and there wasn't any indication of where my clothes were.

That was when I saw her.

She was a shadow in the corner, standing there looking at me. At first I thought she was just my imagination, but as soon as I focused on her, she moved toward me. She didn't walk as much as she floated to my bedside. Her hands were pale white against the rails. "You're okay," she said, her voice barely above a whisper.

It didn't sound like a question, but I nodded just the same. "Yeah, I think so." My voice sounded weird, like it was coming from somewhere far away. "Where am I?"

She put a hand on my forearm, and it was like ice. "You are here," she said, her face still covered in shadows. "You need to be here."

"I am here," I agreed, trying to pull my arm away. "Where else would I be?"

That was when I felt my entire body shake with a racking pain.

The room burst into a brief halo of blinding light before going dark again. Her nails were cutting into my arm like she was holding on to me for dear life. "Danny!" she shouted. "Danny, stay with me."

Now I was scared. My body was getting cold, and I couldn't move. I looked over to the lady, my eyes no doubt wide with terror. "What's happening?"

"Danny," she said, the tone in her voice becoming kinder. "Danny you're going into shock. Stay with me."

I forced my hand to move and placed it over hers. "Where am I?"

"You have to stay here," she said, her voice changing again. "You have to stay here."

There was another flash of light, and the world became bright and unfocused. There were people staring down at me, dark silhouettes that looked more like alien abductors than real people. Just like the last time, the moment faded and the room went black again. In that moment I looked over to the lady in the shadows, and I knew who she was.

My whole body went numb, and I realized I couldn't feel the pain from my leg anymore. My body was shaking from more than fear. My hand gripped hers tightly. "Please, please don't go!"

I don't know if I saw the hint of her smile or just imagined it, but I knew she was smiling at me. Her hand moved across my forehead, brushing the hair out of my eyes. "You have to stay here." She sounded sad. "You can't leave yet."

The pain in my leg was like a fire on the horizon, a small spark indicating a distant blaze.

"Stay here, Danny," she repeated, leaning forward to kiss my forehead. "You have to stay here."

My arm began to throb with pins and needles, like I had fallen asleep on it for days. Again the pain was muted, far away, but this time I knew it was mine. I tried to focus past it to look at her. "I wanna go with you!" I cried as the feeling moved up my arm to my shoulder.

"Stay here," she whispered. "Stay with your dad. He needs you."

As the pain in my chest hiked up, I could feel myself being pulled violently away from wherever I was. From her.

With all my focus, I tried to grab at her, but the darkness was fading, and I was being pulled back toward the light.

I screamed for my mom to stay, but it was useless... she was gone.

I awoke gasping in my bed, a doctor and three nurses surrounding me. I tried to sit up. *"Mom!"*

I felt one of the nurses push me back down to the bed with one hand; it was an indication of how weak I was that she succeeded.

"He's okay," the doctor said in that same clinical way all doctors seemed to talk. "That was close."

"I'm sorry, doctor," one of the nurses said. "The father didn't indicate any allergies—"

"Doesn't matter," he said, cutting her off. "He's obviously reacting to the codeine. Check his scripts and change them. He can't take another one of those." He sounded like a jerk, but something.... I thought I saw his jaw twitch... but I lost the thought as quickly as it had come.

The nurse seemed pissed, but she was doing a pretty good job of holding her tongue. She just nodded at him and said, "Yes, sir," before walking out.

"Danny?" he said, looking down at me. "How you doing?"

"Where is she?" I asked, each word feeling harder than the last. I was exhausted, but I needed to know where she went.

"Who? The nurse?" he asked, flashing a light in my eyes, obviously not listening to my questions. "Danny, you had an adverse reaction to the painkillers we were giving you. I need you to follow my finger with your eyes." He began to move his index finger to the left and right in front of my face.

I tried to slap it away, but lifting my hand seemed almost impossible. "Where is she?" I asked again, my eyelids getting heavier by the second.

"Pupil dilation looks okay," he said to the nurse behind him. "Okay, Danny, looks like you're over the worst part. Just try to relax and get some rest."

"Need to know…," I said as I fell back into unconsciousness.

CHAPTER EIGHT:
DISQUALIFYING FOUL

THE FIRST person I saw when I really woke up was my dad.

He was out cold in a chair tucked away in the corner, and he looked like he was the one who got hit by a car. He was unshaven. To Dad, being unshaven in public was like walking around naked in public would be to the rest of us. It just wasn't done. Every memory I had of him was clean shaven, hair high and tight, and clothes clean and pressed. Seeing him looking like that drove home how bad the accident had been way more than the cast on my leg did.

I tried to sit up, but pain exploded from my knee all the way up to my hip. It was so unexpected I cried out loud before I could stop myself. I bit down on my bottom lip hard as I looked over at my dad, hoping he had slept through it.

"Danny?" he said, instantly opening his bloodshot eyes and pushing out of the chair wide awake, on alert. "Don't move!" he commanded quietly; he knew I was holding my breath to keep from screaming. I watched him as he fumbled in my covers and came up with the nurse call button. He jammed it, like, half a million times. I tried to find a way of lying still that didn't cause me to cry like a bitch. My hands clutched the covers, and I realized there was no way I was going to find an escape from the agony that used to be my left leg.

He grabbed my hand and held it tight as we waited for the nurse.

The pain faded for a second as I looked down at his hand holding mine. My dad had never been the most touchy-feely person in the world, and as I grew older, expressions like this grew rarer and rarer. I moved mine to grasp his and marveled at how small it seemed compared to mine. His hand had always been like a paw that engulfed my hand whenever I had to hold it, but as I held his now and tried not to break his fingers when the pain took over, I saw they were about the same size. When did that happen? He kept glancing at the door as his other hand pushed the button, which gave me time to stare at him and, for the first time in a long time, really look at him.

He was a handsome guy; he rocked that whole military style in a way that looks stupid on other men. What hit me, though, was how young he looked to me all of a sudden. I don't know if it was the naked fear on his face or just the scruff, but I could see the guy my mom had fallen in love with and married all those years ago, and I realized I looked like him. He was still young, younger than the dads of anyone else I knew, but I hadn't realized it until now. My dad was always older and invulnerable in my mind, but I had the feeling I was seeing him for the first time as a human being.

The nurse came in and saw me starting to sweat from the pain and my dad's panicked look and hit the buzzer on the wall. "I need pain management stat," she called into the intercom as she moved my dad aside. "Danny, where does it hurt?" she asked slowly, like I was a retard or something.

"My leg?" I gasped out, trying my best not to scream at her.

"Your leg or hip?" she asked, slipping a blood pressure cuff over my bicep.

To be honest, the pain seemed to be everywhere, but I tried to focus past it to see if there was an actual answer to her question. And there it was—just to the right of my ass, which made it more my hip than my actual leg, though there was a throbbing from my knee that wasn't friendly at all. I tried to move slightly and was rewarded by another explosion of pain.

"*Hip!*" I screeched as I clenched my dad's hand for support.

The nurse's expression didn't waver as she took my blood pressure, but I could hear her cuss just under her breath as she glanced over at the monitor on the other side of my bed. Pulling the cuff off, she turned toward the door and screamed, "*Where are those meds?*"

The pain was getting worse now as it crept from the side of my hip toward the rest of my groin. It felt like my bed had caught fire, and I involuntary tried to raise my hips to get away from it, which only caused it to flare harder.

The nurse's hands grabbed the sides of my hips and pushed them down. Her eyes locked with mine. "Do not move," she commanded in a tone that I was pretty sure could have stopped my dad in his tracks. "I know it hurts, but you have to keep still."

I closed my eyes, and my head fell back onto the pillow as I tried to keep myself as still as possible. Through pained gasps I said, "You should seriously date this chick, Dad." I took a few deep breaths as another wave of pain passed through my hips. "You guys could just order each other around."

I heard my dad say something, but it was lost as the feeling of a hot poker being shoved into my pelvis hit me. I didn't care what she said or who was watching—I let out a howl that was probably heard two states over. I arched my back instinctively, which only made it hurt more. Someone else ran into the room, and I heard my dad calling my name like he was at the end of a tunnel. He sounded worried, but he was so far away.

And then my hand was engulfed with heat, as if someone had put it in a bowl of boiling water. The feeling slowly but steadily made its way up my arm and into my shoulder. When the heat hit my heart, the world ceased to exist. I thought fuzzily that I had jumped up out of my body for a moment from the way the pain ceased to be. The no-pain wasn't numbness; it was much more invasive than that. I was sure I was hovering above the bed and away from my body, which had trapped the pain.

I knew in some distant way they were doing something to me, but it felt like it was happening to someone else entirely. I was lost in that space of no time, and that was when I knew they had dosed me again. I assume this was what doing hard drugs felt like, and I had to admit I hated it. The lack of control and feeling of just floating made me sick to my stomach in ways I had never felt before. It was so beyond the dizzying feeling you get from heat exhaustion, or even getting hard fouled during a game, that it was insane. If this was the feeling junkies chased, I knew at that moment I would never be one of them.

Time must have passed, because the next actual thought I had was that the room was much darker than I remembered. My dad was there looking five years older than he had earlier today—least, I hope it was today. He saw I was awake and put the paper cup of coffee down and strode to my bed.

"Hey, bud, you okay?" he asked in a tone I wasn't used to hearing from him.

I opened my mouth to talk, but it felt like my tongue had been deep fried in kitty litter. I croaked out a barely understandable "Water?"

He nodded quickly and poured me a cup of water from a plastic jug that was just out of reach from my bed. I tried to sit up to take the cup but found myself strapped to the bed. I looked, and there was some kind of belt across my waist holding me down. "You really aren't allowed to move," he said with a slight smile that seemed more sad than happy. He put a straw to my lips, and I sucked the liquid down as fast as I could manage. I know now it may have just been normal, room temperature tap water, but let me tell you, that was the best-tasting water I had ever experienced.

I finished the contents of the cup in one swallow and took a few seconds before asking, "More?"

He chuckled, and this time it sounded more joyful than sorrow filled.

"Take it easy. You have cotton mouth from the meds, that's all," he said, putting the straw up to my lips again.

This time I did take a few smaller sips, but the water was no less exquisite than it had been before. If anything, now I had time to relish its perfection as my throat came back to life. "What happened?" I asked after finishing the second cup.

"Today?" he asked, tossing the empty in the trash.

I shook my head and nodded to the cast. "I mean what happened?"

He followed my gaze and nodded. "Ah, you mean what happened with the car?"

"Oh God! Did I wreck your Jeep?" I felt my stomach do a barrel roll as I thought of even a scratch on the Jeep.

He pulled the chair closer to the side of the bed. "One, it was your Jeep; two, your Jeep saved your life; and three… yeah, it's wrecked."

I didn't know how to process that information and lay there feeling like I had just found out a family member had passed away. Dad had owned the Jeep since before I could remember, and it was gone because of me.

"I'm sorry," I whispered after a few moments of silence. He looked down at me in confusion and saw the tears in my eyes. "I know I screwed up," I said, choking up.

He looked like his eyes were going to fall out. "Danny, the guy jumped into your lane. This isn't your fault."

I had no idea where all this emotion was coming from. I was tired and still woozy from the drugs, sure, but it was more than that. The Jeep was just a symptom of a larger problem, and that problem was me. Everything I seemed to touch got fucked up, and no matter how hard I tried to make things right, I just ended up making them worse by the time I was done. Basketball was supposed to be the thing that made me right, and I'd fucked that up just like I had fucked everything else up.

I felt my eyes sting as I got out a barely audible "I mean the other thing." I forced myself to keep talking. "I know I'm not what you wanted in a son—"

"What?" he said, cutting me off. "Are you serious?"

His voice was angry, and normally I would have been taken aback by it, but all it did was make me feel worse. "I know you would have liked someone who wasn't—" The word refused to pass my lips. "—who wasn't wrong."

He stopped and stared at me with an intensity that made me think he might go off and hit me for a second. In a halting voice that cracked with emotion, he asked, "Did I make you think that? That you weren't right?"

I couldn't even look at him. "I know what I am, Dad. I know what it is."

"Jesus!" he cursed, pulling at what little hair he had in frustration. "I don't…." He stopped and turned away from me.

"Dad?" I asked, feeling light-headed for a moment

When he turned around, there were tears in his eyes. "Danny, I almost lost you like I did your mother. When I got the call…." He stopped, unable to go on. Fighting back the emotion, he continued, "Son, you are exactly what I wanted in a son, and if I ever made you feel anything different, that is my fault, not yours."

He took my hand again, and I felt a weight melt off my shoulders as I began to get sleepy. "I just want to be better…."

I never finished the sentence because I drifted off to sleep.

My dreams were haunted by half-glimpsed images that refused to come into focus but were nonetheless terrifying to my sleeping mind. There was a pack of people just outside my vision who were screaming things at me, but I couldn't understand them. I was wearing a basketball uniform that was too small, and no matter how I tried to pull it down to cover me, it didn't work. I was supposed to shoot a free throw, but every time I picked up the ball, I could feel my shorts riding up, exposing me to the crowd. I could hear the crowd laughing from inside the darkness, and I saw the shot clock running out.

I woke up drenched in sweat, fighting as hard as I could against the band that kept me strapped to the bed.

"Whoa, Danny," my dad said, putting a hand on my chest to hold me down before I hurt myself more. "It's a dream. It was just a dream."

I could still hear the laughter in my head, but it faded away to the sound of my pounding heart as I realized I was awake. "Dad?" I asked, confused about where I was for a moment.

"You were in an accident, Danny. You're in the hospital?" he offered, and it came back to me.

I nodded and lay back as he moved his hand. "Bad dream?"

My mouth opened to answer him, but as quickly as the dream had hit me, the memory of it vanished. I struggled to grab what I could about it, but all I could remember was holding a basketball and people laughing at me, which didn't seem that scary at all. Instead I just nodded and reached for the water before I realized I was still strapped down to the bed.

"How you feeling?" my dad asked, pouring me a fresh cup of water.

I downed it before answering. "Sore but nothing serious." My leg throbbed, but it was a dull ache compared to the knives of agony I had been through before. "How long was I out?" I asked, not sure how much time had passed.

"Not long," he said, pouring me another cup and putting it on the tray closer to me. "So you think you're feeling up for a visitor?"

I paused. Who would want to come see me?

Before I could even ask, the door opened, and Nate burst through with a handful of balloons bobbing over his head. "Man, the things you do to get my attention!" he said with a huge smile on his face.

I could feel my face break into a matching grin when I realized he was really there and not some drug-induced hallucination.

"There's no need to fear," he said, handing me the balloons. "Natedawg is here."

And for the first time since I woke up in pain, I felt better.

I had no idea why my dad had called Nathan, but I got the feeling he thought something "more" had happened between us in Florida. There was really no way to explain to him that Nate and I were just friends, but at that very moment, I didn't care. I hadn't realized how much I had missed him until I started talking to him. He ended up eating my Jell-O as we watched *SportsCenter* during lunch, the entire time telling me how the season was for him and his team. My dad went home, hopefully to shave and change clothes, and we watched football until dinner.

As I ate my tasteless hospital meal, he chowed down on a burger he had bought from the vending machine. "So... tell me this was an accident and not a cry for help," he said as we watched the scores scroll past the bottom of the screen.

I almost choked on my chicken as I looked over to him. "What?"

He kept watching the screen. "I heard about your season and that you got pretty beat up." I felt my stomach start to knot as the thought of my attitude reaching Nate's ears passed through my mind. "Couple of people said you got pretty cocky."

I wasn't hungry before, but now I felt sick to my stomach and put my fork down carefully. He looked over at me, and all I could do was nod.

He took another bite and went back to watching TV. "Yeah, I did that too in high school, was a complete dick." I almost choked as I tried to think of Nathan being as bad as I had been this year. "I thought I was the second coming of Jordan or something and started telling everyone what to do." He shook his head at the memory. "Complete douchebag."

"What did you do to change?" I asked, feeling like we were talking about a fictional character rather than him.

"We got our asses kicked, and I ended up having the best stats on a losing team." He tossed the wrapper into the trash and looked back at me. "And in the end that made me a loser too. Remember that, young Jedi," he advised with a smile. "The team wins or no one does. That's the only way it works."

I felt three kinds of shitty, but there was a light at the end of this tunnel, I realized. There was a way to get out of this. I just needed help. "How long you staying?" I asked him, trying not to sound too hopeful.

"I'm here as long as you need, bud." His smile was infectious. "I ain't going nowhere."

I felt like things were looking up, right up until my dad walked in with the doctor.

The look on the doctor's face was so neutral that it came across as fake. He obviously had his poker face down pat when delivering bad news to patients. If it was just him, I might have missed the way his eyes never lingered on me for long or the way he kept his distance as he talked. But as it was, it wasn't just him, and my dad has a horrible game face.

I suppose my face wasn't all that slick as well, because Nate grabbed my fingers and squeezed them to get my attention. When I looked up at him, he gave me a reassuring smile, which made me more confused than anything else.

"So, Danny," the doctor said, looking at my chart. "How's the pain?"

"Right now? Not bad," I answered truthfully.

He nodded and checked something off. "Turns out you're allergic to codeine," he said, still not looking at me. "Would have been nice to know that before we gave it to you, but it turns out you've never needed it before now." He glanced up at me. "See what being healthy gets you?"

I'm pretty sure that was an attempt at a joke, but I didn't smile.

"So here it is," he said, closing the chart. "The car that hit you impacted the driver's side going somewhere around sixty miles an hour. It was the fact that your Jeep was so far off the ground that you're here to talk about it. Instead of hitting you straight on, it caught you below the waist." He paused and let those words settle in. "I've seen enough car crashes in my time to know, you would have most likely been killed in a normal car. You got lucky."

If this is what lucky felt like, I did not want to be unlucky.

"Now the bad part. Your leg is broken in three different places, and there is a hairline fracture in your hip. I have no doubt that you're going to heal from it completely. You're young and in great shape."

I nodded, not understanding the bad part of the news.

"But there is a chance you aren't going to be able to play ball anymore," he said flatly. "I mean, maybe recreationally, but professionally?" He shook his head as a way of finishing his sentence. "Anyway, we aren't there yet. We have a lot of physical therapy in front of us first. You thought you exercised before? Wait until you try rehab; you'll wish you could go back to just working out."

Nate, who was still holding my hand, looked at the doctor. "You've never done two-a-days, doc, and you're wrong." He looked down at me and grinned. "He's not only going to play basketball again, he's going to kick ass at it."

My dad asked the doctor some questions, but I ignored it as I looked up at Nate. "You really think so?"

He shook his head. "Nope. I know so."

He said it with such conviction I had to believe it myself.

CHAPTER NINE:
REBOUND

TURNS OUT the doctor was not wrong; physical therapy sucked balls.

I was released with crutches and pain killers after a week and a half, a week and a half that Nate spent by my bedside. I asked him if he had other places to be, but he always shook his head no before going back to watching TV. "Nope, I'm where I need to be."

And that was the end of the conversation.

When I got home, I found my dad had replaced my bed with a much larger hospital-style one. "Turns out there were still a few of these in storage on base from when it was a hospital," he explained when I looked at the thing, confused. "You're going to need to keep as much weight as you can off that hip for the time being. This is going to help."

I found it hard to believe that my dad found a free hospital bed just lying around, but I was too tired from hobbling from the car to my room to argue. I sat down on the edge of the mattress, and my dad took my crutches. I saw most of my stuff had been moved out of the way, and my old bed was against the far wall. At the end of the bed stood two suitcases and a duffel bag with the A&M logo on it.

"Nate's using your old bed. You don't mind, right?" my dad asked me. I heard Nate clattering into the house, hauling the rest of my stuff in from the car,

"He's sleeping in here with me?" I asked, panicked.

My dad gave me a small smile. "Relax, it's going to be okay."

Having Nate in my room as I slept was not my definition of okay at all. But I was too tired to argue. Instead I leaned back into the bed and scooted myself up, which brought an explosion of pain from my hip.

"*Fucking shit!*" I screamed. My leg felt like it was being torn off by a shark with a pretty serious grudge against me. I saw spots form in front of my eyes even though they were closed from the pain. I felt my dad's hands grab my shoulders and steady me as he called out to Nate for something.

I had really thought I'd felt pain before in my life. You're talking to a guy who worked out no less than four hours a day and thought he was pretty good friends with pain. I really thought pain and me were on speaking terms and that this was going to be something we could get through together. But as I lay there feeling like my leg was on fire, I realized pain was not my friend. In fact, we barely knew each other.

That and I was going to end up being its bitch for a while.

Telling me the pain would be gone in a little bit, my dad shoved a couple of pills into my mouth and followed them with a drink of water. I didn't believe him because there was no way two little tabs of anything could take away the engulfing agony that made up my entire left leg. I didn't need two tablets of what I'd swallowed. I needed a whole pizza full of serious pain crap, because this was not going to work if I had to....

And then I felt light-headed.

"Oh wow," I said after a few minutes, lying back on the bed.

"There we go," my dad said, breathing a sigh of relief.

Nate's face loomed over mine for a moment as he looked down at me. "Do not try to move like that without someone helping you, dumbass. You want to hurt yourself more?"

I reached up and pinched his cheeks. "You're cute," I said, drunk as I'd ever felt before.

"Leave him for now. He needs some rest," my dad said to Nate. "Ignore what he says. He's out of it."

Their voices started to fade away as my world grew darker, and I finally slept.

When I woke up, it was night. I could see the full moon peeking in through my window. My mind was fuzzy from the meds, but I could hear Nate snoring quietly across the room. I sat up, and I heard a bell ring down by my foot.

"Huh?" I heard Nate say in the dark. "Danny, you up?" I heard the bed creak when he rolled off, and he was next to my bed. "How you feeling?"

"Hungry," I said before I could even think about it.

I saw Nate grin in the darkness as he took the bell off my toe. "Figured. Let me grab you something. Everything else okay?" he asked, pausing for effect.

I nodded. "And maybe something to drink," I added.

"You sure? That's everything?"

"Um, I think so, yeah."

"Okay, 'cause I'm going to be in the kitchen for a while, and you can't get up by yourself."

"Um, okay," I said slowly.

"Do not get up," he repeated sternly.

I gave him a mock salute. "Aye aye, captain."

He rolled his eyes and walked out of the room… and then it hit me.

I had to piss.

I looked out my door and knew there was no way to get his attention unless I practically shouted, which seemed like a bad idea since it was almost three in the morning according to my alarm clock. I didn't want to wake my dad, but I didn't want to piss myself either. Which I was about to do.

"Nate," I screamed in a whisper out the door.

Nothing.

"*Nate!*" I tried again.

All I could hear was running water from the kitchen.

Oh fuck, the water was not a good thing to hear. I looked around in a panic for something to piss in. A cup, a mug—shit, I'd take a water balloon right now, but there was nothing.

"Nate!" I whispered again.

I looked across the hall and could see the bathroom from where I was. I could do this. I could limp across the damn hall. I mean, I used to run miles, for God's sake. Across the hall couldn't be that hard. I winced as I moved my legs off the side of the bed, and my head swam for a moment as I tried to force past the pain coming from my hip.

"Come on, Monroe," I encouraged myself. "You can do this."

The toes of my uninjured foot touched the carpet, and I took another few seconds to catch my breath. I waited to see if Nate was coming, but water was still running in the kitchen, and it was driving me nuts. Taking a deep breath, I steadied myself and tried to stand up.

And screamed as loud as I ever had as I fell to the ground.

I say I fell, but it was more like I threw myself as hard as I could at the floor, because there was no way in hell my foot could support my weight, not even a little. Of course hitting the floor didn't do anything for my hip, which joined in with the pain symphony my leg was belting out and let me tell you, they liked the song something fierce. I couldn't move because everything I did was just more pain, but just lying there was like lying in molten lava.

It was like nothing I had ever felt before.

You think you know pain well enough from all the times you stub your toe or slam into a pole, but man, that pain wasn't even in this pain's league as far as I was concerned. Normal pain was two ten-year-olds throwing the ball around after school. This pain was all-NBA, trust me. Nate came rushing in with my dad hot on his heels. That whole plan of not waking him up? Yeah, that didn't work. They hovered over me, not sure what to do, since every time they tried to get me up, I screamed louder as my hip and leg began to go into the third chorus of "You're a Fucking Idiot and Should Have Waited."

Finally my dad grabbed my shoulders and pulled me up in one motion like I was a scarecrow. "Grab his legs and swing them onto the bed," he barked at Nate, who grabbed my feet as my dad eased me into the position I'd started in five minutes earlier. "Okay, down gently," he said, which was funny because if there were any additional pain from them laying me back down, I was not going to feel it over the blinding clusterfuck that was my left side.

"You goddamned idiot!" my dad roared once I was lying back down. "Do you have any idea what 'do not move' means? The doctors aren't even sure you're going to be able to run again, much less play ball, and you want to try crawling out of bed? What the fuck were you doing, Danny?"

Tears of shame and anger were rolling down my face and, I am not ashamed to say, from pain as well. I just looked at my dad.

"You can't be this stupid!" my dad kept going while I tried not to wince from my hip's aria.

"Mr. Monroe," Nate interrupted timidly. "Can you get his pills? I think he's in pain."

At first the words meant nothing to my dad; between being wakened and being four kinds of pissed, he was not processing language very well. But one by one the words penetrated, and he looked at me and asked, "Does it hurt?"

I nodded.

"Good," he said, shaking his head. "Maybe pain will get the message through that thick skull how hurt you really are." He stomped out and into his room.

Nate walked over to the side of my bed, a sympathetic look on his face. "You could have just said you needed to piss, dude."

I looked up at him shocked. "How did you know…?"

He looked down and then away.

Perfect, I hadn't only woke up my dad and fucked up my leg. I'd also pissed myself.

Perfect, Danny, just perfect.

My dad shoved some pills down my throat, and within a couple of minutes I was out cold, When I woke up, sunlight was coming through the window, and Nate was nowhere to be seen. I looked around groggily, trying to remember last night.

And then it hit me.

I tossed back the covers and saw I was wearing a different pair of sweats.

Falling back into my pillow, I groaned. "Perfect. I had to be changed like a fucking baby."

Nate must have heard me because a few seconds later, he walked in. "So it lives," he said cheerfully. "How you feeling?"

Mortified, I pulled a pillow over my head. "Horrible."

"You in pain?" he asked, concerned. "I have pills, but we have to be—"

I pulled the pillow off. "No, I'm embarrassed, dude."

That made him pause. "Why?"

"Really?" I asked him. "I pissed myself last night."

"Oh!" he said, realizing what my problem was. "Seriously, man, let that go. You couldn't help yourself."

"Says the guy who didn't piss himself last night," I muttered.

"You have to go now?" he asked, holding up a plastic container. "Get it out of the way."

"What is that?" I asked, knowing exactly what it was and hating it.

"It's something to piss in," he explained way too happily. "They sent it home with you." He held it out to me. "So yes?"

The bad thing was, I did need to piss.

"Fine, give it to me," I said, taking it and opening the top. "Just… go in it?"

"Yeah," he said, examining the container intently. "It looks big enough, right?" I had no idea, since I never measured how much I pee.

"I can get up," I said, shoving it away.

"No you can't," he said, putting it back in my hand. "Unless you have to take a dump or need to shower, you're in bed. So learn to use it or piss yourself again. And this time I am not changing you."

My stomach heaved, and I felt like I was going to throw up.

"Oh God! You changed me?"

"Well, I helped your dad, but… dude, it isn't that big a deal," he tried to convince me.

"God, I fucked things up," I said, feeling like I could die right there and then.

Nate sighed and shook his head. "Just go to the bathroom. I'll grab you some food."

He walked out, and I opened the top and did my business. Turns out the bottle was more than large enough.

He came back carrying a plate with some eggs and sausage, and I could hear my stomach make a noise in response. "Well, part of you is happy to see food," he said, putting the plate down and reaching for the container.

"You don't have to do that," I said quickly.

"You gonna eat breakfast next to a container of piss? Dude, just chill out."

I wanted to argue, but the food kept distracting me, and he walked out before I could even try. I inhaled everything in about three bites; nothing had ever tasted so good in my life. I was about to lick the plate when Nate came back in and handed me a huge glass of orange juice. I grabbed it and swallowed it in one huge gulp.

"Damn!" I said, leaning back. "That was the best breakfast I've ever had."

He laughed and took the plate and glass away. "It was eggs, dude. You just haven't eaten in forever."

"You don't have to clean up after me," I said, realizing the instant the words came out how stupid they were, because what was I supposed to do? Hobble to the kitchen myself?

He put the plate down on my dresser and turned around to look at me. "Okay, let's get this over with. What's your deal?"

I had no idea what he was talking about.

"You can't be here by yourself, and I'm trying to help. What's your damage with that?"

"I just feel bad. You shouldn't have to do all that," I muttered, not sure how to answer. "I mean, this can't be how you wanted to spend your summer."

"I planned on spending summer figuring out if I wanted to hear my mom bitch about my dad or visit my cousin in North Texas. I didn't have any plans, and I don't mind doing this. Anything else?" he asked, crossing his arms.

"Why? You barely know me," I blurted out. "I mean, I appreciate you being here, but I just—"

"I had a brother and he died," he said, interrupting me. The words brought me to a screeching halt. "He died, and I have always wondered what it would be like…." His voice got thick with emotion, and I could hear him clear his throat. "Anyways, I've always wanted a little brother, and you seem to be needing a big one right now."

We locked eyes.

"You got it?" he asked.

I felt ashamed. "I didn't mean… I just…." Nothing would come out in the order I wanted it to.

"And your dad told me about you, and I don't give a flying fuck if you're gay, bi, or the world's ugliest woman. It doesn't matter to me, so if that's what you're scared about, you can get over that as well."

The pills didn't make me feel as dizzy as his statement had.

"And no, he didn't just say you liked guys. He asked a series of questions that made it pretty clear he was asking if I was your friend or your *friend*," he said, using air quotes. "I told him we were just friends, and he dropped it, but I think I cracked his code. So, anything else you want to talk about, or we good?"

I nodded.

"Awesome," he said, picking the plate and glass up again. "You're getting ripe, so that means trying to get you vertical, which is improbable, or a sponge bath, which means you getting over the fact I'm seeing you naked. Which I already have. So figure it out."

And he walked out.

Now you have an idea how my summer went.

Nate took care of me when my dad was gone and helped me get to the physical therapist so I could learn to walk again. I really thought that was going to be the easiest part. I mean, how hard could it be to walk again when I was used to working out six times a week? There was nothing this guy could throw at me that I wasn't ready for.

Turns out the list of things I was not ready for was massive.

It was almost a month and a half after coming home, which meant almost two months since the accident, and I was climbing the walls, metaphorically. My hip still ached, but it no longer exploded into earth-shattering fits of pain like it had. The doctor said I was healing really fast, which was good. When he took my cast off, I thought the leg under it belonged to someone else, it was so small. I had always prided myself on my calves; not a lot of guys have good ones, and I had great ones, if I was going to be honest.

Now I had one normal one and one that looked like it was attached to an eleven-year-old boy.

The doctor warned me that having my cast off was no indication that I was ready to do anything strenuous. He said hip injuries were tricky with the healthiest of people, and I shouldn't get my hopes up. He set me up for PT three times a week, which Nate would help me with while my dad was working. The PT guy was this massive black guy who looked like he was a former Oakland Raider linebacker and looked me and Nate up and down when we walked into his gym.

"You Monroe?" he asked. I nodded. "Great. You are not a basketball player in here. You are not a jock. In fact, all you are is someone who can't walk, so I don't want to hear any crap about how healthy you are or what you did before this. We're going to do this my way, and I am not taking any flak just because you used to be able to jump."

"He'll jump again," Nate said, not liking this guy's tone at all.

PT guy swiveled his head toward Nate, and it reminded me of a bulldog orientating on its prey. "You a physical trainer?" Nate shook his head. "You have a degree in health or kinesiology?" Another shake. "Then shut the hell up."

I almost chuckled until he looked back at me. "Laugh it up. We'll see how funny this all is when we're done."

It took all of forty-five minutes for him to get me to cry.

No joke, I had been run into the ground by coaches on two continents, and none of them had made me hurt like this guy. Besides the fact that I hadn't done shit in two months, so I was as weak as that eleven-year-old kid my leg belonged to, it turned out most of my muscles had assumed doing nothing was the way we were going to live from now on and were pretty pissed to find out the vacation was over.

I was drenched in sweat, lying on the exercise mat as he went over and wrote some things down in my file.

"You okay?" Nate asked, coming over to me.

"Hell no, he is not okay," PT guy shouted from across the gym. "He's lying there crying his eyes out like he's been mugged. What part of okay do you think that looks like?"

"I'll be okay," I assured him.

"Maybe," PT guy said, walking over to me and dropping a piece of paper onto my chest. "That's a list of things you should get. Epsom salts, heating pad, normal stuff." He then added a folder. "List of exercises you should be doing every day at home." And then another stack of papers. "And a dietary list you ain't gonna follow, but you can't say I didn't give it to you."

He finally dropped a towel onto me and concluded with, "Next Monday, same time."

Nate helped me limp out slowly before PT guy could come back for some more.

Turns out PT guy wanted me to soak in a tub of hot water to help loosen up some muscles, which sounds like a completely normal request until you realize I was over six and a half feet tall. We had a tub, of course, but it was small for normal people, which meant it might work if I wanted to soak my feet. My dad talked to the school and got permission for us to use the locker room there, specifically the huge tubs we used for icing up or soaking in. Since it was still summer break, no one was using them, so the people Dad talked to let Nate and me go in after therapy so I could cry in private.

Nate stripped down to his trunks and got in with me since there was more than enough room. The first few sessions I actually fell asleep, I was so drained after being mangled by PT guy. The second week the coach came in. He had, of course, heard that I had been in the accident, but this was the first time he'd checked in on me. When he saw Nate and I were in the tub, he made a face but didn't say anything, instead asking me how I felt.

"Sore," I admitted. "I thought I was okay, but just simple leg lifts are killing me."

He nodded, no doubt understanding more about it than me. "Son," he said, looking at Nate. "You mind if we have a second?"

Nate nodded, climbing out of the tub and wrapping a towel around his waist. "Holler when you're ready to get out," he said to me.

Once he was out of earshot, the coach said in a low tone, "Look, Danny, your accident... what happened. That wasn't because of what I said to you, right?"

And here I thought he was going to accuse Nate and me of fooling around in the tub.

"No, Coach," I said honestly. "Everything you said that night was true, and to be honest, I never even saw the other car." I got flashes of memory sometime, but I wasn't going to tell him that. Half seconds where I could hear the other car tearing through the Jeep's door, the red flash as my leg snapped.

I shook my head. "I wasn't drunk or anything. Seriously, Coach. It was just an accident."

He seemed to accept most of that. He wanted to say more, from the look on his face, but he didn't. "Well, get better, and even if you can't play this year, you're still on the team. I expect you to be on the bench cheering and giving them pointers."

Even if I couldn't play? For some reason hearing the coach say it out loud made it real in a way my dad, the doctor, and even Nate hadn't been able to. I didn't say anything, just nodded, and we talked about nothing for a while, but I can't remember what it was. All I could think of was that I might not be able to play this year.

On the way back to base, I asked Nate, "What if I can't play again period?"

He didn't even pause, just shook his head. "Nope, you'll play again."

He sounded so sure it took me by surprise. "I mean play professionally," I amended.

He nodded. "That's what I meant too."

As we pulled off the freeway toward the base, I asked, "And you're so sure, why?"

He took a couple of seconds before answering, gathering his thoughts. "Because God gave you a gift. He gave you basketball, and he wouldn't take that away from you. He might make you work for it once in a while, but he'd never take it from you. You'll play again."

He said it with such conviction that it was startling. "You really think that?"

"That you'll play again?" he asked, glancing over to me.

"That I have a gift?"

He chuckled. "Dude, you're as tall as the Chrysler Building, you have zero percent body fat, and can do a standing jump that most people need a trampoline to pull off. You really think that isn't a gift?"

I didn't have an answer, so I just sat there and stayed quiet.

When he saw I wasn't really convinced, he laughed. "Look, you can think whatever you want, but trust me when I say there are a ton of 'ballers out there who would kill for what you were born with. That doesn't mean you should go and be a douche about it, but it does mean you should thank God every day for giving it to you."

We pulled onto base, and I filed the information away somewhere in my brain to look at again later. I was just too tired to really think then.

When August began to dwindle away, it was becoming clear there was no way I could play that year. I was walking, which was awesome, but anything more than that, and I started panting like I was two Big Macs away from a heart attack. The coach assured me again that I had a place on the team, but I started to get depressed because it felt like I was falling behind.

Falling behind what, I couldn't tell you. All I knew was I was in a race with some fantasy version of myself, and he hadn't been in a car accident that almost killed him, so he was playing this year and I wasn't. Of course, fake me wasn't into guys either and actually liked his girlfriend, so he was ahead of me in more than a few ways.

Which reminds me, I guess I should mention what happened with Carol before we get too far ahead of ourselves.

Carol, of course, tried to visit me in the hospital, but at first they didn't want anyone in my room wearing me out other than my dad. After that, Nate had practically moved into my hospital room, so I had talked to her a few times and assured her I was good and didn't need anything. Which was true, but I guess as my girlfriend she wanted to do something. When I started PT, my time was either spent at therapy killing myself or at home resting up from killing myself, so I had even less time for her to come by and check on me.

Finally, one day her sister Susan knocked on my door. In her hand was my class ring.

I was lying on the couch and tried to get up when I saw her. She glanced at Nate and walked past him without saying anything. "So yeah, this is yours. I know you got in an accident, and I'm glad you're okay now, but using that to ignore my sister is a shitty thing to do."

"I didn't—" I began to protest.

"Tommy told me about you," she said, cutting me off, and I felt myself go pale. "When you came back and apologized to her, I thought you had changed, but obviously I was wrong," she said, looking back at Nate again. "So here, and leave her alone from now on. Got it?"

I nodded as I took the ring.

"I'm not going to tell her because she'd just feel like an idiot that she had no idea, but I should. I should tell the entire school who you really are and see if you're still big man on campus."

As she got angrier, I just shrank more and more inside.

"Okay, we got it," Nate said, opening the door.

She looked over and laughed. "Oh, so you're the new boyfriend? You know he dumped the last one without even telling him why, right? When it comes to Danny, it's all about him, and no one else matters."

Nate took a step toward her and growled, "Bitch, you have no idea what you're talking about. I'm not his boyfriend, he didn't blow your sister off, and if he did dump some guy, do you think he did it with a smile? You think doing something like that would be easy? And before you ride out of here on your broom, the reason he has to lie to people like your sister and dump guys he really likes is because of small-minded fuckers like you, who think threatening to tell people is acceptable."

Her mouth was almost to the floor, she looked so shocked.

"Well, you two should be very happy together," she snarled, storming out.

"I'm sorry," I mumbled, but I'm pretty sure she never heard me.

"I'm not gay, bitch!" Nate bellowed before he slammed the door. "Though chicks like that sure make me wish I was." He looked over at me, and whatever he saw wasn't good. "Danny? You okay?"

The room was spinning as I felt the house of cards that had been my life come crashing down around me. Cody, Tommy, all of it just came slamming into my brain at the same time and I fell back onto the couch, dropping my ring because everything it reminded me of just made me sick.

And that's how my summer ended, sports fans. Not with a victory but with a big old Danny Monroe clusterfuck.

Yeah, I don't know how I couldn't have seen it before. God loves me big time.

CHAPTER TEN:
SECONDARY BREAK

WHEN SUMMER break ended, Nate went back to College Station, and I got ready for a school year that was going to suck in, like, fourteen different ways.

I don't want to say that the guys were happy I wasn't playing that year, but it was pretty obvious they weren't going to be crying rivers of sadness for me. I had done too much last season to alienate myself from them to think they would have some sympathy that I'd busted up my leg and hip. The coach explained I would be acting like a student coach that season, meaning I was going to watch the squad and work with the guys one-on-one to build up the skills they needed to improve. At first it seemed like the shittiest thing I could do for a season, but then something happened.

I remembered how much I loved the game of basketball.

Last year it had been all about points and winning, and I forgot the sheer joy of just playing the game. It crept up on me. I was going over hand placement for free throws when I got up and hobbled over to the free-throw line. I couldn't even jog yet, but standing still, I could do all right. The guy I was showing—I think his name was Simon or something—was watching as I steadied the ball with my left hand, showing him what I'd been talking about.

I dribbled twice and looked up at the basket, and for a brief moment it looked like it was a million miles away. My mind couldn't understand how I had ever sunk a ball into that tiny basket from so far away. Suddenly I felt like I had never played before and everything was completely alien.

Then I closed my eyes and took a deep breath.

Without thinking, I put the ball up. My hip ached as I went up on my toes to give it power, but I ignored the pain and stood there, watching the ball sail away from me in slow motion. It spun over and over as it drifted toward the basket as if it had all the time in the world. I was sweating as I watched that ball climb and climb....

And miss as it ricocheted off the backboard.

I could hear Simon stifle a gasp next to me, because if that had happened last year, it would have been followed by a string of curses blaming everything but myself for the miss. Instead I just laughed and said, "Okay, you want to do it exactly like that except for the missing part." He saw I wasn't upset, and he laughed also.

From there things began to change.

The rest of the guys realized that the accident hadn't only hurt my leg but possibly knocked out the gigantic stick that had been up my ass. It was a good day, and by the end, Simon's posture was better, and he was well on his way to mastering the free throw.

The rest of my day, unfortunately, went downhill the moment I walked into rehab.

Maybe I was limping, or maybe PT guy had some weird psychic sense, but he knew instantly something was wrong. "You playing basketball?" he asked as I began to stretch.

I froze, wondering how he could have figured that out. "No," I said instantly and then looked away from him before he could use his crazy eyes on me. When I glanced back, he was still staring at me. "Not really," I added, and his expression didn't change. "It was a free throw. One free throw!"

His face lit up as he smiled. "Oh, just a free throw. Then that's cool."

I sighed in relief when was he suddenly in my face screaming. "No, it is not cool!" I winced, but he kept on going. "Do you get that you're lucky to be walking without a cane? No, of course you don't, because you think this is all a joke." I opened my mouth to protest, but he wasn't in the mood to let me talk. "Your hip is on the verge of cracking, and when it does you're going to have to have screws put into it, and then you're going to be lucky if you can jog, much less do free throws. Every time you put stress on it, say like coming back down from a jump, you run the risk it will just go, and that's it. No more basketball, no more normal life—you're just a tall guy with a limp. So you wanna think this is a waste of time or that you're invulnerable? Be my guest. Because *my* hips are fine."

I felt so bad I thought I might throw up.

"Don't even bother warming up. I am too pissed right now to do this. I'll just end up hurting you."

Oh my God, he'd been holding back this entire time?

"Be here tomorrow if you're serious. If not, do whatever you want. It's your life."

I hobbled out of there as fast as I could. As I sat at the bus stop and waited for the shuttle that went by the base, I thought about what he'd said. The thought I might never play basketball again really hadn't sunk in. I had been scared I might not be as good as I was, but not being able to play at all was something I couldn't get my head around. What was the point of my life if I couldn't do the thing I loved? What would I do? I couldn't even imagine it. I loved absolutely nothing else as much as basketball. On the bus I swore I would take PT seriously and do everything I could do to get back to basketball.

Because I didn't know any other way to live.

At school I did my best to get the guys ready for the season, and after school I threw myself into PT as if my life depended on it. Because in a lot of ways, it did. PT guy didn't say anything to me, but I knew he was watching me like a hawk. He expected me to mess up again, and I knew it would be the last strike against me. So I focused all my energies into getting better and stopped worrying so much about the season.

It was a couple of weeks before the season started when Nate hit me up on Skype from his dorm.

"So he hasn't killed you yet?" he asked me about PT guy.

"Not yet, but I thought he was going to when I told him about the free throw." I could see Nate's dorm room behind him, and it looked like the coolest place I could imagine. I mean, sure it didn't look like much, but it was his, all his, and that was something I had never had before. Every room I'd had really belonged to the military, so it never felt like it was really mine. I was a renter—no, a squatter at best—since I didn't pay anything. So the dorm looked like it was Willy Wonka's place in my eyes.

"Well, that you deserved," he said, laughing. "You could have messed yourself up bad. And it wasn't even a real free throw."

I gave him a grin. "So if I busted my hip making an actual point, then it would be okay?"

He pretended to think about it for a second. "Well, yeah, that seems fair."

"Fuck off," I said, laughing.

He looked like he was going to say something when a head came into the frame. I didn't know who she was, but she was really pretty. "We're going out to Westgate," she announced before giving Nate a kiss on the cheek. "We'll be at Mad Hatter's if you change your mind."

He kissed her back, and I felt a small chill go down my spine.

"This is Danny," he said, gesturing to the screen.

She looked over and waved into the webcam. "Hey, I've heard about you," she said, smiling.

I smiled back, but I felt my stomach sour. "Hey," I answered, not sure what to say.

She waited a few seconds to see if there was anything else, and then she looked back to Nate and said bye. He watched her leave the room, and I just felt worse and worse. "So yeah, that's Amy...," he began to explain until he saw the look on my face. "Danny? What's wrong?"

It was a good question, one I couldn't answer. I mean, why was I so upset? I knew Nate wasn't into guys. Was there some part of me that was jealous? I mean, I knew I had no right, but my heart apparently thought otherwise. "Yeah, I'm cool," I answered, sounding lame even to myself.

He paused and looked at me through the screen for a long time before he started talking. "Danny, you know I'm not like that."

Awesome, not only am I being stupid and jealous, but I'm being *obviously* stupid and jealous.

"I know," I said way too fast. "It's not that." I lied so badly that I knew I would never be a criminal mastermind because once accused, I'd just look down and deny it so badly they would have no choice but to lock me up.

"Danny," he said, but I refused to look up at the screen. "Danny, look at me." I peeked up, and I saw him staring at me intently. "You know I care for you as much as I can, but I don't want you to get confused about what we are."

"I'm not," I said honestly. "I just...." And my words left me.

"It's just what?" he prompted.

I took a deep breath and readied myself to say the last words I would ever say to Nate, because after this he would turn off his computer and never talk to me again. "It's just this summer I got used to having you all to myself... even as friends, and I just miss you and it kills me I am stuck down here and can't even play basketball and I am just a screwed up guy and I won't blame you when you stop talking to me I just...." I felt my eyes start to sting, and I swore I wasn't going to break down in front of him. "It's nothing, my fault completely." I'd expected a lot of different responses coming from him, from screaming to just unloading a buttload of insults at me, but I wasn't ready for what he actually did.

He started laughing.

My mind didn't quite know how to process that, so I just sat there dumbfounded. When he didn't stop, I had to ask. "What's so funny?"

He wiped his eyes and shook his head. "Dude, you are worse than any three girlfriends I have ever had." I scowled, not really understanding what he was getting at but pretty sure it wasn't good. He had to see the look of confusion on my face, and he sputtered out between laughs, "It's not bad. I'm just—" He caught his breath. "—I mean, I spent my entire summer break taking care of you, and you want more?" Yep, I was right, I now felt even worse. "Look, bud, we will always be friends if I have my wish and no girl will ever change that, and the fact I go to school, like, eight hours away from you sucks, but neither one of us has enough money to commute back and forth just for a weekend. This isn't about me. It's just that you're lonely."

"I know," I said, trying not to sigh.

"Well, then go make some friends. Or better yet, go get some. I mean, you're not a bad-looking guy." I stared at him, and he shrugged. "I mean, I'm guessing here. People say I look okay, and you have the same build as I do. If you were straight, I'd say come up here for a party and I could get three girls on you, but I'm fresh out of gay guys...."

"Your advice is to go get laid?" I asked him, not believing what he was saying.

"Danny, as we spend more time together, you're going to find that's my answer for a lot of things. Depressed? Get laid. Bored? Get laid. Have a test tomorrow? Get laid so at least you have something to think about when you're failing. You're sixteen! For Christ's sake, loosen up."

"It's not that easy to just go get laid," I muttered. "At least with guys. I mean, what if someone found out, and—"

"I get it. There just has to be a way around it." He seemed to think about it for a second and then snapped his fingers. "I got an idea; hold on."

He started typing something on his keyboard and moved his mouse around some. I'm not sure if he had minimized the Skype window, but I could still see him. It took about a minute, and then he said, "Okay, check your Facebook."

I flipped screens over to a browser and pulled my Facebook account up. There was a friend invite from Amy. "What's this for?" I asked, not accepting it.

"Amy is a theater major. Like, all of her friends are gay. Accept the invite and look through her friends. If you see anyone you like, I can be sure he's gay and then see if he's into you."

"Dude, it's Facebook, not a yellow pages to get laid."

He chuckled. "You've been using it wrong. Click the invite."

I did, not knowing what I had just agreed to.

The next few days, I ignored Facebook like a plague. I wasn't sure what I was going to catch being on there, but I knew it couldn't be good. Three more days of grueling PT, along with having to watch guys play basketball when I couldn't, left me completely frustrated by the time Friday rolled around. I took the bus back from PT, once again cussing out the guy who'd totaled my [dad's] Jeep not just for fucking my leg up but for making me ride public transportation.

By the time I got back to base, I was cranky and exhausted. I threw myself into the shower and hoped the hot water would somehow bring me back to life. Most likely I was overestimating the magical power of a hot shower, but at that point I needed something to cheer me up. There was a note on the table along with a couple of twenties from my dad telling me he had duty all weekend and I should order a pizza.

Friday night at home watching TV. It's official, I was living the high life.

So it should come as no surprise that after a medium hand-tossed with extra cheese and three episodes of *Arrow*, I ended up on Facebook. I still had no idea if Amy even knew Nate had friended us, but I was so bored that I had nothing better to do. She had over a thousand friends, which was just silly because there was no way she knew all those people in real life. I mean, I was pretty sure I hadn't even met that many people in my entire life, much less to be friends with. There was no mistaking that most of these guys were in drama and gay from the pics they had for their profiles. I know that sounds shitty, but I mean, there is being gay and then looking *real* gay. These guys looked flammable. I kept flipping through them, my boredom overriding the feeling I was just using a really skeevy dating service.

I was about to give up when I saw his picture in the middle of a dozen others.

It wasn't just his blond hair or ridiculously white smile that made me notice him; there was something more. I clicked on his profile, and I was stunned by the guy I saw. His name was Sam Parker, and I was instantly attracted to him. I can't lie. Anyone would have been attracted to him. He had shaggy blond hair that framed a face that on its worst day would be described as angelic. His eyes were such a bright blue that it looked like he was wearing contacts, though from the numerous pictures he had up, I could tell they were natural. He had a kicking body. He'd posted numerous pics of him with some friends at the beach, and I had to admit I would have stared at him relentlessly if I'd seen him in person.

He went to high school in Dallas, and from what I could tell, he was insanely popular.

I cyberstalked him most of the night. I found his Instagram account along with his Twitter and absorbed as much as I could. He played baseball for his high school, but he was openly gay, which blew me away because we were the same age, and he had already come out? If people had a problem with him being gay, it didn't come up on social media. There was no way a guy like this was real. I left Nate a message on Facebook to call me no matter how late it was and tried to close my laptop.

That lasted, like, ten minutes before I was back online looking at this guy's profile.

He had two older brothers who both looked like they were models too. From his pictures I could see he had been to Disney World twice with his family, and there were a ton of pics of him in Australia surfing. In fact, as I kept digging, there were a ton of pics of him in surfing trunks and nothing else. He had a flat stomach with a decent six-pack that looked like he took keeping in shape seriously. The more I learned, the more I became obsessed. Sam Parker was the perfect guy.

At some point I passed out, because I woke up with my cell blaring "Space Jam," meaning Nate was calling me.

"Hey," I croaked into the phone.

"Man, what were you doing all night?" he asked me in a cheerful tone that was not appropriate for this early in the morning.

"Um... nothing," I said, rolling away from the sunlight coming through my window. "Ate pizza and...."

And I remembered.

I sat up and instantly regretted it as the sun killed me. Covering my eyes, I said, "I found someone."

"Cool!" he said, sounding really happy for me. "Where did you meet him?"

"I haven't yet," I explained quickly.

"Wait, what now?"

"On Facebook, Amy's Facebook. I saw someone on there." Oh my God, this seemed so legit last night, but now I just sounded pathetic.

"Oh," he said, confused, and then I heard him get it. "*Oh!* Yeah? Who's the lucky guy?"

"Sam Parker," I said, trying to push past how stupid I felt.

"Sam?" he asked. "Blond surfer-looking guy?"

"Yeah, that's the one. He's from Dallas?"

"Richardson—he goes to high school with Amy's brother," he confirmed. "Yeah, pick someone else, dude."

"Say what?" I asked, sitting up in bed. "Why?"

From his hesitation, I knew he was searching for the right words. "Sam is... Sam is intense. He came out when he was, like, fourteen, is on the baseball team, I think he's class president. I don't think it would be a good fit."

"Why not?" I asked, trying not to whine.

"Um... he's... he's pretty out" was all Nate said.

"Are you trying to say he acts like a girl?"

"Oh no, I had no idea he was gay until Amy told me. He comes off like a normal jock. I'm just saying he is pretty vocal about being gay. I don't know if that's your thing."

"What would be so wrong with that?" I asked, even though I had a feeling what he was going to say.

"Dude, no one knows about you now, and that's a good thing if you're heading towards getting a scholarship. I'm not sure Sam is a date-on-the-DL kind of guy. I'm pretty sure if he was going to date someone, he would have to be out."

"But he lives in Dallas," I protested.

"Richardson," Nate corrected me.

"He doesn't live *here*," I amended. "If I went out with him there, no one here would know. I mean, how could that hurt me?"

I heard him sigh and knew I was talking out my ass. "Look, man, I know what you mean. Sam's a good-looking guy. I'm not gay and I know that. But he's, like… I don't know, like some kind of weird alpha gay male. I don't know if you're ready for that. Why don't we stick a pin in that and keep looking?"

"Nate, are you saying he wouldn't go for me? 'Cause if you are, just say it."

"It has nothing to do with your looks. I just don't think you're gay enough for him, that's all."

We talked about the upcoming season a little, but my heart wasn't in it. *Not gay enough?* Was that a thing now? I hung up and lay there in bed, staring up at my ceiling, wondering what I had done so wrong that life seemed to delight in kicking me in the balls. I mean, bad enough that I turned out liking guys, but now I didn't like them enough? I just wished I could skip this part of my life and jump to the part where I was out of school and didn't have to worry about what other people thought about this crap.

I put it out of my mind for the next few weeks heading up to the season.

The guys were good, but it was pretty obvious that we weren't strong enough to make it to state this year. If they played their asses off, they might get to the playoffs, but past that, there wasn't much chance. I didn't say anything, of course, because people have a way of surprising you just when you thought you had everything figured out. I just helped where I could and encouraged them the best I knew how.

But it was hard.

As the season started, I saw plays they were missing, opportunities they were passing up on the court, and it took everything

I had not to stand up and scream at them to pay attention. By the third game I was pretty sure I was on my way to an ulcer or a heart attack, and then I saw the coach looking at me, smiling.

"Welcome to the sidelines," he said just loud enough for me to hear. "*This* is the hardest part of the game. Watching it and not being able to affect it."

I suddenly had a huge understanding of how hard it is to be a coach.

I followed Nate's season as closely as our own, and it looked like he was having about as much fun as I was. Their team was getting dominated by the other schools, not because they were lacking in talent but because the other teams had some incredible talent. I wasn't sure how much A&M put into its basketball program, but whatever it was, they needed to spend a little more.

It was no surprise that we didn't make it to the playoffs; we had played our hearts out, but at the end of the day we didn't have the extra oomph that would have pushed us further. I had a sinking feeling that was on me. No one said the reason we lost was because I hadn't been playing, but I knew it, and it made me work that much harder at getting better. By the time Christmas break was over, I was feeling a thousand percent better, and my hip barely ached at all.

"So you're as good as you're going to get," PT guy said on a cold afternoon in December.

I was wiping myself down and looked up at him in shock. "I'm fixed?"

He shook his head. "No, I said what I meant. You're as good as you're going to get. Coming here or just doing it at home, it's all the same from now on."

I felt like it was my birthday and Christmas all wrapped up in one. "So I can play basketball again?" I asked eagerly.

He didn't say anything for a long time while he picked up the mats we had used. The longer he was silent, the more scared I got. Finally he sighed and looked over at me. "Look, Danny." I was shocked he knew my name. "I'm going to say something, and I know you're going to want to argue and fight against it, but don't, because I'm just telling you the truth. I don't think you should play basketball anymore." I felt the ground fall out from under me. "Normally a sport like that will cause repetitive stress injuries. With a part of the body that's already weak, stressing it more is just asking for trouble. Does that mean you can't play basketball? No. It just means sooner or later that hip is going to give out on you, and then you're going to need, at the very least, a cane to walk for the rest of your life."

It was the most he'd talked in the months I'd been coming there, and what he said was even worse than I'd imagined it would be.

"That being said, you're going to do everything you can to play again, so it doesn't matter, but I think you need to hear it at least once. Keep playing basketball, and you're going to destroy your body. Period."

I swallowed hard. "Are you going to put that on my evaluation?" I asked, talking about the piece of paper he needed to sign to let me back on the team.

He sighed again. "I should, but there is no earthly reason to do so. They want to know if you're well enough to play basketball now, and the answer is yes. No one is asking me if you should or not. So I'm telling you. Don't do it."

I said nothing, knowing anything that came out of my mouth would be an argument.

"You still want me to sign off on you playing basketball, don't you?" I nodded like a bobblehead. "Fine, I tried."

He signed the paper and thrust it out at me. "When your hip gives out on you, don't come back here. I hate seeing my all my hard work destroyed by stupid people."

"Thank you," I said, taking it before he changed his mind.

"And don't ever thank me for helping you be stupid again."

I changed and practically ran out of the gym.

I texted Nate on the bus ride back to base, telling him I was cleared to play again.

He texted back, asking if that meant I could come up to College Station for the weekend.

I literally made a *yahoo* noise when I read what he had sent. The old lady next to me moved a few inches farther away from me, but I didn't care. I told Nate it meant exactly that.

My dad, on the other hand, thought it meant nothing like that.

"You just got off of disability," he said as I set the table. "What if something happens up there?"

"Like what, Dad?" I pleaded but not whined, because my dad did not respond to whining at all. "I'll be with Nate the whole time. It's not like I'm going to fall down and not be able to get up."

He didn't say anything, which meant he was trying to find another reason to say no.

"Look, I'll have my cell the entire time, and I promise not to be on my feet a lot." He didn't say anything. "Come on, Dad. You know Nate will be all mother hen on me as well."

He sighed, and I knew I had won. "Fine, but I'm talking to Nate first."

"Deal," I said, jumping up in excitement. Obviously I had forgotten how tall I was in the past few months, because I hit my head on the ceiling pretty hard and almost fell on my ass. Pretty much making my dad's point for him. Instead I rubbed my head and kept putting the plates out.

"Tell him it's going to have to be next weekend," my dad said as he took the roast out of the oven. "We're busy this weekend."

I had already pulled my cell out and was in midtext. "Why?" That was a definite whine, because he looked over and scowled at me.

"Hey, if you want to go up there so bad, you can," he said, putting the pan down. "It just means I'll have to go pick out cars by myself."

I opened my mouth to argue and then stopped. "Cars?"

"Yeah, the insurance settlement came in, but if you aren't interested, you go, and I'll—"

"*A new car!*" I screamed, making sure not to jump this time. Instead I grabbed my dad from behind, picked him up, and twirled him around. "*A new car!*" I repeated as he laughed.

"Okay, just because you're bigger than me now does not mean you get to just throw me around," he exclaimed as I spun us around again. "Daniel Devin Monroe, put me down right now!"

I dropped him like he had burst into flames.

"How much do we have?" I asked him, thoughts of new Mustangs and Camaros dancing in my eyes.

"Enough," he said, smoothing his slacks out. "It covered the Jeep and included your pain and suffering, so we have enough for a new car." I opened my mouth, but he held up a finger. "A car that we will both agree on and use. Deal?"

I nodded, not trusting myself to speak.

"Go clean up before this gets cold," he said, gesturing at the roast.

There was a puff of Danny-shaped smoke where I had been standing as I ran to the bathroom.

After dinner I got on Skype and talked to Nate, telling him about PT and the new car.

"Well, that's even better," he said, taking a bite of something. "Amy and I are going to Dallas next weekend. Meet us there."

"What?" I said, suddenly feeling way out of my comfort zone.

"Her brother is in some talent show thing, and she wants us to go for support. We're leaving Friday morning. Meet us up there, and you can crash at her place with me all weekend."

"But I don't know her!" I said, wondering why meeting Amy was bugging me so much.

He shrugged and took another bite. "So? You're going to have to sooner or later—she's my girlfriend and you're my little brother. You guys are going to have to meet at some point."

I felt that tingle in my chest when he called me his little brother. "What if she doesn't like me?" I asked, laying my cards out on the table for him to see.

He laughed. "Dude, I want the two people I love in the world to meet. Come on. Just show up and see how it goes. We'll burn that bridge if we come to it."

I had never had someone besides my dad say they loved me before. It was a good feeling. "I'll have to ask my dad."

He nodded. "I'll call him too, let him know it's on the up-and-up."

"You have my dad's number?" I asked him, surprised.

He gave me a sideways look from the computer. "Dude, you don't know it yet, but we are family, so get over it."

I had to laugh at that.

"Dallas?" my dad asked later that week. "Danny, that's, like, eight hours away."

"So?" I said, ready for that argument. "We'd need to give the new car a test drive anyways. Why not to Dallas?"

"What if something happens on the way up there?" he argued back.

"I already called AT&T and got their car thing put on our phones. They'll send a tow truck wherever I'm at, and it's only, like, five bucks a month." He opened his mouth, and I added quickly, "Which I am willing to pay for a free tow."

"What about gas?"

"Well, you said some of that money is for pain and suffering. If there's anything left after the car, can't I use it for gas? Just this once?"

He sighed, and I knew I was wearing him down.

"Danny, we can't have you driving eight hours every weekend. We cannot make this a habit."

"I won't," I said, pouncing on the moment. "This is a one-time thing, and if I want to go to College Station, I'll pay for it myself."

"How?" he asked, knowing I had no answer.

"I'll get a job," I shot back.

He rolled his eyes. "Fine. If we find a car this weekend, and there is money left over, you can go." I began to get up to celebrate, but he cut me off. "But I am warning you, if there is anything wrong with your leg or hip and you don't tell me, I will take that car away from you so fast you'll think you dreamt it up."

I nodded. "Yes, sir."

He sighed. "You know you've done the 'sir' thing since you were six, and it doesn't score you any points, right?"

"Yes, sir," I said again, smiling.

He shook his head. "Go get ready for bed. And no talking to Nate all night on your cell. I can hear you through the walls."

I gave him a small salute as I ran off to take a shower.

Once my dad was safely in bed, I texted Nate. "I'm in."

All he sent back was one word.

EPIC!

Chapter Eleven:
Advance Step

I WANTED a Mustang; he wanted an SUV. I wanted another Jeep; he wanted a Volvo. I wanted a convertible; he wanted a minivan.

"Did you get turned into a forty-five-year-old soccer mom when I was in the hospital?" I asked him at the third lot we looked at.

He didn't say anything, but he had a sour look on his face.

I thought car shopping would be like actual shopping but for much cooler things. Instead it turned out to be a lot of numbers and safety figures that did not take into account how cool metallic red with a deep clear coat looked. I wanted something stylish, something flashy. He wanted something practical, something that would save on gas.

But there was more to Dad's shopping than that.

He was asking way too many questions, doing so much more than just kicking tires. I'll admit it took me till the fourth lot until I noticed it, but give me a break, I *did* notice it.

"What's going on?" I asked him as we looked over another mess of cars we weren't going to agree on.

"What?" he asked me back. "I want to make sure we get the right car."

"Right for what?" I said, not letting him off the hook that easily. "I mean, what's your criteria here?"

He didn't say anything at first; he just walked around this ugly Geo like he was really thinking about buying it, but I knew he was just stalling for time to put the right words in order. Finally he sighed and looked up at me. "The last car I bought ended up saving your life. Do you think I'm going to ask anything less from this one?"

That shut my big mouth up in a hurry.

Finally we were able to come to a compromise. We got a Ford Fusion—one, because it looked the least nerdy of the cars he liked, and two, because it got great gas mileage along with that emergency thing on the mirror that lets you talk to someone. So if I broke down or had an accident, I could push a button and get help. The car wasn't cheap, but the insurance settlement covered it with very little to spare.

Just enough to get to Dallas and back, it turned out.

"You do know I should take what's left and put it towards insurance, right?" my dad said as we drove back to base.

"Yeah, but you wouldn't do that because I'm your only son and just got over a debilitating car accident, so you want me to be happy." I glanced over at him during a red light and gave him the widest-eyed, most innocent look I could muster. "Right, Daddy?"

He burst out laughing as the light turned green. "Okay, okay! If you *never* call me Daddy again, I'll drop it."

It was a fair deal all around.

"So no texting in the car," my dad began, reciting to me his version of the Ten Commandments when we got home. "No drinking, no speeding, no anything you would not do if I was in the car. If I find you've broken even one rule—"

"You will take the car away and throw me in the dungeon I'm sure you're in the process of building," I finished for him.

"You'll be lucky if you're alive to get to a dungeon," he warned.

"I promise," I said to him, texting Nate. "I am a complete angel in the car, no second chances."

"Danny," he said, getting my attention. "You had a second chance—you almost died. Let's just act like there are no more do-overs, okay?"

I nodded, realizing he really was worried for me. Or, more likely, scared out of his mind.

The next week was like living in slow motion.

School sucked, but that was the same as it always had been. Except with no basketball, it seemed even worse. Every single second was another second that kept me away from the weekend. Nate had e-mailed me directions to Amy's house, and I plugged them into the car's GPS. I was so ready.

I threw enough clothes into my duffel to last me a week because I had no idea what we were going to be doing up there, and I wanted to be ready. My dad made sure he had the numbers of someone living everywhere I would be, and even called Amy's parents to make sure they knew I was coming. I mean, the president went places with less fanfare than this.

Finally Friday arrived, and I had been wrong. *This* was the longest day in the entire world. First period was, like, a week and a half, and by the time it was over, I was close to gnawing my own arm off to get away. Second period was even worse, so by third I texted my dad and asked if I could just bounce during lunch to get a head start.

He texted me back that I could, but only if I didn't have any work for those classes.

Luckily for me, I had already thought of that.

I texted him back that I was good, and he said to call him every hour or so on the road.

My feet never touched the ground as I flew to my car and took off.

As soon as I was out of Corpus, the world I knew as Texas fell away. There was nothing as far as I could see on either side, just a flatness that, I had to admit, was a little overwhelming. Not many people really understand how huge Texas is until they're in the middle of it and have to stare it down. I mean, you could put, like, four other states in here and still have room left over, and most of it was a lot of nothing. Just land and land that went on for miles with nothing to break it up but the horizon. As I drove, the nothing was just something to get through to spend time with Nate. But as the hours went on and on, I realized the nothing was larger than I had thought. I had driven four hours straight, and I was barely halfway there. I pulled over and got myself some much needed caffeine for the next part.

I completely ignored the fact my leg was aching when I walked the minimarket, grabbing a couple of Monsters and a Snickers bar to go. I desperately wanted to lie down and let my leg relax, but the fact I was over six and a half feet tall made that an impossibility. The small benches in the minimart would have barely fit me if I was normal sized, so I was shit out of luck. I absently rubbed the side of my leg as I waited in line to be rung up.

Which was when I saw the guy across the store staring at me.

I was so shocked this guy was intently looking at me that I didn't even notice he was halfway cute. A little older than me, he looked like he was in college and was trying to bore a hole through my head the way he had locked eyes with me. When he saw me looking, he smiled and nodded. I nodded back and looked away, confused. Did I know him? He didn't look familiar, but that didn't mean anything. There were days I'd forget my name if it wasn't written on my driver's license. I glanced over again, and he was pretending to look at something on the shelf, but his eyes were still looking up at me.

He motioned his head to the right.

I had no idea what he was talking about.

He jerked his head again, and I looked to the right and saw the bathrooms.

When I looked back at him, his smile got wider, and he nodded.

"You're up, stretch," the cashier called out to me.

I paid for the gas and my stuff quickly as my mind began to decipher what was going on. Was that guy hitting on me? Like, for real? I got my change and looked over again, and he wasn't there. He had no doubt gone to the bathroom to wait.

I almost ran to my car in fear.

My hands shook as I tried to put the key into the ignition. I wasn't an idiot. I knew there were guys who cruised rest stops and bathrooms like that. I'd just never thought it would happen to me. I mean, did he know about me? Was I giving off some kind of sign he could tell? I almost stalled the car as I tried to race out of the parking lot. I got maybe ten miles away before I stopped checking my rearview mirror to see if he was following me. I knew it was stupid, but I was still terrified.

I suppose I should have been flattered, but I felt the same way I had in Germany when my dad asked me if I'd done what Joshua had said. Dirty, ashamed…. I pulled over and threw up on the side of the road.

I washed my mouth out with a Monster and continued toward Dallas a few minutes later. I made sure not to stop again.

An hour from the city, I got a text from Nate asking me where I was. I pulled over to call him back and explained where I was. "It says, like, an hour with traffic," I explained, talking over the cars that rushed past me on the freeway.

"Yeah, once you get through Dallas it's, like, just north of it," he explained. "Just keep on I-75 and you'll be fine." I heard someone ask something in the background. "Yeah, you're going to be cutting it close for the show. You want to just meet us there at the school? 'Cause we're going to dinner after."

I'd finished my last Snickers about fifty miles back, and dinner sounded good. "Yeah, text me the address to the school, and I'll put it in the GPS."

His voice got high. "Oh, look at you with the sophisticated GPS. Aren't you special?"

"I am," I quipped back. "But it's okay, Nate. I'll still tell people you're my friend."

He laughed. "Whatever, smartass, just get here already."

He hung up, and a few seconds later he texted me the school's address. I punched it into the GPS and took one last stretch before getting back into the car. I was almost there—one more hour and I could stop fucking moving. Dallas was a huge city, and I had to admit I wasn't ready for it at first. I had been lulled by Corpus, and Texas in general, to believe that it was more a sprawling mass of nothing than an actual modern place, but as I drove into Dallas proper I found I was completely wrong.

More than just big, it was modern, sleek—in a word, exciting.

The traffic was horrible, of course, but even that was cool to me, since the most traffic we ever saw in Corpus was when some dumbass couldn't figure out how to get off the freeway correctly and tied up traffic for a whole ten minutes. This was actual traffic from too many people all going somewhere at the same time. It was kind of cool.

For about twenty minutes, and then I was over it.

I honked my horn a few times and even screamed at a few people as I slowly but surely made it through downtown intact. I followed Nate's directions faithfully, and within a half hour, I was through the mess and on my way to Richardson. I pulled up in front of the school and realized I might have actually read the directions instead of just blindly following them.

It was a Catholic school.

Well. I assume Catholic because that was the beginning and end of everything I knew about religion. It looked like a nice place, all things considered, but as I parked, I couldn't help but feel like I was sneaking into enemy territory. I texted Nate I was there, and minutes later he came out of the school with a huge smile on his face.

"Magellan has arrived!" he called out to me. "I had even odds you would get lost somewhere downtown."

I hugged him and took a second to relish the fact I was with him again. "Almost, but the thought of food kept me moving."

He patted me on the back and walked me into the school. "It's about to start, and then, trust me, Amy's parents always go to this kickass BBQ place that will fill you up."

The halls we walked looked just like a normal high school except for the religious imagery all over the place. There was a case with sports trophies just like ours, except there were a crap ton more trophies. "So her brother goes here? Like, for high school?"

He nodded as we walked into a huge auditorium. "Yeah. Amy went here too. It's a great school if you can get in." When he saw I was confused, he explained, "It's a private school, and not a cheap one either."

I couldn't imagine, having gone to high school for free; paying for it seemed insane.

There were almost a hundred parents in the auditorium, all of them dressed like they had way more money than my dad ever made. Nate walked us almost to the front, where there was a collection of people sitting waiting for the show to start. I recognized Amy from her appearance on Nate's Skype sessions.

She gave me a huge smile and stood up quickly. "Danny!" she exclaimed like we had been friends forever. "You're taller than he said you were." She hugged me, and I hesitated for a second before hugging her back. You ever meet those people who are just so happy, they make you happy by osmosis? Amy was one of those people.

"Yeah, trust me; 'little brother' is a joke on many levels," Nate said from behind me.

"Mom, Dad, this is Nate's brother, Danny," she said after we hugged. Her parents gave me warm smiles, and her dad shook my hand.

"How was the drive? Had to be tiring," he said as we sat down.

"It wasn't bad," I lied, my leg throbbing from being still for so long. "I had a lot of caffeine and music, so it was all good."

They nodded and laughed, and I looked over to Nate. "Brother?"

He shrugged. "Might as well be," he said, smiling. "'Sides, what do they care?"

The lights went down, which was good because it hid the huge smile that had broken out across my face.

The first few presentations were from younger guys, like freshman doing some lip syncing and one guy doing a violin thing that looked like it was hard as shit to play. Next were the sophomores, and you could see the routines were getting a little more involved with costumes and set decorations. Some were cool, but it was mainly parents who were digging it.

Then the juniors came out and did their thing, and the difference was like night and day. Where before there were just groups of guys going up there lip syncing, these guys were actually singing and doing a pretty good job at it. After the normal kids sang, the football team came out in their letterman jackets and sang an a capella version of a One Direction song. It was better than it sounds, and the girls in the crowd went ape shit as the jocks bumped and ground to the beat.

Nate nudged me and said the guy on the end was Amy's brother.

They got a standing ovation, of course, because who doesn't like seeing jocks sing and dance in rhythm? The juniors cleared off and the announcer introduced the varsity baseball team, and the crowd got quiet in anticipation. The lights went down, and the familiar guitar thrum from "Stacy's Mom" came blaring over the speakers. I heard a couple of girls scream when the lights flashed once and a spotlight hit a jock who was singing. At the next beat, another light and another jock. Three beats, then the song started, and the lights came up on stage, revealing the baseball team.

In board shorts, sunglasses, a pair of socks, and nothing else.

If I thought people went crazy over the football team, it was nothing compared to the sight of a dozen shirtless baseball players singing on stage. They were all ripped and hot. I mean, that was obvious, but all of them together just multiplied the effect tenfold. They looked like the youngest troupe of male strippers in the world. My mouth went dry, and I felt myself get a little hard as the song began.

I watched the guys on the end push around fake lawnmowers while the guy in the center sang, and I was just blown away over how hot these guys were. They were all wearing white socks, which made the whole effect even hotter for some reason. My eyes had no idea where to look, but when I focused on the guy singing, I knew I had been looking at the wrong guy this entire time.

The guy was Sam.

I want to say "my Sam," but that's silly, since I had never even said one word to him. But it was still how I felt. That was my Sam, and he was shirtless up there being the hottest guy in the world. His hair was wild, the shaggy blond locks glowing under the stage lights making him look like an angel. His body was even better than the pics had shown. Every single cut of every muscle was perfectly defined as he stalked the stage, singing to the audience. He owned that song and the crowd. He grinned at the girls, singing how Stacy's mom might need a guy like him, and I knew if there was a universal symbol for sex, Sam's grin while he sang was it.

The guys behind him kind of swayed together to the beat, but trying to watch them was useless, because I couldn't tear my eyes off my Sam.

He pushed his sunglasses up onto his head, and I could see the bright blue of his eyes glimmer at me from the lights. He was leaning forward, and I could see a string of *puka* shells around his neck that made him look like the perfect surfer boy. Girls ran up to the stage and waved their hands at him as he passed by, like he was an actual rock star.

This guy was openly gay? How did that happen?

He paced the stage as he asked if Stacy remembered when he'd mowed her lawn, and even more girls screamed in response. I looked around and no one had anything less than a huge smile on their face. People were standing up and swaying with the music. Most of them women.

What was going on?

I looked over at Nate, and I caught him staring at me with a small smile. He leaned closer to my ear and whispered, "Don't ever tell me I didn't get you anything."

He sat back, and I just gaped at him in shock. Erotic shock, but shock nonetheless.

A few people performed after the baseball team, but I don't recall them. Every time I closed my eyes, I could see my Sam's body in front of me, like I had been staring at the sun too long. If I had thought he was perfect after looking at the pictures on Facebook, I was assured he was more than perfect by seeing him in person. Midway through the senior presentations, Amy's brother, Conner, came and joined us, his letterman jacket under his arm since he had looked like he was ready to pass out on stage.

Amy introduced me to him in whispers so as to not interrupt the people on stage.

"Oh yeah," he whispered, shaking my hand. "The basketball guy, right?"

I nodded, wondering what Nate had told them about me.

He looked me up and down for a few seconds and then chuckled. "Yeah, Sam's going to love you."

I felt my heart skip a beat as he went back to watching the presentations.

Turning to Nate, I grabbed the front of his shirt and asked, "What did you tell them about me?"

He looked a little worried by the intensity of my question. "What, dude? You wanted to meet him, right?" I said nothing. "I talked to Amy who talked to Conner who talked to Sam." When he saw I wasn't even breathing, he patted me on the back. "Calm down, man. If we can get a man on the moon, we can get at least one under you."

If he thought he was being funny, he was sorely mistaken.

The rest of the show passed in a blur. My stomach threatened to climb up my throat and out of my mouth in protest.

No *way* could I meet Sam tonight! I'd just gotten done driving for like a year and a half, and I hadn't been able to really work out in forever. Not that I would have had a chance if I'd looked my best. Guys like him could have anyone in the world, and he had to know that. Why would he even bother looking at some skinny freak like me in the first place? Somewhere in the middle of some seniors doing a really bad version of "Call Me Maybe," I felt my stomach kick one last time, and I raced out of the auditorium to find a bathroom.

Luckily there was one across from the doors, and I raced into a stall just in time to see everything I had eaten in the last week come spilling out of my mouth like an upside-down geyser.

On my knees, I kept heaving and heaving as I felt tears falling from my eyes. I hated throwing up under normal circumstances. This was anything but normal. A couple of minutes later, I felt a hand on my back and Nate's voice telling me it was going to be okay. "Come on, man," he said quietly. "Get it all out."

I know it should have made me feel better to have him there, but honestly it just made me feel ten times worse. Bad enough I was having a panic attack over meeting a guy, but worse that my best friend had to see me crying like a little bitch. I knew he was trying to help me, but it was doing anything but.

I heard someone else's voice in the bathroom, and Nate said to them, "He's cool. Get him some water, okay?"

I heard the bathroom door close, and we were alone again.

"Dude, what's wrong?" Nate asked quietly. "Are you that upset about meeting Sam?"

I nodded, face still over the toilet.

"Why?" he asked, his voice straining because he obviously didn't understand my distress. "Danny, he's going to like you, and if he doesn't, that's cool too. I mean, you can't stress out so much about meeting one guy."

Wiping my mouth, I looked over at him. "You don't get it, Nate. Guys like Sam, they have the entire world in front of them. There is no one who wouldn't go out with him. You only get one chance to make an impression with someone like that, and on my best day I'd be iffy. But like this?" I said, gesturing to myself. "Like this I'm just a freakishly tall geek who has never gone out with a guy for real. Why would he even bother?"

"Because you're a great guy," Nate said without hesitating. "And if he can't see that, you don't want to be with someone like that anyways."

"You don't get it," I said, feeling my stomach finally unclench. "It's different for guys."

He helped me up as Conner came back in with a bottle of water. "You okay?" he asked me, obviously having no clue what was wrong.

I nodded and took a huge gulp of water. "Yeah, just feeling a little sick. Shouldn't have eaten gas station hot dogs." It was complete bullshit, but he seemed to accept it.

"Conner, tell Danny here about Sam."

I glared at Nate, but he ignored me. Conner started to talk.

"Sam is a trip," he explained. "On the surface he comes off like a self-absorbed asshole and most people think that's all he is, but he's not like that at all. He's really smart, even though he never shows it. He really gets tired of people just liking him for his looks. So far it's been mostly girls since he's the only gay student we have, but the quickest way to piss him off is to just go on about his looks, because they're the last thing he values."

Sam sounded like no one I had ever met before. "So then what does he value?"

"Integrity." Conner answered without even thinking about it. "If you knew his brothers, you'd get it, but Sam lives his life by this weird code, like a knight, and people who don't, he blows off pretty fast." He paused for a second. "Wait, you're not throwing up because of meeting Sam, are you?"

I didn't say anything.

"Dude, you can't stress over that. He knows what you look like. He may not be shallow, but he's not going to meet up with someone he isn't attracted to. And trust me, he's attracted."

"How does he know what I look like?" I asked while glaring at Nate.

"What?" Nate said after a few seconds. "Only you can Facebook-stalk someone? I told him you were into him and he looked you up. Not my fault you have, like, a thousand pics on your wall."

"They're from games." I said lamely. I got tagged by guys on the team all the time when someone posted pics from a game.

"Yeah, well, he liked what he saw," Conner assured me. "So just chill, it's all good."

"You seem pretty open-minded about him being gay," I said, finishing the last of the water.

"I've known Sam and his brothers forever, and trust me, him coming out as gay didn't even faze anyone in our class. Almost everyone likes him; besides, who cares? So you're gay. Why should it matter?"

I looked over at Nate. "You really set this up for me?"

He chuckled. "It was this or invest in a lot of porn for you. This seemed to be the cheapest route."

I looked over at Conner, and he said, "Sam is, like, the loneliest guy I know because most gay guys who come at him are only in it for his body. Nate said you're a stand-up guy, so I talked him into meeting you."

That guy was lonely? It made no sense whatsoever.

"So come on," Nate said, putting his arm around my shoulder. "Man up and meet this guy already, because all your whining about being single...." He locked eyes with me and finished, "You're killing me, Smalls, just killing me."

I had been Sandlotted, so I shut up and went with them.

People were coming out of the auditorium, which meant the show was over. I looked over to Nate and mumbled, "I'm sorry; I ruined the show for you."

He shook his head. "I was here to see Conner and I saw him. You saved me from falling asleep in front of Amy's parents, so it's all good."

Amy and her parents met us at the door. They looked at me like I was a sick puppy or something. "You okay?" Amy asked. "You ran out of there pretty fast."

Before I could answer, Conner chimed in with, "Gas station hot dogs are bad, mmmm'kay?"

Obviously he watched *South Park* too.

"Oh, you poor thing," Amy's mom said, putting her hand up to my forehead. "You need to lie down?"

Having someone pretend to be my mom even for a second was weird. On one hand, it was incredibly reassuring, but on the other, her automatic temperature check was like an electric shock, and I felt myself pull away before I could stop. "I'm okay, just a long drive."

"You still up for eating?" her dad asked. It sounded like he was warning me that I'd better not screw up his BBQ plans.

"I'm good," I assured him. "It passed quickly."

"Okay, well, follow us," he said, pulling his keys out. "We'll lead you to the promised land."

"We should drive with him," Amy suggested to Nate. "You know, in case he gets lost."

Nate nodded, and Conner said, "I want to go with them."

Amy's dad sighed and just gave up. "Fine, everyone go with whoever. I am going to go eat."

As we all walked down the hall, I asked Conner, "Sam knows where we're going?"

He laughed. "Yeah, he's meeting us there. Relax, man."

We got halfway to the parking lot, and I looked over at Nate. "This is a mistake."

He just smiled at me and growled, "Killing. Me. Smalls."

I shut up and led them to the Fusion.

"Dude!" Nate said, walking around the whole car. "You made out like a bandit."

"It was a compromise," I said, unlocking the doors. "I wanted a Mustang."

Nate laughed. "No way in hell your dad was letting you get one of those after that wreck. I'm shocked he let you drive, period."

Nate and Amy got in the backseat while Conner took shotgun. "This is sweet," Conner said, buckling up.

"How is your leg?" Amy asked from the back.

"It's better," I said, not bringing up how much it hurt driving up there. "I'm not a hundred percent, but it's getting better."

"Next year," Nate said, clapping my back.

I nodded, not caring about next year right now.

We pulled up to a huge BBQ place. The parking lot was crammed with cars all over the place. It was a Friday night in Dallas, and the food here was obviously good. We parked and found Amy's parents in the lobby, waiting to be seated. The smell from the kitchen was insanely good, and I felt some misgivings fade away as the thought of food came to mind.

"Told you this place was good," Nate said, elbowing me. I nodded and he laughed. "Hard to be nervous when it smells so good, right?"

I hated everything about my life at that moment.

There was a commotion behind me, and I saw Conner talking to someone as a pair of adults pressed past them. I stared, waiting for the people to get out of the way, when I heard one of the adults say something to Amy's parents.

And then they moved, and I saw Sam talking to Conner.

He had clothes on now and looked even better to my mind. He had a pair of jeans on with a green button-up shirt and a skinny blue tie on over it. Anyone else would have looked way overdressed for a place like this, but instead he looked like he was a model showing off this year's entries in preppy fashion. I found myself staring a little too long when Nate nudged me. "Mouth closed, tongue in, soldier. You're drooling."

I shook my head and looked away when I realized he was close to being right.

"Dude, I cannot do this," I whispered to him. "I mean, look at him."

He shook his head, laughing. "Look at you," he shot back. "Trust me, dude, you're in this guy's league."

I didn't even feel like I was in the same race as he was, much less league.

"Chin up," Nate said, taking a half step away from me. I turned to see where he was going when I felt a tap on my back.

"Danny, this is Sam," Conner said as I looked behind me.

He looked up at me and gave me a half grin that made my heart skip a beat.

"So you're not small," Sam said, holding his hand out to shake.

"Um... thanks," I stammered, shaking his hand.

"How tall are you?" he asked, staring at me intently. "I mean, I'm six one, and I feel like a shrimp standing next to you."

"Six six," I said, feeling way self-conscious. "But everyone is small standing next to me. I'm a freak that way."

His smile got a little wider. "So you're a freak? Is that a good thing?"

My mind locked up as I tried to figure out what to answer.

"Relax," he said, finally breaking out into a brilliant smile. "We're all freaks; it's what makes us interesting." Before I could answer, the waitress said our table was ready and everyone started to follow her into the restaurant. "I am starving!" Sam exclaimed, excited.

I followed hesitantly, not sure if meeting Sam had gone well or not.

The two people who had blocked my view were his parents; along with Amy's, Conner, Nate, and me, it was a huge table. Conner sat next to Sam, which meant I was next to Nate. I was disappointed but kind of relieved, since I had no idea what to say to Sam. As I was putting my napkin in my lap, Nate leaned in and whispered, "How'd it go?"

I shrugged. "No idea. He seems fine, but I sounded like an idiot."

"So then normal?" he joked.

I kicked him under the table.

There were various conversations all around me, but I just sat there, since I didn't know anyone but Nate. I sipped my iced tea and tried to remain invisible when Sam's dad looked at me and asked, "So you play basketball too?"

I was so shocked to be talked to, I almost dropped my glass.

"Yes," I answered quickly and then followed it up with "No," which was then finished by an "I will."

Now everyone was staring at me.

Sam leaned over and looked at me. "That only makes sense if you're in a 'choose your own adventure' book."

My face was red, and all I wanted to do was crawl under the table, but I'm pretty sure they would have caught on to where I was hiding. Instead I just blurted out, "I did play basketball, but then I got in a car accident, so I haven't this year, but I will next year."

"God willing," Nate said quietly.

"God willing," I amended.

Sam was still staring at me with that same quiet smile. "Well, that makes more sense." He sat back.

"What's your father do?" Sam's dad asked next.

"He's a Marine."

"And your mom?"

I was starting to feel like I was on trial.

"She died when I was young," I said, trying to keep the hurt out of my voice.

Sam's mom hit his dad on the arm. "Happy?" She looked at me with sympathetic eyes. "I'm sorry. I'm sure she would be proud of you."

I know this lady was a stranger, and she had no idea what she was talking about since she didn't know me from the guy who took our drink order. But I felt my eyes sting a little, and I smiled back at her. "Thank you." And I meant it.

I heard Sam say something to Conner, and the next thing I knew they were trading places. Now Sam was sitting next to me, and I was flustered all over again. "I'm sorry about your mom," he said once he was settled and the conversation had moved on.

"It was a long time ago," I said, hoping it made me look a little less like a whining bitch.

"Still hurts," he responded, not taking the bait. "And it's okay to be sad about it." I looked over at him, and the blue of his eyes was like a swimming pool on a blistering summer day. "It really is."

I smiled back and felt a tightness in my shoulders fade a little.

"So a car crash?" he asked, grabbing a roll from the center of the table. "That had to have sucked."

"Yeah, I don't remember it, but they said it was pretty bad." I watched him spread a huge amount of butter on the roll and then shove it into his mouth.

When he saw me watching, he kind of smiled and chewed some. "Sorry," he said around the food. "Didn't really eat today."

I laughed and grabbed a roll myself. "You don't have to excuse eating in front of me. I love eating." I put on as much butter as he had and popped it into my mouth.

He swallowed his roll and took a drink of water. "Well duh, I can't even imagine how many calories it takes to keep you moving."

It was the first time someone had complimented me on my height that I didn't feel like a freak. I nodded as I swallowed. "I'm always hungry."

"Well then, you're going to love this place," he said, grabbing us both another roll. "Their portions are insane." He handed me the roll and then held his up like a glass. "To eating like pigs."

I touched his roll with mine. "I will *so* eat to that."

We both consumed the bread instantly.

We made small talk during the meal, but it wasn't a place to really talk since we were surrounded by a mass of people. He was easy to talk to, and I couldn't help but stare when he told me about how long it had taken for the baseball team to learn that routine. It wasn't just his looks, though he was hotter than any guy I had ever seen in person before; it was the way he talked so enthusiastically. He sounded like a little kid describing his day. Each and every fact was just the best thing in the world, and you couldn't help but get excited with him.

At least I couldn't help it.

"There is no way I could get up there in just board shorts," I told him after we'd finished a dinosaur-sized plate of ribs.

"Why not?" he asked, gnawing the last bit of meat off a bone. "You look like you have a kicking body under those clothes." I felt my face go red as my mind struggled to find words to answer that. He must have seen my hesitation, and he added, "Oh come on, you have to know you're in great shape."

"What about you?" I asked back. "You looked like a model up there."

He shrugged. "I like staying in shape, but you look like an actual athlete."

"You're not?" I asked again. How could this guy not know he was, like, fifty different kinds of hot?

"Nah," he said, putting the bone down. "Being a jock is, like, the family business. Both my brothers played baseball, my dad played baseball—it was play baseball or be disowned. So I play baseball, but it's just a game, not a life choice." He leveled a look at me. "Not like you and Nate with basketball."

I sat there and said nothing, trying to figure out how much he knew about me. It was like he'd been briefed all about me, and I was just sitting there trying to guess who he was. "You don't like baseball?" I asked after a few seconds.

He shrugged again. "I play water polo too. I prefer swimming to anything. Baseball is fun as a game and all...." He kind of trailed off. "You know, let's talk about something else, okay?"

I nodded, not sure what had just happened.

"You ever surf?" he asked.

I laughed. "Um, no. Have you seen me?"

"Tall people can surf," he said, ignoring my question. "You ever skate? Like on a board?" I shook my head. "Oh well, I always say if you can skate, you can surf."

"Where do you surf in Texas?" No wonder his Facebook photos had made him look like the perfect surfer guy.

"Padre Island, Corpus has some baby waves.... There are places," he answered as the waiter came over to ask the table if anyone wanted dessert.

Or course, Sam and I wanted some.

Conner asked Sam something and Nate took the second to lean closer to me. "So, better?"

I looked at him and nodded, the smile on my face no doubt making me look dumber than I normally did.

"Told you," he said, nudging me. "You're not half as ugly as you think you are."

"I don't think I'm ugly," I whispered to him.

"Oh...," he said, making a face. "Well then, someone should tell you you're ugly."

I nudged him back, and we both started to laugh.

"Well, this has been fun," Sam's dad said, standing and not making it sound like it was much fun at all. "Are you coming home with us, or you staying the night at Conner's?"

Sam looked at Conner, who nodded. "I'm good."

"Call your mother in the morning," he said, helping his wife on with her coat. "The dinner is on me. Pleasure seeing you again, Frank." Amy's dad nodded, and they walked out.

"Your dad just paid for this whole meal?" I asked, kind of shocked.

Sam nodded. "His way of apologizing for being an antisocial asshole, I'm sure."

I hadn't gotten that vibe from him at all, but then again, all I had been paying attention to was Sam.

"It's getting late," Amy's dad said, getting up himself. "Anyone grabbing a ride with us?" No one said a word, and he laughed. "Okay, just remember there is a curfew." He tossed some bills down for the tip. "You guys stay out of trouble."

Amy and her mother said something to each other, and then we were alone.

Sam leaned over and looked at Amy. "So, Purgatory?"

Her face lit up. "You're damn right, Purgatory."

I was once again lost.

Nate explained to me as we walked out to the parking lot. Purgatory was an eighteen-and-over bar in downtown Dallas that was considered the best place to party for kids our age. It was an all-sexuality club, so there were a ton of straight, gay, and bi people there, and on a Friday it would be packed. I pointed out I was only sixteen, and he pointed out I looked like I was twenty-two.

"You're coming, right?" Sam asked me as he stopped at a cherry red BMW convertible. He leaned on the trunk and gave me a grin that looked like it was ten different kinds of illegal. The Beemer had vanity plates on it that said SYMBA.

"You just can't wait to be king?" I asked him, smiling.

"Not even a little," he answered. "So you're coming with us?"

I took a second to examine his car and buy myself time to think of an answer. It was tricked out with silver rims and a leather interior. If the BMW cost less than eighty grand, I would eat my hat. "This is really yours?"

He stood up, like he was still trying to joke, but I could hear the seriousness in his voice. "Don't change the subject. Are you coming out with us or chickening out?"

"Chickening?" I asked, moving closer to him. "You think I'm Marty McFly or something and you can goad me into going?"

He got even closer to me. "I think you're scared silly of me, and you'll use any excuse to bolt."

"What did Conner tell you?" I asked suddenly.

The tone of my voice must have been drastic, because the playful smile left his face. "Nothing, I was just joking."

This was a mistake. I was just doomed to fuck this up. What did I know about flirting with a guy, much less one like this? I was better off going back to Amy's and watching *SportsCenter* before I passed out.

"Hey." He spoke so quietly I'm sure no one else could hear him. "Just come with us. I'm not ready to say bye to you yet." Nearly pouting, he looked up at me, and I wondered how anyone in the world ever told this guy no.

"Fine," I said with as much confidence as the Washington Generals had when they went up against the Globetrotters. If you were wondering how much confidence the Generals had? None at all, because they knew they were supposed to lose.

CHAPTER TWELVE:
SHOWING TO THE BALL

PURGATORY SAT on an entire block of downtown Dallas, and it was packed from what I could see.

Nate and Amy had agreed to drive with me as we followed Sam and Conner in Sam's car. They had both drilled me the entire time about Sam.

"Did you like him?"

"What did you guys talk about?"

"What did he say to you in the parking lot?"

It was kind of insane.

"What's his story anyways?" I asked Amy as we circled around the block again looking for a parking spot.

"Sam? His great-grandfather found oil back when Texas was still Mexico or something, and his father sold all of it off to BP for a VP spot and more money than God. He has two older brothers and, for people who are richer than God, they all turned out really cool. The oldest, John, is like a god around town. I mean, if it turned out he was Captain America, no one would blink."

And that feeling of throwing up suddenly came rushing back.

"And you thought it would be a good idea for us to meet?" I asked Nate.

"What?" he asked, confused. "You're the one who said you wanted to meet him."

"Yeah, before I knew he was like Richie Rich."

Sam had pulled up to the valet parking spot and motioned for me to follow.

"How much does this cost?" I asked, looking for a sign that had a price.

Sam had left his car and walked over to my window. "Just leave it—they'll park it."

I shifted into park and started to pull out my wallet. "Do I just leave the money in here or give it to them?" I didn't want to admit I had never used valet parking before.

"It's cool," he said casually. "It's paid for already."

The parking attendant appeared and handed Sam a credit card. I tried not to gawk at the fact he had plastic. I guess I did a crappy job, because he saw me staring and showed me the card. "Isn't that cool?" he said, handing me the card. "They make them special order."

I looked down and saw that it was a MasterCard with Lion King characters on the front, the picture of the monkey holding the baby lion on the rock. I shouldn't have been, but I was shocked to see it had Sam's name on it. "You have a credit card?" I asked stupidly, since I was obviously holding it.

He nodded and slipped it into his wallet. "Yep yep." It was pretty obvious it wasn't a point of pride with him.

"I'm sorry," I said quickly. "I know you're not supposed to ask about money. I've just never seen someone my age with their own card."

He gave me a smile that could have parted the clouds on an overcast day. "No, it's cool. I was stoked when I got it, but my dad has made sure to remind me that it's not an invitation to just spend money whenever I want." In a lower voice he muttered, "Even if it's my money."

"I've never seen a card with *Lion King* on it," I offered as we walked up to the door, trying to change the subject. "It's very cool."

He smiled and nodded, but I could tell he was upset. He handed the doorman a wad of bills for all of us, and we were let in despite the line of people behind the velvet rope. "Um, can we just walk in?" I asked Nate, who was behind me.

He nodded. "He's a VIP member or something—no lines."

I walked in but couldn't help but glance at the people who were waiting to get in.

Amy and Nate had been right; the place was packed. The music hit us like a wall as we walked into the club proper, and I winced, since I'd never been in one before. I turned to Nate and shouted, "*Is it always this loud?*"

He just shot me a grin and nodded, and we followed Sam as he walked through the crowd.

It wasn't obvious, but people kind of moved out of his way as he walked, not like they were afraid or anything, but like they didn't exactly believe what they were seeing. Like they had heard of him but never expected to see him in the flesh. A girl came up and threw her arms around Conner, and he hugged her back like they were friends. He began talking to her, and she glanced back at us for a second. We made our way through the mass until we reached a back room where another doorman was standing in front of another velvet rope. I could see some kind of lit-up room behind him, but a thick gauzy curtain blocked my view. It wasn't heavy enough to stop people from getting the idea there was a room beyond it, but more than enough to prevent them from seeing what was going on inside.

The doorman nodded as Sam walked in. Sam paused and looked back at us and told the doorman something. Conner and the girl walked forward, and Conner passed through. However, the bouncer guy put a hand in front of the girl and shook his head. Conner looked at her and shrugged apologetically as we walked past. I paused to look back at her, but Amy grabbed my elbow and pushed me forward. "Don't look back," she ordered. "She's a status leech, always trying to glom on to someone coming back here. Trust me, leaving her behind is a good thing."

I wasn't going to argue with her, but I didn't feel any better than I had when we cut in line.

The music in the VIP lounge wasn't as loud, and the floor wasn't as crowded, so I could actually see about five smaller lounges with leather couches surrounding lit-up glass tables. Sam walked over to an empty one and sat in the center of the couch farthest from the dance floor. I'm not kidding, he looked like he owned the place. He motioned for us to sit down with him, and I felt like I was way, way out of my league. Everyone in there looked sophisticated and cool, and I was anything but. I was a tall gangly guy who was wearing clothes his dad bought at Walmart. I doubt the people in here had ever heard of Walmart.

As soon as we sat down, he looked at us and grinned. "Shots?"

Conner whooped in agreement, but I looked at Nate. "I can't drink. I'm not twenty-one, and I'm driving."

He gave me a reassuring smile and said, "You can drink in here, and you want me to drive instead? I'll stay sober."

I trusted Nate with my life, but I also knew if anything happened to that car and I wasn't driving it, my dad would just take me out to the boonies and shoot me in the back of the head, mob-style. Shaking my head, I said, "I'm going to just have a Coke."

He nodded and looked at Sam, pointing to him and Amy. Sam looked at me, and I gave him a no.

He paused for maybe half a second and then shrugged. He leaned forward and pressed the top of the table with one index finger. I realized I was looking at a computer's touchscreen. It lit up and a menu popped up where Sam had touched it. He started tapping buttons to order drinks for all of us. He pulled his wallet out and tossed his card on the table. I watched the system identify the card and scan it superfast. I leaned in, never having seen anything like this before.

Sam leaned closer so I could hear. "It's called a Surface," he explained over the music. "Fucking cool, right?" I nodded, fascinated, when the screen asked him if he wanted to open a tab. When he pushed yes, it asked how much. The number he entered had three zeros after it. My mouth went dry at just the thought.

"How can you drink in here?" I asked after he placed the order. "It's, like, illegal in Texas."

He shook his head as he put his wallet away again. "The front of the club is an actual business. Back here is a private club that has a membership, which means it has completely different rules."

"That doesn't sound legal," I said.

He grinned. "Oh, it's legal, just not cheap."

Yeah, I was right; I was in way over my head.

"So why not drink?" he asked after a few minutes of silence.

"I'm driving, and it's a new car. My dad would kill me if something happened to it."

"So drink," he said, not seeming the least bit concerned. "I'll call you a cab, and you can get the car in the morning."

"I'm good," I said, thinking that sounded expensive too.

"You don't drink?"

"I do," I lied, since I'd never really gotten drunk.

He laughed. "It's okay if you don't. Seriously, I think it's cool."

I looked over at him, and he was giving me a smile that made me think of a cobra hypnotizing its prey. "I'm just paranoid about the car," I assured him.

The waitress bought an expensive-looking bottle with something tan in it. I assumed it was tequila. There were five shot glasses around the bottle. I ignored the one for me and tried to get her attention so I could order a Coke.

"You just type it," Sam said, seeing her walk away from me. "Just pull up the menu and scroll down to whatever you want." I followed his hands as Nate poured a shot out for everyone else. It was at the end of the menu for drinks, and it cost seven bucks, but there it was. Coke in a glass.

"Seven bucks?" I asked, shocked. "I could go get one for a buck at Circle K."

"Dude, I got it," Sam assured me and pushed the order button for it.

"I don't feel good about ordering a Coke that costs more than a movie."

He smiled as he took his shot from Nate. "Then don't worry. I ordered it."

I was about to say that wasn't the point when the waitress handed me a glass with Coke and ice in it. Once Nate saw we all had a drink, he held his shot up and said, "To new friends."

"To getting shitfaced," Conner announced right after.

Sam nodded. "I can drink to both of those." And they all downed their shots while I took a sip of Coke. Seven bucks and it was still watered down. Typical.

I seemed to be the only one who wasn't having a good time. Nate and Amy looked like they were blown away to be in a VIP area, and Conner wasn't missing any opportunity to scope out the girls who were trying to peer in and see who was inside. Sam seemed happy, but something told me it was an act. Maybe he wasn't as taken with this place as everyone else, or it could be there was something on his mind. Whatever it was, I seemed to be the only one who noticed.

"So you like this place?" I leaned over and asked him.

He seemed surprised by the question and gave me a half smile. "Why? Don't you?"

Looking around, I saw a lot of drunk people trying too hard to look like they were popular, and a couple of people doing their best to act like they were bored. For a second I thought about just lying and going along with it but then thought that was a bad idea. I mean, if I don't like something, why do I have to lie about it?

"No, not really," I finally said.

The answer seemed to amuse him, and his smile grew larger. "Why?"

I shrugged. "Because it's a loud place where drunk people are, and drunk people are too loud and too dangerous for my taste. What's there to like?"

He scooted closer to me slightly. "So then what do you do for fun?" I opened my mouth to answer and he added, "Besides basketball."

I closed my mouth and thought about it. "I like comic books," I admitted quietly. "And I love sci-fi movies, though I don't understand much of them, and I watch a lot of Disney movies. Which is why I think it's cool you like *Lion King*."

He started laughing but covered his mouth to hide the fact.

"What?" I protested, feeling like I missed a joke.

When he could talk, he looked at me, his eyes the brightest blue I had ever seen in my life. "You're a nerd." I felt a scowl drop over my face, but what he said dispelled it. "I mean, you're cute as hell and look like a hot-ass jock, but inside you're a nerd."

He kept laughing, but I was no longer paying attention. Cute? Me?

"What about you?" I fired back jokingly. "You have *Lion King* on your credit card."

He nodded proudly and pulled his phone out. "I don't hide the fact I'm a nerd," he said, putting the phone down on the table. The table lit up for a moment and then an outline of his phone appeared, flashing around the device. "Look, I have proof." He touched the table and a menu opened up with a list of commands. He pushed one, and half a dozen folders popped up. He pushed one labeled Disney Vacation and the folder expanded, showing about fifty different pictures.

I peered at them and saw they were of Sam and his two brothers at Disney World. It looked like they couldn't have been more than two years ago. The oldest wore a Captain America shirt that looked like it was painted on him, it was so tight. He was built like a linebacker and was almost as hot as Sam. He had a full-sized shield in one hand, and he was striking a pose next to the middle brother. He was taller than Sam but smaller than Captain America Junior, and he wore an Iron Man shirt as well as two gloves that had lights in the palms. He was cuter than the oldest one but not even close to his younger brother. Sam had on a Thor helmet and was holding a replica of the hammer. The three of them were posed together, looking like a trio of hot-ass frat guys playing superhero.

"That's John." Sam pointed to the oldest. "And he is Captain America in real life. That's Eli." He pointed to the middle one. "He wishes he was as cool as Tony Stark. And of course I'm the only one with the hair to pull Thor off."

There were dozens of photos of them all over the park, still with their props. The three of them acted like they had no fear of looking silly in public and more than a few pictures had them posing with what had to be strangers. They looked so happy, so carefree, that I was instantly jealous of being an only child.

"So I'm not only a dork but a proud dork," he said, closing the folder down. "While you, sir, are in the closet."

I glanced over at him, and he realized what he'd said.

"I mean about being a nerd," he amended. "As for being gay, that's your business."

The tone of his voice made it pretty clear that he didn't agree with my choice to be in the closet, but he wasn't going to dwell on it. "I don't know what I am yet," I said after a few seconds.

He picked up his phone. "That's too bad," he replied, putting it in his pocket. "Because if you did know, it would be hard for me to resist you." Before I could respond, he grabbed Amy's hand and pulled her out to the dance floor.

He didn't say anything to me for the rest of the night.

I tried to a couple of times, but he was either on the dance floor or talking to one of a dozen people who seemed to hang on his every word. It was obvious people knew who he was, and they treated him like a celebrity. It got close to last call, and Nate and Amy were ready to leave, while Conner was in a corner booth making out with some girl he'd been dancing with all night.

Nate walked Amy and Conner out to the car while I walked over to Sam, who was talking to a group of people who looked like they had money as well. "Hey," I said, interrupting the conversation. "We're going to take off."

He glanced over his shoulder at me and nodded. "Cool, get home safe."

I felt the urge to reach over and kiss him, but I was pretty sure that was not the smartest thing I could do. There were a thousand things I wanted to say, but none of them made any sense outside my brain, so I just ended up saying "Was cool meeting you" and walking away.

When I got in the car, Nate and Amy were in the backseat, looking like they were about to fall asleep, while Conner was texting someone. I pulled out into traffic, and Amy asked me, "So did you get his number?"

"He didn't give it to me," I answered, following Conner's directions back to his house.

Nate leaned forward. "Did you ask him for it?"

I admitted I didn't.

"Then you're an idiot," he said, sitting back.

I could not argue the fact I was indeed an idiot.

Amy and Conner's home was pretty big, a two-story house with a cellar, which was pretty rare for Texas. The entire lower level had been turned into a den/guest room, and they had a fold-out couch where Nate and I would sleep. As with everyone else I had met today, it was obvious Amy's family had more money than my dad and I had ever or would ever possess. Nate kissed Amy good night, and we headed downstairs.

I let Nate use the small bathroom across from the foot of the stairs first while I changed into a pair of sweats to sleep in. When he got out, I went in and brushed my teeth as he took off his clothes and pulled on a pair of trunks. I'm sure the pullout bed was more than big enough for normal people, but Nate and I were far from normal. Our feet stuck out way past the end of the frame, and there was no way for us not to bump up against each other lying there.

"I don't think he liked me," I said after a few minutes of silence.

"I'm pretty sure he did, dude," he answered sleepily.

Sighing, I felt the same gnawing depression I had been fighting all summer begin to grow again. I really felt like I was going to cry. "What's wrong with me? I mean, I like guys, but I'm so afraid of telling people...." My eyes began to sting. "I'm pretty sure he didn't like me."

"Come here," he said, putting an arm around my shoulder and pulling me into a hug. I leaned into him and just cried while he held me close. Normally being this near Nate would have horned me up fast, but there was nothing sexual in the gesture. He stroked my hair and whispered to me quietly, "There's nothing wrong with you, dork. You're just different, and there's nothing wrong with being different. You haven't figured that out yet, but you will."

"What if I figure it out too late?"

"There is no too late," he reassured me. "God makes sure everything happens when it's supposed to. Until then, just keep faith."

"I don't think I have any faith," I admitted, sniffling.

"Then I'll have enough for both of us." He hitched back a little, and I felt myself shift instinctively into the crook of his arm. "Just go to sleep, bud. Things will be better in the morning."

"I love you, Nate," I said distantly.

I felt him kiss the top of my head. "Love you too, bro."

I don't remember anything after that.

We spent the rest of the weekend at Amy's house. Her dad fired up the grill, and we all enjoyed their pool in the hot Texas sun. That night we went to the movies with Conner and the girl from the club. If I was feeling lonely before, sitting between two couples just drove it home even more.

I got up early Sunday morning to drive back. I did my best not to wake Nate, but I was tossing my clothes into my duffel when he mumbled, "You're leaving already?"

"Yeah," I said, grabbing my stuff from the bathroom. "I want to get home before it gets too late, 'cause I know my dad is going to make me go to class on Monday no matter how late I get in."

He sat up and ran a hand through his hair. "So you're just going to take off without even getting his number? Not even a try?"

I shoved my deodorant into the bag and turned around. "It's not like it is for straight people, okay? You guys have it easy. You see each other, and it's all 'hey, let's get coffee, okay,' 'hey, let's date, okay,' 'hey, let's get married and have a kid, okay.' I don't even know what I am right now, and Sam does. He knows exactly who he is and what he wants and, trust me, Nate, it's not me!"

It was the first time I'd ever raised my voice to him, and I felt a little shocked I had.

He looked down and sighed. "You're right, I don't know how it is for you, but I know this." His eyes locked with mine. "You're a great guy, Danny, and if I could be gay for you, I would. I knew you were special when I saw you in Florida, and if Sam can't see that...."

Something inside me snapped. "Why? Why me?" I asked, letting the bag drop from my hand. "You've treated me different from day one, and I'm sorry, but it comes across a lot like flirting, and it's just messing me up. So what is it, Nate? What is your thing with me?"

All the anger about Sam, about liking guys, about missing a whole season of basketball, all of it came spewing out of my mouth onto Nate. Even though I was pissed, it didn't change the fact that he had treated me weird since Florida and never told me why. I'd just accepted it because Nate is exactly the kind of guy I would go for, but he wasn't gay, he wasn't into guys. So why me?

"Did I ever tell you about my brother?" he asked me.

"You said he died, but that was about it."

"He was four, and he got hit by a car...." I felt the blood drain from my face. A tear rolled down his cheek, and I felt even worse than I had before. "Anyways, he died, and I just had this hole in me where he was supposed to go. I had this whole way of how life was supposed to be with him, and then he was gone, and I never got over it."

I sat down on the edge of the bed.

"You think you're broken, Danny? I see my brother everywhere I look. I see someone his age, and I wonder if that's what he would look like. I see brothers fucking around, and it's like I lost a limb but can still feel it ache." He was really crying now. "You were what I thought he would be like," he finally admitted. "Funny, shy, into basketball, so damn talented but no faith in yourself. It's not fair to you, I know, but that's why. Because God took my brother too early, and I've spent my entire life looking for him."

I reached over and grabbed him. He pulled me into a hug, and we sat there grieving for a life that never was. We bawled for a whole existence that was only imagined, a parallel world where his brother lived, and I was normal and not some freak who liked guys. A place where he and his brother were a pair of basketball-playing brothers who made recruiters shit themselves, and I had a girlfriend and my dad didn't think I was a huge, gay disappointment.

"I'm sorry," I finally said. "It isn't you, it's me. I'm just messed up inside and can't get it together."

He pulled back and wiped his eyes. "No you're not. You're not messed up at all, Danny. So you like guys; that isn't messed up, that's the way God made you. I don't think there's a thing wrong with it, and you shouldn't."

"I'm a freak," I said, still not able to look him in the eyes.

"Dude, we're all freaks inside. Normal is just the lie we all agree to tell the public."

I hugged him again, and I felt a small part of my pain drain away for a moment.

"Go to church with us," he whispered to me. "Please, just go once with me. Let me introduce you to our Father."

I nodded, knowing I would have run into a fire if he told me to.

Luckily all my khakis needed was a hot iron to make them presentable, and one of Nate's shirts fit well enough for me to wear. But the tie was another thing altogether. I glared into the mirror at the tie, wondering who the idiot was who came up with this crap. I had always worn clip-ons to school for game day. Tying an actual tie was beyond me.

Nate walked into the bathroom and said, "Look at me. Chin up. Stand still."

I turned, and he made the limp piece of blue cloth dance in his hands; it went from a snarl of fabric to a perfectly knotted tie in nothing flat. He smoothed it out and smiled at me. "I always wanted to do that."

The feeling was so intense it just came out of me. "I love you," I said, reaching out to hug him. He hugged me back, and I knew if I never found a guy to go out with in my life, just having Nate as a friend would be enough for me.

There was a flash of light, and we looked over to see Amy standing there with her phone, taking a picture. "Sorry, that was just too freaking cute for words." She gestured at us. "Now stand next to each other and smile."

Nate stepped over next to me. I put my arm around him and felt his arm circle around my back. "Say cheese," she said.

We both smiled and said cheese.

It was the first picture I ever took with my big brother. I know I'm not supposed to do this, but I need to tell you this before I forget. Amy sent me that picture, and I printed it out at home, and I took that thing everywhere with me. It was in my locker at school, when I went to college it was taped next to my computer, and past that even. That picture was my talisman, my good luck charm. It wasn't a picture; it was a light against the darkness that always seemed to surround my life. It was a candle that never went out no matter how hard the wind blew.

I loved him that much.

Okay, so back to the story.

We all got dressed and went to Amy's church, which was this huge glass building in Dallas. Everyone who was there looked like they had more money than... well, I was going to say God, but if God owned this church, then he had some bank of his own. We found a seat in one of the first few pews, and I sat with Nate as Amy and her parents said hello to their friends.

"So do you know anyone who is, like, normal or are all your friends, like, millionaires?" I asked him in a quiet tone.

He grinned at me and said, "Well, I know you."

"I hate you," I muttered, knowing I had been burned.

After a few minutes everyone sat down, and the service began. There was a prayer that I didn't understand and a lot of "amens" before an older, white-haired priest walked up to the podium. "Normally this is where I would say my sermon and most of you would fall asleep." There was a spattering of chuckles from everyone. "But today we have a treat. I'm sure most of you here remember Thomas Mulligan. His family were members here years ago. He had two sons, and one of them has just returned from doing missionary work in Africa. Since you are expected to sing for your supper here, we asked him to give the homily today." He stepped aside and a handsome guy, who looked around thirty, walked up to the podium.

Did I just say the priest was hot? Yeah, I'm going to hell.

"Thank you, Father Jimms. I don't know about singing, but I'll see what I can do about earning my way." He looked out at us, and I could see his eyes were a light green that made me think of fresh-cut grass.

"Morning," he said, smiling. We all said "morning" back. "I know I'm supposed to be up here talking about scripture and the good book and all, but I just don't have it in me today." He walked from behind the podium and sat down on the carpeted steps that led up to the altar. "Instead, I just want to talk. About the world, the stuff happening in it... you know, life." I looked over at Nate, who shrugged. This was new to him too, it seemed.

"What is the greatest challenge to the church today?" he asked the crowd. "What is the biggest threat to the word of God?"

"Perverts," someone cried out.

"Murderers," called out another.

"Faggots," someone from the back yelled, and the place went silent. I felt my heart begin to pound in my chest as my stomach soured. I guess it showed, because Nate reached over and put his hand over mine and squeezed it.

Father Mulligan stood up slowly. "Perverts, murderers, and faggots." He paused for effect. "Oh my."

The crowd nervously chuckled.

"So these people, these sinners are the problem, then?" he asked rhetorically. The crowd agreed halfheartedly. "Those who have strayed from the path of the righteous are the greatest threat to the church today? Why?" he asked, looking at the crowd. "Because they hate what they can't understand? They try to tear us down because we show them how flawed they are?" A few more cheers of agreement. "So then it's jealousy? They attack us because they're jealous we are assured the keys to the kingdom while they will, at the very best, spend the rest of their godforsaken lives wandering the desert looking for water?" More agreement from the crowd, who seemed to be getting into it.

"Well then, how do we stop it?" he asked. "How do we keep these sinners from tearing down our faith? Do we condemn them? Do we punish them for crimes against the Holy Father? Do we try to outlaw them? Stop them from marrying each other? Make it legal for people to not serve them if they want?" The crowd was quiet now. "Do we take away their rights as citizens and make sure that even if they don't believe in our way, they will live their life by it?"

No one said a word.

"If these people are the problem, then shouldn't we do anything we need to stop them? Isn't it our responsibility as Catholics to stand up and fight back? Are we not warriors of God?" The crowd started to agree with him again, but I could see the look of speculation on a few people's faces.

"If this is a war for our souls, then shouldn't we use every weapon at our disposal? Our words, our votes, and our actions? Shouldn't we stand up and make sure that these perverts, murders, and faggots are made to pay?" More agreement from some, but a few more people were scowling now.

"Does it not say in Ephesians, 'put on the full armor of God, that you may be able to stand firm against the schemes of the devil'?" A few more cheers of agreement. "'For our struggle is not against flesh and blood, but against the rulers, against the powers, against the world forces of this darkness, against the spiritual forces of wickedness in the heavenly places.'" A few more cheers and a couple of amens. "'Therefore, take up the full armor of God, that you may be able to resist in the evil day, and having done everything, to stand firm.'" Now almost the whole place was cheering with him.

I, on the other hand, felt like I was seconds from being lynched.

"So we have to do everything in our power to stop these people, right?" he asked. The crowd this time readily agreed. "These people are the problem, right?" More agreement.

"Well, I'm sorry, but you're wrong," he said. He'd walked as he'd talked and stood at the pulpit once again.

The mood of the crowd came to a screeching halt.

"You're dead wrong. The greatest problem facing the church today is not perverts, murderers, or faggots." He stared intently out at everyone. "The greatest threat to the church today is you."

Now people were vocally upset. There were some boos and a couple of protests, but Father Mulligan just stood there and waited.

"The greatest threat that faces the church today is the startling lack of love and acceptance by the people in it." You could have heard a pin drop. "You people didn't name three things that were threats to the church. You named three groups of people who need the love of God the most." I saw a few people staring at him with their mouths open in shock. "The church is not a sports team. We are not one side that is arbitrarily picked to be against another. You see perverts, and I see sick people who need to be healed. You see murderers, and I see fallen brothers and sisters who have never needed love more in their lives. And you see faggots, and I see a group of God's children being hated for just being. And you say you are faithful Christians, and I see a group of hateful people masquerading as children of God."

People were murmuring to themselves, and I could tell this was not the homily they were expecting today.

"If we are servants of God, and I mean true servants and not just in name, then we have an obligation to love everyone in the name of the Lord. Not just the people we agree with and not just the things we can understand, but everything. Saint Augustine said it best when he wrote '*Cum dilectione huminum et odio vitiorum.*' It translates as 'With love for mankind and hatred of sins,' but nowadays we just say love the sinner, but hate the sin. And though it is true we must love the sinner, I think Augustine got it right the first time. With love for mankind. That is the point, for all of mankind. Not the white folks or the straight ones or the nice ones, for all mankind. There are times when I think the Statue of Liberty has the right idea. 'Give me your tired, your poor. Your huddled masses yearning to breathe free. The wretched refuse of your teeming shores. Send these, the homeless, tempest-tost to me.'"

He paused to let the words sink in.

"She got it. The woman who wrote that got it. Why can't we? We are supposed to be God's chosen. We are his servants here on Earth, and it is our job to bring his love to those who don't know they are loved. Our job is not to hold others in judgment. Not to belittle the people we don't agree with. You think there is evil in the world? So do I. You think there is wickedness abundant in the air? I agree. You think the answer is hating them? You're wrong, dead wrong. And I assure you, if you think the fact you are here, dressed up on a Sunday, is a golden ticket to heaven, it isn't. You want to quote Corinthians and tell me that the sexually immoral, idolaters, adulterers, or men who practice homosexuality will not inherit the kingdom of God, then be sure to finish the quote with thieves, greedy people, drunks, revilers, and swindlers too. You think having money and wanting more is good? Not according to that quote. You want to think getting the best out of a deal is good, you're better off finding another passage to defend it."

He began to pace as he talked. "People are so quick to say what will keep you out of heaven, but they forget we have guidelines covering how to get in too. He left us a lesson plan, and all we have to do is follow it. Judge not, that you be not judged. Matthew 7:1. You shall love the Lord your God with all your heart and with all your soul and with all your strength and with all your mind. *And your neighbor as yourself.* Luke 10:27. Love your neighbor as yourself. It is right there. Why can't we see it? You want to say those people are a threat to the church, and I say it's the people who forgot that last part. Love your neighbor as yourself. You want to talk about who isn't getting into heaven? What about Romans 3:23? For *all* have sinned and fall short of the glory of God. *All,*" he repeated loudly. "Not just the ones in here, not the ones who are straight, but all. It isn't our job to say who will and will not get into heaven. All we have to do is the very best we can and let the rest fall to our Father. And I swear to you, he will take points off for pointing fingers at others and telling everyone what they have done wrong."

The crowd was coming back around now, and I could see they were agreeing with him, myself included.

"So let me start over," he said, smiling at us as he got behind the podium again. "What is the greatest challenge to the church today?"

I spoke up before I even knew what I was doing. "Love."

He looked over at me and winked. "See? This young man has it."

I felt my face grow red as I looked over at Nate, who was looking at me with a huge smile.

"Now let us pray," he said as we all put our heads down and closed our eyes.

It was the first time I understood what people got out of going to church.

After the service, people were walking around talking to people. I asked Nate if I could go to Father Mulligan and say something. We walked over and waited as he talked to an elderly couple who seemed taken with his sermon. When they were done, he turned to us and looked at me with wide eyes. "Well now, I didn't know God still made them this big anymore."

I looked down in embarrassment as Nate said, "Father, this is Danny. This was his first time at a mass."

"Was it?" he said, sounding pleased. "And what did you think?"

Looking up at him, I felt a million warring emotions in my heart. "I loved it, I really did."

That seemed to make him even happier, and he clapped my shoulder. "That is humbling to hear, Danny. Nowadays getting to kids your age is the hardest part. If God had a Twitter account, it might be easier."

I chuckled at the joke. "So how do I do it?" He looked confused. "I mean, what do I do to go to a church? I mean, is there an application or something?"

He shook his head. "No, it's a lot like buying a good suit. You need to shop around until you find one that will keep you warm, that is comfortable, and most of all doesn't feel like it's suffocating you. Every church is different, even though we all have the same boss. He's pretty lax with the franchise."

I laughed again. Were all priests this funny? "So I just show up and, what? Ask questions?"

"I bet you there are hundreds of people out there who would love to answer any question you have about God and his plan for you, Danny. All you have to do is ask."

"I will," I said quickly.

His face got serious. "I'm not going to lie to you, Danny, it isn't easy all the time. God asks a lot of us, and all we can do is endure. Some people think church is just a social thing to see friends and to feel better about themselves, but if you're serious, if you want to really do it, it will take some work."

"I'm not afraid of work, sir," I said, thinking of how hard I worked to be good at basketball.

"Neither is he," he said, pointing up. "What you give, he will repay a thousand times over."

Nothing in my life had felt this right before, and I was almost giddy with emotion. Overcome, I reached over and hugged him. "Thank you so much for talking today."

I felt him hug me back and say, "No, Danny, thank you for listening today."

And that was when I became religious.

CHAPTER THIRTEEN: B.E.E.F. (BALANCE, EYES, ELBOW, FOLLOW-THROUGH)

THE COACH yelled to me on the sidelines, "Monroe, are you even listening?"

Indeed I was not even listening. I was too busy looking across the court at the end of my world and wondering how I got there. No, scratch that, I knew exactly how I got there. I was actually wondering how to get the hell out of there.

I had been trying to will my heart to stop beating for most of the game so far, but no dice.

Nodding at the coach, I tried to force myself to pay attention to the game. After all, this was the playoffs for State. I was a senior and about to graduate, and all I could think about was how badly I'd screwed everything up. That and how hot he looked.

It had started out such a good season too.

Since I was a senior, no one even blinked when I was named team captain; in fact, it was expected. I had a dozen guys looking at me asking how they were going to win State this year. Fortunately I had an answer for them. BEEF.

No, not like meat, B.E.E.F.

It stands for Balance, Eyes, Elbow, and Follow-through. It was the technique they taught me in Germany when I was first learning to play, and I realized we all needed a refresher in the basics. That summer break we all headed up to Austin. The coach had booked us a week of basketball camp, where we were all taught the game again from the ground up. Most of the guys needed it, because they had learned to play the game on the court. They hadn't gone to any school or had special lessons in it. It was a game you played with a ball and a hoop, and that was it. The tactics behind the game were a mystery to them, and they needed to solve it. I needed it because I was badly out of shape. Not in regards to my body—I had gone back to working out like I used to—but my skills on the court needed some help. I hadn't played with a real team in almost a year, and from the way I was tripping all over the court, it showed.

That and the fact that my hip would not let it go.

It's not like it always hurt or anything, but it did not seem to share my love for basketball. I knew this because after any game, it screamed at me for at least an hour, no matter how long I iced or applied heat to it. I began downing Advil like it was candy, telling myself to just man through because there was no time to worry about a little bit of pain.

I so wished it was just a little bit of pain.

After the camp we began to really gel as a team, and it was an epic thing to watch. What had started out as just another group of high school guys was slowly becoming a unit. We all became obsessed with getting better, and for a couple of perfect weeks, we weren't just a basketball team but a band of brothers. We ate, talked, and slept basketball. It was the center of our universe as the summer shambled slowly toward fall. But for the first time in forever, I wasn't hesitant about the coming school year. I was eager for it.

I was ready for this season.

The first few games, we blew past the other team so badly that they might as well have been junior high kids. By the third game, there were college recruiters in the stands, and they were all watching us. I had never been so proud of the team. They didn't get cocky, they didn't get overconfident, they didn't let the wins go to their head. We had one goal collectively and that was winning State this year. Nothing else mattered. We ran as a team in the morning, our breath fogging with the early chill as we lapped the football field again and again. No one talked, no one complained. We all ran in unison, knowing in our mind's eye we could see the same finish line.

The only other thing I did during this time was go to church.

Nate had been right about faith: it was everything. I read the Bible, which was okay, but honestly contradicted itself more than it made sense. I listened to the youth pastors who spoke to us every weekend, and one cold Sunday morning in the middle of August, I was baptized as the sun broke over the dark sky. I had never felt so at peace in my entire life. I worked out, I went to school, and each night I prayed for God to allow me the strength to win this year.

By the middle of the season, I had come to realize someone up there was listening to me.

We had lost one game, and the crowds were getting larger and larger. It made us popular, but I have to admit, I didn't pay attention to it. I was too busy with homework, running, and reading scripture to worry about something as silly as popularity. My dad noticed the difference and brought it up during dinner one night.

"So what's up with you?" he asked as I gnawed at a chicken leg while skimming over my trig worksheet. I gave him a questioning look, and he gestured to the books on the table. "With you, all you do is work. I haven't seen you go out once since you went to Dallas."

A shadow crossed my mind when I remembered meeting Sam and all that nonsense.

"I've been busy," I said, dismissing the ghost of Sam's smile. "I want to win this year."

"Well, yeah," he said, trying to get my attention back. "But, Danny, all work and no play makes one a dull boy."

I glanced up at him. "Whoever works his land will have plenty of bread, but he who follows worthless pursuits lacks sense."

He gave me a look. "Did you just try to Bible me?" I looked down. "You did, you seriously tried to Bible me with verse and crap." He got up and tossed his napkin on the table. "Okay, you're done," he snapped, closing my book.

"But I have to finish…," I began to protest.

"I'm sure it's due later this week, which means you have time now," he said, making it obvious he had no patience for me trying to convince him. "Get up, get changed, and we're going out to do something."

"Like what?" I asked, wondering if other kids had this problem.

"Anything but schoolwork or reading the Bible," he replied, grabbing our plates. "Go," he said, seeing me still standing there. "I'm not kidding, we're going out now."

I grumbled as I stomped off to my room and changed.

When I got out, he had put on a windbreaker and was checking his phone. "You have a choice between minigolf, bowling, or a movie, but I warn you, there's nothing good playing."

"Dad, I'm fine," I said, sitting down to pull my shoes on. "Seriously, I don't need—"

"Minigolf. Bowling. Movie," he repeated firmly.

"Bowling," I said, choosing the least of the three evils.

We ended up at a local bowling alley, renting shoes and finding a lane. My dad's shoes fit perfectly, and he was ready to go in minutes. I, on the other hand, was not so lucky. I had just turned eighteen, and I was now six seven in bare feet, bare feet that were a size sixteen. The guy behind the counter thought I was joking when I told him my size, but when he leaned over the counter to look at them, he realized I wasn't. He gave me the biggest pair they had and wished me good luck getting them on.

I wasn't going to need luck. I was going to need some kind of shrinking potion.

"Dad," I said, with my heel still out of the shoe. "I don't think this is going to work."

He looked down and hid the smile on his face with a hand. "That's what you get for having clown feet."

I gave him a dirty look just as I heard a female voice behind me say, "You can bowl in your socks." I turned around and saw a girl who looked familiar. "My friend is weirded out by wearing other people's shoes, so she always just bowls in socks."

"I know you," I said, not realizing how stupid that sounded.

"I've seen you on base at the chapel," she replied. "We're in the same youth group."

Now I didn't just feel stupid but stuck-up, since I hadn't noticed her at all. But truth be told, I wouldn't have been able to ID anyone from that group. I had been so focused on school and the season that I hadn't even tried making friends.

"I'm Danny," I said, holding my hand out.

She kind of laughed. "I know, I'm Emma." Her hand looked so tiny in mine that I felt like I was going to crush it. "Is that your brother?" she asked, looking at my dad.

My dad was looking for a ball so he hadn't heard, and I laughed. "That's my dad, but please don't tell him he looks young enough to be my brother. He'd never let me live it down."

"I'm here with some friends," she said, gesturing a couple of lanes down. "If you guys want to bowl with us, it's cool."

"I'll ask my dad," I said hesitantly. "I'm not sure if this is like a bonding thing or we're here to actually have fun."

She laughed again, confused. "Okay, well, if you decide to join us, that's cool."

"Who was that?" my dad asked, watching her walk away.

"She's in my church group," I said, confused by the way I was so confused.

"Pretty girl," he said, putting his ball down. I looked over at him, and he shrugged. "What? She's attractive for a girl her age, just a fact."

I gave up on the bowling shoes and went over to find a ball. When I came back, my dad kept glancing over at Emma and her friends. "You know, if you want to go hang with them, it's okay," he said, smiling.

"You wanted to come bowling. I can't just ditch you."

"No, I wanted to get you out of the house before you went nuts. You interacting with kids your own age in a recreational activity is, like, the whole point of tonight."

I looked over at them, and Emma smiled and waved. My hand waved back before I could stop it.

"Go on," he insisted. "When a pretty girl waves at you like that, it means she wants you to come over and talk to her. Trust me."

I looked at her and then back at him. "You sure?"

"Oh, just go!" he said, shaking his head. "Before I push you over there."

Taking my ball, I walked—well, more slid—the of couple lanes over to where Emma was sitting. "Room for one more?"

Her face lit up, and she nodded. "Guys, this is Danny. He goes to my church."

I waved and smiled, trying not to feel like I was invading their night.

That was how I ended up realizing I wasn't completely unattractive to girls. Emma admitted after a few times of going out with friends that she thought I was cute but never had the nerve to talk to me at church. At first I was shocked because cute was not the word that popped into my mind when I thought of myself, but that was followed by the fact that I didn't instantly reject the idea of liking her back. I mean, it wasn't fireworks or the same animal urge I'd had when I saw Sam, but she was a nice girl, and I liked hanging out with her.

And at the time, it was exactly what I needed.

Emma's dad was in the Navy and stationed on base as well, so we had a lot in common when it came to always being the new kid in town. She went to a different school in town, which made sense, since my dad had chosen my school because it was the high school that took basketball the most seriously, not because it was nearby or the newest. Emma had picked a different school. I liked having a girlfriend. It was comfortable to be able to put my arm around someone and have them tell me they thought I was attractive. She had been raised religious and was reserved when it came to sex, so she was thrilled to find I wasn't in a hurry to get into her jeans.

The only person who didn't seem happy about Emma was Nate.

"A girl?" he asked me over Skype. "Did I miss something?"

"No," I said, trying to laugh the question off. "Maybe I'm bi and not gay. You ever think of that?"

He just stared at me through the computer screen for a few seconds. "I never thought about it at all, dude, because you like guys." He saw the look on my face and sighed. "Look, Danny, if you're really into this girl, that's cool, and I'm all behind you, but if you're doing this to cover something up, then you're an asshole. That girl really likes you, and you—"

"I do like her," I said quickly.

Too quickly.

"Okay, cool, man," he said, a little dismissive. "If you like her, that's awesome. I'm happy for you."

"You don't sound like it," I shot back.

His eyes locked with mine through the screen. "That's because I've seen what it looks like when you really like someone."

My mouth went dry, and I started to feel queasy.

"Okay, I need to finish this homework," I said, looking away from my laptop.

"Yeah, me too."

"Talk to you later."

"Sure." And he logged off.

I ignored him and began dating Emma.

The season only got better and better. There's something about having someone in the stands cheering for you who isn't your dad that makes you want to do better. Emma and her friends started coming to games and cheering for us, and I found myself playing better for them. It was about this time that recruiters started approaching me about college. The first was from Oklahoma, and they offered me a trip up to their campus to look around and see if I liked it. I was blown away, but my dad said to try to calm down and wait. They wouldn't be the only ones.

He was right.

As the season progressed, different college recruiters came knocking on my door, so to speak, each one trying his best to convince me their school was the best fit for me. The amount of effort these guys put into trying to convince me just to go to their school to look was staggering, and I was overwhelmed.

My dad, on the other hand, was completely whelmed by the attention and fielded the offers as they came in. It was like a dream come true as brochures started to litter our kitchen table. One night he just stood there and stared at them all, a huge smile on his face, as I felt a warm glow in my chest that I had done it. I had finally done something that made him proud of me.

The fact that all these colleges were watching made me play even harder.

As each game passed, we got closer and closer to State, the pot of gold at the end of this rainbow. I trained harder, prayed more, and just hoped I had enough to get what I wanted. Emma was supportive as hell. She was stoked to be dating "a real live basketball star," as she put it. I didn't want to get a swelled head from all the attention, but it was getting hard not to. Every week there was an assembly in the gym, and the entire school cheered us on. There were signs with my name on them. For the first time in my life I was someone, and it felt great.

We took the championship for our district and headed to the playoffs for State, where the real fight would begin. We went to Austin and spent the next couple of days getting used to the gym while holed up in a hotel. My dad took some leave and rented a room a couple of blocks away. It was after an afternoon practice that he pulled me aside and said there was a recruiter here wanting to talk.

"Right now?" I asked, wiping the sweat off my forehead. "It can't wait until after tonight's game?"

He gave me a Cheshire cat smile and said, "You're going to want to talk to this one now."

I showered and changed out and met him in the parking lot. We drove to a pretty nice Mexican place to eat. When we showed up, we were told there was a private table already reserved for us. I gave my dad an impressed smile as the waiter walked us to the back of the place to a sectioned-off dining room. He slid the doors open, and there were three men in suits talking, but I didn't even notice them.

Nate was sitting at the end of the table, smiling like a loon at me.

I looked back to my dad. "These guys are from A&M?"

He nodded and turned me around to face the men. "Gentlemen, this is my son, Danny."

They all stood up and shook my hand, patting me on the back and saying they'd heard a lot of nice things about me and all that. I just kept glancing over at Nate, and he winked at me once as he took a sip of tea. They introduced themselves as Mr. Peterson, head of the athletics department; the oldest one was Bud something, who was from the alumni committee, whatever that was; and the last was Patrick Nunnely, head coach of the basketball department at A&M. Once we got settled, Mr. Peterson said, "So, Danny, hell of a year so far."

I nodded. "Just playing my hardest, sir."

Nate snickered slightly but covered it with a cough.

Nunnely glanced at Nate for a second, giving him a silent warning, and then looked to me. "Well, I'm not going to beat around the bush here. We want you for our team, and depending on how tomorrow's game goes, we'll be able to tell you how much we want you." I cocked my head, confused as to what that meant. "You win tomorrow, and I not only guarantee you a full ride, including room and board, but Bud here can make sure you never need anything again. Your car from this year?" I shook my head. "Well, you'll never have that problem again."

Bud smiled and nodded. "If you can make it to State tomorrow, I'm pretty sure I can convince the alumni association to make sure you're more than taken care of. Our players need to concentrate on things like school and practice, so we make sure everything else is handled."

"And if the team loses?" my dad asked.

"If he loses, I'm certain we can still find a place for him on the team, but it will be harder to convince them to be so generous with an untested freshman. Players are rewarded on skill, merit, and loyalty. Something Nathan here has told us you possess in spades."

I glanced at Nate, who shrugged and said, "In all honesty, I was pretty drunk when I said that, so I could be wrong."

We all laughed at the tension breaker.

Peterson waited until the laughter died down. "The bottom line is this, Danny. Play your heart out tomorrow, and you'll be rewarded on your performance."

It sounded so simple at the time.

After dinner my dad talked with the men while Nate and I took a walk outside. "Thought you were mad at me," I said as we took in the Austin night.

"Mad?" he asked, not looking at me. "No. Maybe disappointed but not mad."

"Why can't I like a girl?" I asked him, stopping right there on the sidewalk.

He looked back at me, and I could see the profound sadness in his eyes. "If you really liked her? You could, but we both know you don't."

"But you know what the Bible says about being gay," I countered. "It's a sin, and I would be—"

"Stop," he said abruptly, and I realized I had been wrong. He hadn't been mad at me before. Now he was mad at me. "I did not take you to church so you could learn to hate yourself. That place is not a place of hate, and if all you got out of that book was that you were an abomination, then, boy, did you read it wrong."

"Are you telling me God didn't say that being gay was wrong?"

"I'm saying there is a lot that Leviticus says is wrong. If all you can see is gay, then you're trying too hard. Come on, Danny, why is this such a problem for you?"

"*Because I'm tired of being a failure!*" I raged at him. "*I don't want to be seventy feet tall and I don't want to be the guy who never knows anyone and I don't want to be the faggot who disappointed my dad!*"

I could see the shock on his face as he realized how much being like this was killing me.

"I can't do it any more, Nate, I can't. I just want to be normal. I just want to be another guy." I felt a sob shudder through me. "I'm tired of all of this. I just want to be normal."

He looked shocked as I broke down. His arms surrounded me, and I leaned into him. "Okay, Smalls, I'm sorry. I'll drop it. If you're happy with this girl, then be happy. That's all I want for you."

It was all I wanted for me too, but I didn't think I was ever going to get it.

I went back to the hotel and slept like the dead. All my hopes and dread for tomorrow canceled each other out, and I didn't even remember if I dreamed or not. I woke up at the alarm and for a few precious seconds could not remember why today was important. It was like the greatest gift the universe could have given me, because everything had fallen away in the mists of sleep, and I was just a guy waking up.

"You ready to win this?" my roommate asked, and it came rushing back.

Oh yeah, life.

We worked out a little in the gym, stretching out the kinks and getting warmed up. So far we hadn't seen the other team. There was a whole other gym they were given to work out in. We had avoided each other the whole week, so it was kinda cool. The auditorium began filling up as we retreated back into the locker room to get ready.

We all sat in silence as the roar of the crowd filtered in. We were all nervous, but we were ready. As ready as we were going to get.

"So we're here," the coach said five minutes before the game. "This is it. I'm sure I'm supposed to tell you this is just another game and to go out there and play your asses off, but I can't. This is it, boys, this is the whole ballgame. You win, and we're on to State, and win or lose, we're in the big time. We lose, we go home and get to watch these idiots play the game we're supposed to be in on TV. So go out there and destroy them. They've made a few changes to their team, but we should be ready." He looked at me and asked, "You sure you can do this?"

I gave him a confused look. "Yeah, I'm ready." Was he doubting that I could handle this?

"We know our game—let's go play it," the coach assured us.

A guy knocked on the door and poked his head in. "Corpus, you guys are up."

We all stood in a huddle, and I put my hand in the middle of us. "Tigers on three," I said.

"One, two, three."

The echoing of us all screaming "Tigers" as loud as we could was deafening as we ran out onto the court. The noise of the crowd hit us like an explosion when we entered the court. There were lights everywhere, and I could see a bank of cameras off the court reminding me this was being televised. It was hotter than any court I had been on. I couldn't even see the people in the stands, so finding my dad and Nate was impossible. We gathered on our side of the court, and the coach reminded us of some last minute pointers.

As the big man on the team, I was the one to tip off for first possession.

"You're sure you can do this?" the coach asked me before I walked out onto the court. "Because I need your head in the game, not in the past."

Again I looked at him, confused. "I'm here to win, Coach."

"Good," he said, slapping my back. "Go do this."

I walked out and tried to get my eyes used to the huge floodlights they had set up. There was going to be a lot of playing time watching the floor instead of looking up unless I wanted to be blinded. I got up to the line and took a deep breath.

"You know, I'd say I was surprised, but I'm not going to lie," the guy from the other team said in a voice that sent chills down my spine. I looked up and saw Cody glaring back at me. "So I'll just say it's going to feel awesome kicking your ass."

My mind froze as the ref blew the whistle and tossed the ball up.

"*Time!*" I screamed as Cody jumped up for the ball, and I just stood there.

Half the crowd groaned as the other half began to boo. Cody had, of course, tapped the ball toward his team, but he realized the game was not on and stumbled to a stop. "What the fuck?" he growled, looking over at me. "You come here to play or to fuck around?"

He looked good, really good. I could see he had filled out the same as I had. What was once cute was now clearly hot. I tried to banish those thoughts as I walked over to him. "What...?" I was about to ask him what he was doing there, but that was a stupid question.

"Are you playing, twenty-two, or what?" the ref asked me.

"Where did you come from?" I asked, knowing he wasn't on any of the tapes I'd watched earlier.

"Transferred," Cody said with a bitter smile. "What? Not happy to see me?"

I took a step toward Cody. "What I did to you was wrong, and I'm sorry for that, and you have every right to be pissed at me." His eyes narrowed. "And any other time I would fall down on my knees and beg for you to forgive me, but that isn't going to happen right now." I took another step until I was right in his face. "Right now I'm going to play circles around you and go on to State. If you want to talk after that, you know where to find me."

Before he could even blink, I turned back to the ref and said, "Yeah, I'm ready to play."

And I was.

We both went up for the ball, but it wasn't close. Cody was a little over six feet, and from what I could see, he had great calf muscles, but I had seven inches on him standing still. Jumping? It was a joke. There was a brief moment where I felt his arm slam into my gut as I came down, but we both knew the refs had no chance of seeing it, so I ignored it. Instead I came down on his left foot as hard as I could, making it clear I was not going to back down from him.

He chased after me with a slight limp, but it was no use, I had the advantage, and I was going to press it.

The first quarter wasn't as overwhelming as I thought it would be. They had done their homework on our team, no doubt with the information by their new teammate Cody. He knew how I used to play, and it showed by the way he crowded me with every step I took.

It was like having a mouthy shadow who obviously hated my ever-loving guts. "So come on, fag, what you think you're gonna do?" he said under his breath, just loud enough for me to hear as I waited to see where Evans was going with the ball. "So which one of these guys are you screwing? Or do they not know what you are?"

I took a step back into him, knocking him on his ass instantly.

"Oh, sorry, man," I said, looking down at him. "Didn't see you down there."

He looked over at a ref, but even if they'd been watching me, it would have looked like an accident. Cody got up and chased after me as I tried to banish his words from my mind. He was so pissed at me, you could hear it in his voice, and it was like daggers in my ears. This is what I did to people. I made them hate me like no other.

"I miss you."

My head spun around to look at him. His voice had broken, and for half a second he sounded so real, so in pain. The ball hit me in the small of my back as I completely missed the pass. Laughing, he tore around me, took the ball, and scored, while I just stood there, staring like an idiot. That was the moment I began to worry that we could lose this.

This went on until halftime. We were better than them, but I was playing so badly that I was actually fucking other people up on the court, so it was closer than anyone wanted to say. We jogged back to the locker room. I was in the back, and before I could get off the court the coach grabbed my arm. Hard.

"I am going to go in there and give a speech about how we need to play harder and think faster. But what we really need to do is replace you out there. I asked if this was going to be a problem, which meant I assumed you'd gone over their roster changes. Obviously I was wrong. Go talk to him, go scream, go take a walk around the arena, but when halftime is over, if you aren't playing any better, I swear I will bench your ass."

I can't imagine they give many scholarships to guys who get benched 'cause their ex-kinda-boyfriends were taunting them on the court. Instead of going back to the locker room, I scanned the stands and found Nate and my dad, looking back at me with concern. I waved them down because if I didn't talk to someone, I was about to scream, and once started, I don't know if I could have stopped.

"What's wrong?" Nate asked the second I was within earshot. He knew how I played, and he knew when I was playing badly.

"That's Cody," I explained. I had told him the basics during that summer when he was my kinda nurse, so he understood the name instantly.

"Oh shit," he said, looking shocked. "Well, in that case, you're playing a hell of a game, 'cause if my ex-girlfriend was shadowing me all game, I would have lost it already."

"That's the boy who moved away?" my dad asked, looking back to the other team's locker room.

I nodded but kept looking at Nate. "This is punishment. This is what I get for even trying to satisfy those—" I paused as I tried to dig up the correct words. "—unnatural impulses. Do you see now? I'm not supposed to be like that."

He opened his mouth to argue but then paused.

"Okay, you know what? Let's go with that theory. You think this is punishment from up high because you dared to like a guy? And you think the Almighty takes time from his schedule to fuck up a high school basketball game, great. Then there's only one way to make this right." I looked at him, waiting for him to give me the answer. "If this is God's punishment, the only way you can get out of it is going and apologizing to Cody. You have to ask forgiveness for your sins, and then it's done. He doesn't have to give it, but you have to ask. It's that simple."

It was so simple an answer, it had to be the right one.

"Wish me luck," I said, walking toward the other team's locker room. My dad called after me, but I ignored him because this wasn't something I could be talked out of. Nate was right. I needed to ask forgiveness for my transgressions against whatever and move on. It was a sign.

Security looked at me weirdly for a moment when I walked up to the locker room, but they waved me through; after all, I was a basketball player. There were a score of assistant coaches and trainers standing outside the actual locker room, with the coach inside giving a speech about how the game was going, no doubt.

Their jaws literally dropped open when they saw me walk in.

"I need to talk to Cody Franks, please," I asked as politely as possible.

"You can't be back here," one of them said, trying to reestablish the rules of normalcy.

"It won't take a second," I assured them.

When it was clear I wasn't going anywhere, one of them knocked on the locker room door and stuck his head in. There was a loud bellow of "Who the fuck is out there?" before the coach came barreling out, more than a few players on his heels. "You need to get the hell out of here before I call a ref and have you thrown out of the game."

"I need to talk to Cody Franks for a second, sir, and then I'm gone."

Cody was peering out of the locker room behind the coach. I could see the shock on his face when he saw I was standing there.

"I'm not kidding, son. Get out of here now," he warned.

Ignoring him, I looked at Cody. "I seriously need five minutes, or I can say what I want to say in front of all these people."

"I'll talk to him, Coach," Cody said quickly.

"What?" he asked, now confused as to what was going on.

"Please, Coach, it'll be quick."

Seeing he had lost control of whatever was happening, the coach dismissed me with his hand and screamed for the team to get back in the locker room. They walked in, but it was obvious everyone wanted to hear what was about to go down. Cody and I walked back toward the court, far enough from anyone who might hear us.

"Okay, talk," he said gruffly.

I took a deep breath and just let it go. "What I did was wrong. I was attracted to you and that was wrong, and I should have never even tried anything with you, and for that I apologize. I'm not like that anymore, and I understand why you might not care, but I'm telling you here and now I was wrong, I fucked up, and I'm sorry. Truly. I'm asking you to forgive me, but I understand if you won't. Right now I'm more concerned that God might not forgive me, but I'm still asking."

He glared at me, speechless, for almost a minute. Finally he shook his head and said, "You're fucking crazy. You're a fruitcake, Danny, and you can try to pray to every God who will listen, but it isn't going to change. I know that because I have to tell myself that every morning when I wake up. I don't know what happened between us, but if you think I'm going to just drop it so you can win a game—"

"I don't care about the game," I said, surprised to find I wasn't lying. "I just don't want you to hate me anymore."

His anger faded for a moment, and he said in a quiet voice, "I don't hate you, Danny. I wish I could."

"I am so sorry, Cody," I said again, feeling tears coming to my eyes. "If I had it all to do again—"

Which was when my coach kicked open the door and saw me in the other team's locker room. *"Goddammit, Monroe! Are you trying to get us disqualified?"* I looked at Cody, and I could see him wanting to say something, but there were too many people around now. Instead he just gave me a sad smile and nodded.

And just like that, a weight was lifted off my chest, and I could breathe again.

The coach dragged me back to our locker room, and there was much screaming and yelling, but I was oblivious to it. I had been forgiven, and that was all I needed in that moment. When he realized I wasn't listening, he stopped yelling and went back to his dry-erase board and began going over plays. When he was done, he looked at me. "You have anything you want to say?"

I stood up and looked at the team. "This is my fault, and I know it. The second half won't be like the first, and we're going to win this. That I promise you." I saw a few guys smile in response. "So let's go out there and show these guys whose house it is. Whose house is it?" I asked.

"Run's house," a few guys said back.

Louder, I shouted, *"Whose house?"*

They all screamed back, *"Run's house!"*

We all got up and cheered as the energy in the room started to rise again. With a roar we charged out onto the court, ready to do battle no matter what the cost.

We won 94-82. Cody didn't say a word to me on the court. It was official; I was going to A&M to play basketball. But more importantly, I was done liking guys. That part of my life was over.

CHAPTER FOURTEEN:
24-SECOND VIOLATION

THE WEEK before graduation, I signed the papers and became the newest member of the A&M basketball team. They gave me a cap that could have been made out of gold and not been as valuable to me. I had worked my ass off since Germany for this, and now here it was; it was really happening.

My dad was fifteen kinds of proud. He bought a sweatshirt that proclaimed him as the proud parent of an Aggie, which he wore every single moment he was on base out of uniform. Nate was overjoyed; we were going to be playing on the same team, and I was stoked. Emma was happy for me too, even if she understood after graduation we were done.

I was moving to College Station, and she wasn't.

It made things weird between us, but in a good way. Knowing that this was it, that there was nothing more, freed us a little bit, and we just decided to enjoy the time we had. She became more affectionate, and I was horny enough not to protest. I had tried not to jerk off since finding God, but let me tell you, I have no earthly idea how he expected us to follow that one. I mean, no sex until marriage and no jerking off? People must have been married and knocked up by the time they were fifteen in the old days. I also didn't want to jerk off that much because no matter how hard I tried to picture girls, it never turned me on enough to do the trick.

So one night after a movie, when she moved her hand over my crotch and squeezed, I couldn't care less that she was a girl. Fuck, at that moment, she could have been a chimpanzee, and I would have groaned like that. She smiled and asked, "How long until you have to be back?"

"I got time," I blurted out quickly.

"Find us somewhere private," she said with a small smile.

It took all my control not to peel out of the parking lot like the devil himself was chasing me. One of the many advantages of living on a mostly closed-down base was the abundance of private places one could find. Whole chunks of space that had once served some greater purpose were now abandoned and just asking to be used by bored kids who wanted to get away from everything. I parked us on the south side of where the hospital used to be. It was covered in the shadows cast by the full moon and gave us complete privacy.

I turned off the car, and we faced each other in the front seat. My heart was racing, and I felt myself starting to sweat.

"Have you ever done this before?" she asked me with a wry grin. I shook my head, since I had indeed never done a thing with a girl. "I didn't think so," she said, taking a step toward me. "I was wondering why you hadn't made a move yet."

Say what?

"I-I thought…," I said as she leaned forward and kissed my neck. "I thought you were saving yourself for marriage."

She scoffed as she nibbled my ear. "God, you really do believe that church stuff, don't you?"

I was about to answer when her hand came to rest on my crotch, or more specifically my member, even more specifically my rock-hard member. Just her touch, through two layers of clothes, was enough to make me moan. It had been so long since I had come that I was on a hairpin trigger and pretty sure I wasn't going to last long enough to get my pants off.

"Wow!" she said, looking down at my bulge. "I never believed that whole big-feet thing before, but now…." She rubbed its length, and I felt myself press back against the car door in nervous excitement. "You are a big boy all over, aren't you?" she asked, her voice dropping lower into a teasing tone. She unbuckled my belt, and I looked down to watch her work. She popped open my khakis and unzipped them in one fluid movement.

"You *have* done this before," I said, realizing I had completely misunderstood who she really was.

"I'm a Navy brat," she said, looking for the gap in my boxer briefs. "You're telling me that you never messed around with girls on other bases?"

I shook my head, telling the God's honest truth.

"Well, then," she said, finding the slit and smiling. "Let me be your first." She reached in and grabbed the shaft of my cock and pulled it out. "Sonofabitch," she said, gripping my manhood firmly. "You're going to make some girl very happy someday."

Before I could respond she leaned down and put it in her mouth.

It was easily the best feeling I have ever had, hands down. A million times better than jerking off, a billion times better than just grinding into my mattress, and though I was delirious at her mouth's ministrations, one thought bubbled up loud and clear in my head.

This will show Nate I'm straight.

It was so out of place, so completely wrong for the moment, that I almost lost my hard-on.

Almost, but not really.

When we were done, she sat up and wiped her mouth with a napkin that seemed to come out of nowhere. I just lay there against the car door as she dropped the vanity mirror down and checked her hair. "Well, that clears that up," she said as she grabbed her lipstick.

I cracked one eye open. "What?"

She applied the makeup and then puckered her lips. "Most of the girls on base said you were either a virgin or gay. Now I can say for sure you're just a virgin." She looked over and smiled at me. "And normally I'd change that before you took off to college, but seriously, Danny, that thing is getting nowhere near me."

I followed her gaze and realized she was talking about my softening cock, still lying out of my boxers. I sat up and tucked it away. "They said I was gay?"

She nodded and flipped the mirror up. "Well, you are cute as fuck, in fantastic shape, and obviously you aren't ashamed of what you got down there. You never hit on a girl, never even looked at one. People talked." She saw the look on my face. "But it's cool. I mean, it's not like you're gay."

I lunged across the car and kissed her hard.

At first she was shocked, but then she began to kiss back. "I'll show you who isn't gay," I said, unbuttoning her blouse. She laughed as I pulled it open.

Before I began to kiss her breasts and ignored everything else, the fact was, I felt like I was playing to an audience I couldn't see. The feeling that all the girls on base were outside the car looking in at me, seeing how I really acted around a girl, was overwhelming. I began to ravish her, focusing all my efforts on replicating what I had seen in every sex scene in every movie I had ever watched. Maybe it was because I was trying so hard or because I was so rattled by what she'd said, but this was doing nothing for me. I wasn't turned on, and I wasn't even the slightest bit hard, but I still went to town because I had something to prove. To her, to the girls on base, to Nate....

To myself.

By the time I had her pants slipped down to her knees, she was panting hard. She grabbed my hair and pulled my head back to hers. "Do you have a condom?"

I did, but the thought I was going to have to be hard to use it panicked me.

"No," I said, trying to sound disappointed. "I thought I wasn't getting close to you," I said with a fake smile.

"I was thinking just the tip," she said. "It's no big deal...."

It was, and I couldn't lose her now. I needed to send her back to her friends with a story that killed every rumor once and for all. I needed to plant my flag of manhood here and now, and I needed to do it as forcefully as possible.

"I can do better than the tip," I said, moving back to pull her pants off completely.

"What are you going to do?" she asked, giggling.

"My feet aren't the only thing I have that's big," I said, sticking my tongue all the way out.

Her eyes got wide, and I lowered myself on her... praying to God that I didn't throw up.

I didn't throw up, though I can't say I enjoyed myself, but then again I wasn't down there for my own good. I was down there to bury an ugly rumor once and for all and make sure it never crawled to the surface ever again. This wasn't a zombie movie. This was a mistake I was tired of having to pay for. Luckily Emma wasn't quiet about what she liked and didn't like, because I was clueless about what I was doing, if I was honest. Slowly but surely I figured out where I needed to be, and when I did, her entire body spasmed around me. Her legs closed hard on either side of my head as I felt her start to react.

And then she reacted again.

And again.

And then she came.

Hard.

She was glistening from a good sweat, and I could see the look of utter bliss on her face. Her eyes were closed, and she was sporting a huge smile. "Okay," she said out of breath. "You are in no way gay."

I grabbed a bottled water from my gym bag in the back and congratulated myself on a job well done.

I dropped Emma off, and she gave me a long and passionate kiss as she got out. "I hope we can do that again before you leave."

Nodding, I gave her a wink. "Count on it." I watched her walk away, wishing my body would react in some way to hers, but it didn't.

I dispelled that thought as I drove back home. Doing my best ninja impression, I crept into the house hoping not to wake my dad. Of course, he was awake in the living room watching *SportsCenter*.

"Someone can't tell time," he said, not even glancing over at me. "You're lucky you already have a scholarship, or I'd—" He stopped and looked over at me. "Did you have sex?"

My jaw hit the ground.

"Seriously, Danny, you stink like sex. What the hell?" he said, getting up.

"I-I mean...."

"With Emma?" he asked. I nodded, and he sighed. "Please tell me you were safe."

"Um... we didn't really do that. I mean, we didn't do something that needed a condom *per se*." This was worse than anything I could have ever imagined.

"Jesus Christ," he cursed, pacing in front of me. "I cannot believe I'm wishing you went back to liking guys." I felt a flush on my face, but he kept talking. "Danny, you have to know that hands down you're the best thing that has ever happened in my life. I in no way regret having you, and I know your mom felt the same way." I nodded slowly, not understanding a word he was saying. "But you cannot ruin your life getting a girl pregnant as young as I did. You can't. You have a whole life ahead of you that can only be complicated with a kid right now."

Oh, well, all of a sudden this made sense.

"Dad," I said, trying to interrupt him. "Dad, listen." He stopped talking and looked at me. "We didn't actually have sex. It was more oral than anything...."

He made a face and shook his head. "Please, Danny, do not describe what you did with her."

"I'm trying to tell you we didn't do that because we didn't have a rubber, okay?" He looked up at me, and I smiled. "I thought you'd be happier that I got it on with a girl."

His expression grew grim for a moment, and I thought I was in trouble. "I didn't have a problem with you when you liked guys. *If* you liked guys. I don't even know now." He sighed and looked down for a moment. "Seriously, Danny, if you're having sex with girls to prove something—"

I lost it.

"I'm having sex with girls 'cause I'm horny, Dad, and I happen to like them, okay?" I fired back. "You know you made me feel like shit in Germany about guys, and now you're doing the same thing about girls. Do you have a problem with sex or just with me having it?"

It was a completely unfair thing to say, and I knew it the moment it was out of my mouth, but I couldn't take it back now. It was out there now, and there was nothing to do but deal with it. We'd never talked about what went down in Germany; instead we'd navigated around those mental icebergs, trying our best not to sink this ship we called a life. But I had just steered us into the biggest one out there, and there was no way to turn back now.

He sat down and turned off the TV. The look on his face was half pissed and half hurt. It was killing me to look at him. "You think there isn't a day I don't think about how I handled that? Do you honestly think I'm happy with what I said to you then?" I didn't say a word. "I wasn't upset about you liking guys, Danny. I was upset about the fact that kid was saying you forced yourself on him."

I sat down across from him as he kept talking.

"I get it now. You guys were fooling around—everyone does at that age—and I should have handled it better." He gave a mirthless little laugh that was like nails on a chalkboard. "This was supposed to be one of the things your mom was supposed to help me with. I have no idea how to handle something like that without fucking you up for the rest of your life." He looked up at me, and I could see tears in his eyes. "Danny, you can be anything you want to be, and at the end of the day you need to do two things to make me happy. Be the best man you can be and come home safely every night. I don't care about anything else."

"But you wanted me to be straight," I said, my voice sounding like I was about to cry too.

He half sobbed. "No, son, I wanted you to be happy."

That was when we both started crying.

We hugged it out and tried to talk around the subject some more, but we were both drained, and there was nothing left to say. I took a shower while he went to bed. I looked down at my dick and closed my eyes as I took it in my hand. I imagined Emma naked in the car, just laid out for me as I stroked.

Nothing.

I clenched my eyes closed harder and tried to imagine a million different girls, all types, there for my taking.

More nothing.

I let go of it and leaned my head against the cool tile of the shower, cursing my life. I wished Nate was there. A flash of him crossed my mind, shirtless in the hide-a-bed in Amy's house, the way he'd smelled as I hugged him, the feeling of him next to me.... Looking down, I saw my cock almost fully hard, and I felt the shame in my chest as I glared at it. Why didn't anything work out the way it was supposed to? What was wrong with me?

The night of graduation, Emma and I finally had sex.

We went to a party at one of her friend's houses and midway through, she pulled me upstairs to celebrate me leaving. Though buzzed, I wasn't drunk enough to actually forget I was with a girl and enjoy the fact I was having sex. Luckily she had no idea how drunk I was, so when I didn't get hard no matter how hard she tried, she blamed it on the alcohol. She told me to wait and went downstairs for something. I wondered if I should get dressed and leave. I mean, what was the worst that could happen? She could say that we were going to seal the deal and then I'd run away like a little baby, and she'd tell every single person she knew that I couldn't actually fuck her.

There was nothing at all pleasurable about this moment to me.

She came back and handed me two pills and a bottle of water. "Here," she said. "Take those." She popped another pill into her mouth and dry swallowed it.

One of the pills was blue, and the other looked like one of those kid's aspirin except it had an apple imprinted on the surface. "What's this?" I asked her, trying not to sound nervous.

She grabbed my hand and put it up to my mouth. "Fun. Swallow," she ordered, watching me the entire time.

I took a sip of water and thought about spitting the pills into the bottle, but she was watching me like a hawk. Swallowing, I wondered what exactly I'd just done. She took the bottle from me and set it aside. I leaned back as she kissed me. Again it wasn't horrible, just not pleasurable. It was a set of lips on mine and a weight on top of me as she lay on my chest. I went through the motions, moving my hands across her back and over her ass, but it did nothing for me. It was like giving a real ineffective massage.

About ten minutes into it, I started to feel flush.

My face was warm, and not from being embarrassed or anything. I was just warm. I tried to ignore it, but my legs started to tingle, and I knew something was happening. "What was that?" I asked as my body began to react to something.

"Calm down, silly," she said, trying to nibble on my ear. "It was a Viagra and a hit of X. In a few minutes, you'll be feeling no pain."

"What?" I said, grabbing her shoulders. "You gave me Ecstasy?"

She giggled. "Danny, you need to lighten up."

My heart began to race, and I felt my fingers start to tingle as she kept trying to distract me. "Can you feel it?" she whispered.

I didn't say anything as my vision got blurry and the room spun around me. I laid my head back on the pillow and closed my eyes to stop from getting sick. She kept moving on top of me, her hands rubbing my unit in hopes of getting me hard. It felt like I was falling for a second, as if the bed had dropped out from under us, and I was tumbling down into a hole I was never going to get out of.

I opened my eyes, and I saw Emma staring down at me, smiling.

"You're feeling it," she said rather than asked.

I opened my mouth to say something, but there was nothing wrong. No doubts, no cares, nothing at all. I felt happy, really happy, and it was insane. I smiled up at her, and she rubbed me again, and now I started to get hard. "See?" she said. "Fun."

I kissed her, not because I wanted her but because the way her skin felt on my lips was, like, the best thing I had ever felt. Everything was a thousand times better than it normally was. The bed was softer than a cloud. Her on top of me was like a million small sparks of electricity moving over me. She pulled her blouse off and tossed it across the room.

"Touch me," she breathed. "You never touch me."

I put my hands over her breasts, and they seemed impossibly small compared to my hands. She unbuttoned my jeans and pulled them off me as I looked up at the ceiling, wondering how it floated above us so easily. "Did you bring protection this time?" she asked.

I nodded, still staring up. "Wallet," I said, my voice sounding like a cartoon mouse.

I heard the crinkling of a package, and then I gasped as she put it over my dick. I had thought her blowjob in the car was the best thing ever, but her touching me was, like, a billion times more than that. I wondered why I wasn't cumming yet, but I didn't care. She got it on and then moved up to kiss me.

"You don't do anything, okay?" she said. Her hair dangling down tickled my face. "The only way this is going to work is if you let me do all the work, okay?"

I nodded, not even knowing what she was talking about.

She straddled me, but I didn't care. Nothing bothered me right now, and I doubt anything could. It didn't matter that she was a girl and I wasn't sexually attracted to her. I didn't care that the main reason I was doing this was to prove my masculinity to people I didn't even know. I didn't even care that there were half a dozen other people I'd rather be doing this with.

Right now everything was perfect.

She lowered herself on to me, and once again my mind was blown. You imagine how great sex is going to be when you're growing up, but let me tell you, nothing prepares you for the actual feeling when it happens. I might have made a sound, but I was too out of it to even notice. I just had flashes of her moaning and telling me I was huge, but it seemed like it was so far away. The room had become nothing but her, and I felt like my head was going to explode. For a second I thought she was calling out my name in passion, but I could see she was no longer on top of me but instead slapping my face, trying to get my attention.

Not even that mattered as I blacked out.

I woke up in a hospital room. From where I was lying, it looked exactly like the last one I had been in. This time I had tubes running into my arms, and there were actual machines behind me beeping with each of my heartbeats. I looked around and saw my dad talking to one of the nurses, and he didn't look worried at all. In fact, he just looked pissed—really pissed.

They noticed I was awake, and the nurse came over and gave me a smile. "You with us, Danny?"

I nodded, my head feeling like it would float away if I moved it too quickly.

"Thirsty?" she asked.

And I was, like, crazy thirsty.

She began to pour me a glass of water and my dad stopped her. "Can you give us a second? I'll give him the water."

She nodded and gave me another reassuring smile. This one was a "Good luck with this, kid" kind of deal, and I knew I was in for it.

As soon as the door clicked shut, he glared at me. "You know, I let it go when you started getting into God." His voice was rough with emotion. "Did I think you were doing it for the right reasons? No, but I let it slide because I thought, how much damage can faith do to someone? I didn't say a word when you started dating Emma, because what do I know about being gay? I mean, in my day we said it was just a phase so I thought, well, maybe it was just a phase." He locked eyes with mine. "Do you realize how bad you screwed up tonight?"

I really just wanted some water.

"Not only did you pass out because your blood pressure was through the roof, but when they brought you in, they took blood. What do you think A&M is going to say when they find out you were on X? You think that's something they let slide with guys they're spending thousands of dollars to play for them? You didn't think that doing drugs might fuck up your free ride?"

I could hear the machine behind me begin to beep faster as his words began to terrorize me.

"Let me tell you some truth, Danny. You're eighteen years old. That means the sound of running water should give you a hard-on. Thinking about linoleum should give you a hard-on. There is no reason someone your age needs something like Viagra to get hard unless they're trying to fuck something they aren't interested in."

His words slammed like sledgehammers into my head.

"When you get out of here, we are going to talk about your sexuality, and I promise you, if I don't like the words coming out of your mouth, I'm going to tell A&M they can shove their scholarship up their ass, because I'm at the point where I no longer think you have your best interests in mind. If liking guys is screwing you up this much...."

He paused, not sure how to follow that statement up.

"I'm sorry," I croaked.

He sighed and handed me the glass of water. "Drink up and pray this doesn't ruin your life."

What happened at the party didn't ruin my life, but it was close. Turns out that since I wasn't an actual student yet at A&M, they couldn't punish me for doing drugs. There was a clause in the contract that said before I actually signed up for classes they could drop me for any reason whatsoever, but they were going to give me a break, since I wasn't the first guy they'd recruited who took X at a graduation party.

Emma never called me again, which was good, since I was pretty pissed at her and the situation I had let myself get involved in. I mean, no, it wasn't all her fault. I was the idiot who took the pills, but she was the one who went and got them, and I wasn't going to forget that for a while. The other person who didn't call me was Nate, which hurt far more. My dad said he had called Nate and told him what happened, and all he said back was to let him know if I got worse.

So all in all, I screwed the pooch in about fifty different ways.

There was a basketball camp for the team during the summer, so when I got out of the hospital, I had about a week to get my stuff packed to head out. It was the most uncomfortable week I could remember, since my dad was still pissed at me but knew I was a couple of days from leaving for most of the summer, and he didn't want to waste any of the time we had left screaming at me.

We agreed I would drive up to College Station and catch the team bus from there, so I had to leave sooner than later, which meant he had one dinner and half a breakfast to say what he wanted to say before I was gone. We sat at the table with a bucket of fried chicken and eighteen years of emotional baggage between us. I would say I was so upset I couldn't eat, but I'd be lying. There was rarely a time I couldn't put something in my mouth.

Wow, that sounded kind of dirty.

"When do you get back from camp?" he asked without emotion.

"August," I answered between bites.

"I'll take some leave and meet you up there, so we can buy you whatever you're going to need for your dorm." Again, his voice had all the emotion someone describing the weather might have.

I couldn't take it anymore. Putting my chicken down, I looked at him. "Dad, I'm going to be all right."

He looked up at me, and it looked like he hadn't slept for weeks. The dark circles under his eyes made him look a thousand years older than he already was. "No, you're not, Danny," he said in that same controlled tone that made the words that much worse. "You ended up in the hospital and almost lost your scholarship, all to prove to yourself you liked girls. That is about as far away from all right as you can be."

He shook his head, and I had never seen him look so sad before. "I know it's my fault, but I have no clue how to make it better. I can't get it through to you that you need to be who you are without worrying about all the rest of this crap."

"That's over, Dad. I'm okay and I'm still going to college. I won't use anything like that again, I promise."

"Do you honestly think it's the fact you used drugs that has me bothered, Danny?" I paused because I had been thinking that exact thing. "Yes, I'm upset you used X, but I'm more concerned about how far you're willing to go to try to change yourself. You don't drink, but you're willing to swallow a handful of strange pills just to pretend to be straight for a night?"

"It was two pills, and I am straight."

His expression went from sad to furious in seconds flat. He opened his mouth to say something and then closed it with an expression that made it look like he was close to slugging me. "I don't know what to do with you anymore, I really don't." He got up from the table and stomped out of the room, his hands still clenched into fists. I finished the chicken and went to sleep, wishing desperately I was someone else for once.

When I woke up, he wasn't there. An envelope of twenties was on the table next to a note that said to call him when I got there. I had never felt more miserable as I put my stuff in the car and drove off base. This should have been the best day ever, but instead it was one more in an ever-growing pile of days in which I'd made my father regret ever having a kid.

Once I got out of Corpus, I turned up the radio and tried to clear my mind. I was eighteen, owned my own car, had a wad of cash, and was on my way to play basketball for A&M. There was nothing so wrong in my world that I couldn't fix it later. This was my life right now, and I vowed to enjoy every second I could of it.

When I was younger, I never understood the allure of driving. I mean, sure, it was cool to be able to take off whenever you could, but the love of it, the whole mystery about hitting the open road and just driving, made no sense. But as I passed Victoria and headed north, I finally got it. The feeling of freedom, the motion, the music, everything was perfect no matter how bad I had fucked up. I was driving away from my problems, not toward them, and that made all the difference in the world.

The parking lot wasn't that full, since it was only the basketball team along with the support staff—people like trainers, coaches, equipment managers, everyone who was working toward making this the best season we'd ever had. That was one of the best things I liked about basketball. No matter how badly you did last season, it was all brand new the next. A chance to redeem yourself from whatever failures you had last time. I parked and grabbed my bag and headed toward the bus, a growing feeling of euphoria coming over me.

One of the assistant coaches was holding a clipboard and checked off my name when I introduced myself.

"Monroe?" he asked. "Yeah, you need to go see that lady," he said, pointing to a middle-aged woman sitting on a folding chair, looking bored.

I was going to ask why, but he just went back to checking people in, so I wandered over to her. "Hi, I was told I needed to see you?"

She looked up at me. "You Pitman or Monroe?"

"Monroe," I answered, confused.

She reached down and handed me a plastic cup with a cover on top. "I'm going to need you to go in there and fill this up," she said, pointing to the building behind her.

I looked back at the bus and saw guy after guy getting on after they checked in, no problem. I looked down at the cup and realized I hadn't driven away from anything; I'd been driving toward a whole new set of problems.

The Stuff at the End of the Book

IT'S FUNNY how stories turn out.

For those of you keeping score, this story was started before *Tales from Foster High*. I had begun to dabble in Danny's story based on a couple of friends I knew who were struggling to be gay and on a sports team. I had no idea what I was going to do with it—again, this was before I ever decided to submit Brad and Kyle's story at all. It's one of those things writers do, and it bugs the hell out of other people. We start stories and then put them away, never to finish.

Right now my friend Gina is reading this and growling because of a *Doctor Who* story I owe her.

So instead I wrote *Tales from Foster High* and then *Lords of Arcadia*, and before I knew it, I had books to write. Once started, *Foster High* had to be finished. The moment I realized the arc, there was no way I could not write those books, and thankfully people read them. I wrote *Lords of Arcadia* as a palate cleanser of sorts. I needed Nine Realms and changelings to get high school boys off my mind.

Wow, that sounded way dirtier than I meant it to.

So working on Danny's story seemed redundant to me. I was writing a story about high school kids who were struggling with their identities; writing another at the same time was courting disaster. And then *151 Days* came around.

As I was writing it, I realized that I had Brad meeting a guy at A&M, talking to him about being gay, and then making this choice on whether to go to school there or not. Didn't think about it—I mean, it was a guy in a story Brad was going to talk to. No big deal.

And then it became a big deal.

Danny, the one in my head, politely pointed out that *he* wanted to play basketball at A&M, and if he was at the school at the same time Brad went to go check it out, couldn't he be that guy? I realized, why not? I mean, it was a great way to make a nothing character suddenly someone, and I got to add Danny, who I really, really like. So I handed the rough draft over to the friends who read it for me before I submit it to be published, and they all asked the same thing.

Who was that Danny kid?

I explained quickly, and they nodded and then asked, "So where is his story?"

To which I gave the worst answer a writer can ever give.

"It's half-done on my hard drive."

You can guess from there what happened, and so after writing *151 Days* I went back and took Danny's story out and began to write some more.

There are three books in this series: the one you are holding now; the next one, which is him in college; and the last one, which is him as a young adult. This I promise you, because I know some people don't like to invest their time in a book series unless they know it's going somewhere.

This is definitely going somewhere.

So now you know.

THE NEXT thing I want to talk about is A&M, the university.

As with *151 Days,* I thought about making a fictional college for Danny to attend and for Brad to check out. I did this because I didn't want to paint the actual college in a bad light as being homophobic. They are not, and anything in these pages is purely fictional and has nothing to do with the real A&M.

In fact, A&M has an openly gay diver named Amini Fonua who holds two school records there. So please do not read this and go, "Oh well, I knew Texas was intolerant and homophobic," because that's not true.

Well, it is true, but it's true for the entire United States.

There are horrible people everywhere who think that being gay is a sin, that gay people are abominations, and that we're all going to hell for it. They all do not wear cowboy hats, trust me. Not everyone in San Francisco is liberal and tolerant, and not everyone in Texas is a red-meat-eating, gun-toting, homophobic Republican. This book is not here to make that stereotype. It's here to tell you that if you have to judge someone, and please don't, judge them on their words and actions and not what popular media tells you they are.

I know many Aggies, and they are awesome people. Really, they are. They smile at you and say howdy—it's a very cool thing—and to think that because they come from Texas they automatically think a specific way is like thinking all gay people have to be sexual deviants. It's an assumption that does no one good in the end. So there, end of lesson. The more you know and all that. Knowing is half the battle. This message was brought to you by the Kyle Stilleno Foundation to Minimize the Number of Asshats in the World.

John Goode
November 2014

JOHN GOODE is a member of the class of '88 from Hogwarts School of Witchcraft and Wizardry, specializing in incantations and spoken spells. At the age of fourteen, he proudly represented District 13 in the 65th Panem games, where he was disqualified for crying uncontrollably before the competition began. After that he moved to Forks, Washington, where against all odds he dated the hot, incredibly approachable werewolf instead of the stuck-up jerk of a vampire, but was crushed when he found out the werewolf was actually gayer than he was. After that he turned down the mandatory operation everyone must receive at sixteen to become pretty, citing that everyone pretty was just too stupid to live, before moving away for greener pastures. After falling down an oddly large rabbit hole, he became huge when his love for cakes combined with his inability to resist the commands of sparsely worded notes, and was finally kicked out when he began playing solitaire with the Red Queen's 4th armored division. By eighteen he had found the land in the back of his wardrobe, but decided that thinly veiled religious allegories were not the neighbors he desired. When last seen, he had become obsessed with growing a pair of wings after discovering Fang's blog and hasn't been seen since.

Or he is this guy who lives in this place and writes stuff he hopes you read.

Twitter: @fosterhigh
Facebook: https://www.facebook.com/TalesFromFosterHigh

Tales from Foster High

Tales from Foster High:
Book One

By John Goode

Kyle Stilleno is the invisible student, toiling through high school in the middle of Nowhere, Texas. Brad Greymark is the baseball star of Foster High. When they bond over their mutual damage during a night of history tutoring, Kyle thinks maybe his life has changed for good. But the promise of fairy-tale love is a lie when you're gay and falling for the most popular boy in school. A coming of age story in the same vein of John Hughes, *Tales from Foster High* shows an unflinching vision of the ups and downs of teenage love and what it is like to grow up gay.

End of the Innocence

Tales from Foster High:
Book Two

By John Goode

Kyle Stilleno is no longer the invisible boy, and he doesn't quite know how he feels about it. On one hand, he now has a great boyfriend, Brad Greymark, and a handful of new friends, and even a new job. On the other hand, no one screamed obscenities at him in public when he was invisible.

No one expected him to become a poster boy for gay rights, either—at least not until Kyle stepped out of the closet and into the limelight. But there are only a few months of high school left, and Kyle doubts he can make a difference.

With Christmas break drawing closer, Kyle and Brad are changing their lives to include each other. While the trials are far from over, they have their relationship to lean on. Others are not so lucky. One of their classmates needs their help—but Kyle and Brad's relationship may be too new to survive the strain.

151 Days

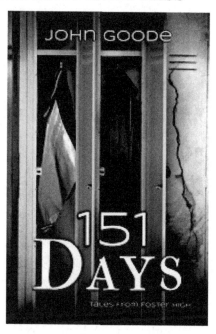

Tales from Foster High:
Book Three

By John Goode

With just 151 days left until the school year ends, Kyle Stilleno is running out of time to fulfill the promise he made and change Foster, Texas, for the better. But Kyle and his boyfriend, Brad Greymark, have more than just intolerance to deal with. Life, college, love, and sex have a way of distracting them, and they're realizing Foster is a bigger place than they thought. When someone from their past returns at the worst possible moment, graduation becomes the least of their worries.

Distant Rumblings

Lords of Arcadia: Book One

By John Goode

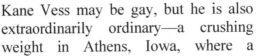

Kane Vess may be gay, but he is also extraordinarily ordinary—a crushing weight in Athens, Iowa, where a person's worth is measured by his uniqueness. But when he meets the school's newest student, Kane's ordinariness seems to evaporate. He is desperate to get to know the mysterious stranger… and that leads him into danger.

Hawk is an exile from his homeland, an otherworldly traveler with impossible abilities and a changeling bodyguard. He's generally disappointed in Earth, which seems common except for Kane. But while Hawk and Kane explore their mutual interest, the forces that made Hawk an exile are busy tracking him down. Kane's newfound feelings pull him into Hawk's shadowy fantasy world, where he learns he needs to grow up fast. Kane's life may now be extraordinary, but if he isn't careful it could cost him everyone he holds dear—including Hawk.

Don't miss this series from HARMONY INK PRESS

Eye of the Storm

Lords of Arcadia: Book Two

By John Goode

Kane Vess thought his life in rural Iowa was mind-numbingly boring. Then Hawk, a prince from another world, appeared and turned Kane's life upside down. At first Kane welcomed the adventure and the chance to be with Hawk—but then a shape-shifter named Puck kidnapped Hawk and dragged him back home.

Now Kane is caught up in another planet's magical civil war, searching for the boy he loves in a place he knows nothing about. With the help of a gem elemental, an ice barbarian, and a clockwork woman, Kane has to find Hawk and stop Puck before he can destroy the Nine Realms.

Don't miss this series from HARMONY INK PRESS

The Unseen Tempest

Lords of Arcadia: Book Three

By John Goode

Kane used to be a normal boy with normal worries. Now he fights alongside his boyfriend, Hawk, and an unlikely group of allies as they attempt to reclaim Hawk's throne and save the Nine Realms. With time running out, Hawk decides to raise an army against the evil shape-shifter, Puck, and his army of The Dark. The adventurers split up in search of a force that will join their cause and help restore order to the Nine Realms.

New allies aren't as easy to find as they hoped. Kane, Hawk, and their friends face unforeseen danger as centuries-old grudges threaten their quest. Nothing is what they thought it was, and Kane and Hawk must find the truth in time to defend against Puck's encroaching army. But the truth about who their true foe is will change everything.

Also featuring this author

FIRST TIME FOR
EVERYTHING

A HARMONY INK PRESS ANTHOLOGY

http://www.harmonyinkpress.com

Made in United States
North Haven, CT
03 June 2022

19801903R00117